ACKNOWLEDGEMENTS

First and foremost, I'd like to thank my family for supporting me and making fun of me all at the same time, for their endless love and encouragement. My grandmother Soraya, the matriarch (who I named the protagonist after), told all her friends that the family drove me so crazy I ended up writing a book about them!

This book would never have happened if it wasn't for the greatest man in the entire world, my Uncle! For if it wasn't for his 1 year deadline to find a husband with the £1m prize as an incentive to get his nearly 30 year old niece at the time moving, this project would have never happened!

Thank you to my amazing mother, for always defending the black sheep of the family and supporting me in pursuing this dream of mine.

I'd like to thank Christian Howgill who was one of the first friends to help me embark on this dream.

A special thank you to one of my oldest and dearest friends Ali Matar, without him this dream would never have come true. He was visiting his niece Prada and nephews Romeo and Leo in the South of France (my 3 fur balls) and accidentally discovered I had written a book! Thank you Lulu Al-Sabah for believing in this project and thank you to Republiks Publishing (Ali Matar and Lulu Al-Sabah) for making this happen.

Thank you to all my incredible friends and family for suggesting that I start working on book number 2, it's in the works...

Sheeva

The Cupid Index

SHEEVA MOSHIRI

REPUBLIKS

The Cupid Index

2021 REPUBLIKS

Republiks.co.uk

First published in Great Britain in 2021 by REPUBLIKS

ISBN – 978-1-8384827-2-5

Typeset by Claudio Rosas
Cover design by Claudio Rosas

PROLOGUE

Sunset Boulevard,
Los Angeles

It's true, you can run in heels. But you can't run in six-inch heels for an Uber that has already left Chateau Marmont on Sunset Boulevard. Soaking wet from a fall of angry rain, Soraya paused and thought about taking the Metro but didn't fancy the idea of walking all that way in the rain in her Louboutin's. Her mother's voice resounded in her ears, mocking Soraya's attempts to slot into a westernized LA life — one so far removed from her own cloistered Persian inheritance of Tehrangeles. There are so many Persians in LA that some funny person came up with the idea of calling it 'Tehran-geles' after the city in Iran.

"Take the car, take the driver. But public transport? Why bother if you don't have to?"

Yes, her mother considered Uber to be public transport, probably because everyone in LA uses it to get around as it's so convenient. Looking back, Soraya wondered why she didn't take the car that day. Maybe because her mother constantly worried about her driving in LA traffic, as well as the 'very real' possibilities that she could get kidnapped in the car park at night or carjacked at traffic lights. Sometimes, she thought that a kidnapping may actually save her from her overpowering Persian family. So, she figured taking an Uber would give her more freedom, despite the rain and all her meetings.

However, when she checked her account, she found she was unable to get a ride because her Uber score had dramatically dropped below acceptable levels after her latest escapades, as well as the fact that she was pathologically late for everything. She really needed to open a new account and start being on time.

Defiant, Soraya walked towards the station, glancing at her watch and with her feet aching from her stilettos. If she hurried, she could be back home in time for the family dinner. Her mother, uncle, and grandparents were all going to be there as usual, but there was something in her mother's tone that morning that had been unnerving, providing an intimation that trouble was brewing just under the surface.

Catching the next train that entered the station, Soraya clambered on board the crowded compartment; her cheek pressed against the cheap material of the strap hanging from the passenger next to her. Trying to get some more room, she turned, only to wedge herself further against the glass partition in the carriage.

Sighing inwardly, Soraya let her thoughts drift. And they did – right back to the subject of her marriage. Her good marriage, her wealthy, well-connected marriage. Her phantom marriage – so far… Soraya felt an elbow jab her in the shoulder and winced. Her friends were all dating, but only one was already married. Happily, to a man of her own choice. Which was how things were in LA. In the USA. Her family liked to tell her about the old days in Persia, when arranged marriages were commonplace, and the Khastegari (when the khastegar's – the suitor's – family meets with the potential bride's family to discuss marriage) took place. But what had that got to do with Soraya? The East's traditions were her heritage, but not the blueprint to her life. She wanted love.

Her mind shifted to Jean-Luc, as they always did when Soraya thought of love. She had believed she was in a perfect fairytale relationship. Then, without warning, they broke up. And that's when the analysis started. The postmortems with girlfriends, family, hairdressers, psychiatrists, and dog groomers. The whys echoing without answers. However, on reflection, Soraya should have seen the writing on the wall. She had been going out with Jean-Luc for five years on and off. They first dated for six months, broke up for a few days, got back together for another four months, broke up, got back together, repeated this a few more times, and then, *boom*! It was over.

The night before had seemed so cozy and normal. They hadn't made love but, other than that, there had been no tell-tale signs but then Jean-Luc had dumped her the next day. It had been the worst night of her life. If

Homer Simpson had been around, he might have added philosophically, "Worst night of your life. *So far.*"

Soraya felt the elbow jab into her shoulder again and glared at the man beside her, turning away as the train drew to an unexpected halt. Here she was, ten months later, and she could finally say that she was over Jean-Luc. Well, to be precise, twelve months, a huge consumption of vodka on the rocks, Xanax, chain smoking, a bit of useless therapy, kissing numerous frogs, new friends, and an uncompleted novel about her stupid ex. Talk about toxic relationships and toxic exes – that one almost killed her.

Swearing under her breath, Soraya glanced at her watch again. Oh shit, don't let me be late, she thought as she stared through the window into the dark tunnel. Not tonight. She wasn't looking forward to dinner. Her mother had been snappy all day and Soraya had a headache that wouldn't lift. So much for Tylenol. Why call it a painkiller if it doesn't kill the pain?

The hum of the lighting in the carriage was making her head throb even more as she glanced around at the other passengers. She studied their faces and wondered which of them were married, which were having affairs, and which were alone. She wondered if the couple talking in whispers in the far corner were lovers. And she remembered how it felt and wanted to feel the same way again. She reckoned that finding love had to be one of life's hardest challenges, even worse than securing a job she liked. Everyone was obsessed with the current financial crisis, which was one of the toughest the world had ever seen, but why was no one talking about the Love Crisis? How come that never made the headlines? The FTSE Index may be plummeting by the day, but surely there should be an index to measure love as well? The Cupid Index. Soraya reckoned that was plummeting by the hour.

Romeo, Romeo, where the fuck art thou?

Uneasy, Soraya glanced at her watch. The minutes were creeping past, the carriage getting hotter and more oppressive, mirroring her feelings that day. Something was coming. Something unwelcoming and threatening. Something that would topple her world overnight.

Shit, why hadn't she taken another Uber?

The Deadline

ONE

In silence, Anahita sat in the drawing room, staring at her manicure. She had struggled with her temper all day, and Soraya's lateness intensified her irritation by the minute. She barked at the staff that dinner would be delayed. Her brother, Amir (also referred to as 'The Godfather') had walked away, which only increased her fury. By the time another twenty minutes had passed, Anahita was incandescent. Having caught the mood of the hour, and her parents long since left the room, Anahita smoldered as she remembered the events of the morning.

It had begun so well. Prepared for a day-long shopping trip along Rodeo Drive followed by lunch at The Beverly Hills Hotel, an immaculate Anahita had been pleased to see two of her oldest friends approach her in Barneys' makeup department. Poised with Chanel's latest coral lipstick and heady from a splash of Prada's newest perfume, she smiled her welcome. A moment later, her teeth were clenching tighter than a dog's canines around a bone.

"Your daughter's getting married?" Anahita had replied, her voice light and her heart creaky. "How old is she now?"

She knew, but she had to check.

"Twenty-one."

Twenty-one, Anahita thought. And Soraya was turning thirty soon. The disgrace…

"She was lucky to find the right husband so young," Anahita snapped, rising to the implied challenge.

"My daughter was married at twenty-four," the other friend chimed in. Anahita's fingers tightened around the lipstick in her hand. "And she's just found out she's expecting her first baby."

Anahita's good mood ended in that instant. She was from a powerful and wealthy Persian family, who had considerable influence and prestige. She had been lucky and envied all her life but, over the last few years, a mild worry had deepened into a suffocating obsession: Soraya, her pretty, intelligent, and appealing daughter, was still single. Despite her best efforts to find a suitable match, Soraya hadn't settled down. Her affairs had been short lived, and her one serious relationship had veered dangerously from comedy to tragedy over a period of five years. There had been no marriage, and no grandchildren. Anahita worried that all that might come of it would be rising psychotherapy fees. Persian women who aren't settled by the age of 30 are said to be about to 'sour.'

Aware that she was gripping her lipstick like a drowning man grasping a cork, Anahita smiled at her friends.

"Well, actually I have some news. Soraya's seeing someone." Her lie caught her off guard the moment it slipped out between her lips. "In fact, we'll be announcing an engagement very soon."

Anahita was swept along with their squeals of excitement. Within minutes, a wedding had been imagined and possible names for the first-born offered up. Her lie had taken on a life of its own and was rapidly becoming a monster that could give Frankenstein a run for his money. Anahita tried changing the subject, but it was pointless. The fizzy joy of imagining her daughter's nuptials was too potent to resist.

By the time the coffee had been drunk, Anahita – without giving any real details – had Los Angeles' Persian society back in her thrall. She relished being envied again. It was only when she had parted company with her friends that Anahita remembered her honeyed fairy tale was bullshit, and that Persian society would spread the news around LA, Laguna Beach, and San Diego within hours.

The lie would mushroom like an atom bomb and, if exposed, would prove as deadly, which was why Anahita's head jerked up as the door opened and her daughter finally walked in.

"Where have you been? And what have you done to your hair?" She rose to her feet imperiously and stared into Soraya's face. "You're late."

"I'm sorry. The train was delayed."

"The train?" Anahita snapped, her temper flaring at the first available moment. "You're not poor! You knew everyone was waiting to have dinner."

"There's no one here." Soraya replied, looking around. The clammy sensation that had followed her all day was intensifying.

"Everyone got tired of waiting for you," Anahita complained, "You should have more consideration for other people. No wonder you can't find a man."

Soraya's eyebrows rose. "Because my train was delayed?" She put her handbag down and pushed the sleeves of her jacket up. Tired and unsettled, Soraya did not want another argument with her mother, and so she tried to appease her. "Look, I'm sorry I was late."

"You have to get married."

Soraya's eyes widened. "Excuse me?"

Slowly, Anahita looked her daughter up and down. After several hours thinking about the lie she had established, she had managed to convince herself that this 'marriage' would be in both their interests. Soraya had played around for too long. Perhaps applying some real pressure might finally get her moving in the marriage market, with the added benefit of stopping anyone from discovering Anahita's deception. The embarrassment would be excruciating.

"You have to settle down. You're not getting any younger and beauty doesn't last forever. No man wants a woman who's past it. You don't want to be left on the shelf. You know how tough it is in Persian society when you're past thirty and still single."

Soraya could feel her face turn pale. The argument was an old one and formed the basis of a hundred disagreements with her mother, her grandmother, Parvaneh, and her uncle, Amir. It was as if they thought that she didn't want to get married, even though nothing could be further from the truth. She just wanted to be married to someone she loved. Someone who cared about her, and who understood that it was damn difficult to live with a foot in both Persian and Western cultures.

"You've fooled around long enough," Anahita went on, mistaking Soraya's silence for passivity. "I love you and I want the best for you," she said in a gentler tone. "But you have to concentrate – and that's something you're not good at."

"Concentrate on getting married?" Soraya baulked. "This isn't some kind of exam."

"Don't argue with me!" her mother countered. "I know better than you do about marriage."

"Which is why you're divorced, is it?"

Her face blazing, Soraya felt the slap before she had time to react. The sense of foreboding she had felt all day had been real. This wasn't just one more argument; this was something else entirely.

"We mustn't fight," Anahita said, trying to calm herself. After all, she had to get her daughter to do what she wanted, rather than alienate her.

But Soraya was already alienated. In fact, the slap had brought all the resentment she had felt for years to a head: the pressure to find someone suitable, the irritation of her family because she wasn't married, and the incredulity of most of her friends who couldn't understand why any woman felt harassed into marriage. *What's the rush?* They asked her, in direct opposition to her family who believed that time was running out. The relentless pressure had intensified to such a point that arguments about Soraya's marital status occurred weekly, while LA's Persian society treated her dismissively. Her mother did have a point: it wasn't easy being single. People talked behind your back and gave you funny looks. In fact, Persian events made her feel so uncomfortable she always ended up at the bar downing vodka shots until she was numb to the discomfort of being scrutinized by almost every woman in the place.

But how was she supposed to behave? Soraya said angrily. "I'll find the right man in my own time."

"No, Soraya," her mother replied, firmly but kindly. "You've been saying that for years."

"But it takes years to find the right person!"

"Unless others find the right person for them."

Stung, Soraya snatched up her bag and coat and made for the door. But, to her surprise, her mother reached it before she did and blocked her exit. There was a hardness about Anahita, which Soraya had never seen before. Her mother often got angry, but this was different. There was an urgency, almost a fear, about her.

"You've got four months."

"What?" Soraya replied, aghast. "Am I hearing you right? Do you seriously believe that if I'm not married by a certain age that no one's going to want me? Why don't you just auction me off at the next charity to the highest bidder? I can't believe you're doing this to me."

"You need someone who's nice and loving, who'll take care of you. You're just too fussy! Why is it so hard for you to pick a man and stick with him?"

"If the majority of men weren't assholes then maybe I would stick with one of them," Soraya replied.

Up until a few years ago, she had been in search of Prince Charming and even thought she had found him in the guise of Jean-Luc Martinez. The world's stock market had been strong, shares in the Cupid Index were at an all-time high, and Soraya had been more than willing to invest heavily in a handsome French man…

Her mother's voice cut through the memory.

"You have four months," Anahita repeated, "which should be enough time to find someone suitable."

Soraya paled.

"Are you joking? If I can't find the right man after years of looking, how can I find him in a matter of months?"

"Because if you don't, I will." Anahita's arm was still stretched across the door, barring her daughter's exit. "There are two men known to the family who would marry you tomorrow."

"Business deals, not love matches."

"A good marriage is like a good business deal."

"Yes, yours was – and it failed," Soraya said quietly, with her eyes fixed on her mother. "You don't want that for me. You can't. You can't want to see me with someone I don't love."

"People grow to love one another."

"And if they don't?" She caught her mother's hand, desperate for Anahita to understand what she was feeling. "I know the right person is out there. I know I haven't made good choices in the past. I know that. But he's out there, the right man. I know he is." She tightened her grip on Anahita's hand. "It's not like when you were young. It's different now."

Anahita shook off her daughter's hand impatiently. "Hah! Some things remain the same."

"To you. Not to me." Soraya battled on. "I live now. Most of my friends don't have the pressure of getting married. They don't feel worthless unless they're with a man. It's not like that anymore."

"And this wonderful new world you live in, Soraya. Are you happy?" her mother asked. "This new culture, this emotional free-for-all, has it been good to you? Have you enjoyed your love affairs? Your career? Hardly. You've never settled down to either. You can't hold a job for longer than a few months." She paused, staring hard at her daughter. "You want to think and live like a Westerner, but your heart's Persian, and it always will be."

"No." Soraya replied, her temper rising. "I live in this world."

"But they don't accept you fully in this world any more than they do in the Persian world! Why? Because you want to live a modern life but you're a traditional girl."

"That's what you want me to be!"

"It's what you are!"

"No!" Soraya snapped. Her tone was fierce. "I might not have a big career or my uncle's fortune. I might not have found the perfect husband and had a child. But I will—"

"—Anyone can fool themselves into thinking that! But remember your apartment, your car, and your clothes. Everything is provided for you. Persian money makes your life comfortable. It would be a very different matter if you had to live in LA like a Californian girl. With a job to pay the rent. If you had to do work you disliked to cover your expenses, it would be quite another thing. You've never seen the real world, Soraya!" Her mother was losing her patience. "Your world is rich and cocooned. Out there it's tough. *Too* tough for you. And don't tell me you wouldn't be alone because you have friends. Most of them are friends because you're rich, Soraya. See how friendly they are when you've lost your allowance."

The two women faced each other. Soraya was breathing heavily as her mother looked her up and down. Slowly, Anahita smiled and touched her daughter's cheek.

"I love you, darling, and I want the best for you. That is why I say these things. I know you. I understand you. I want you to be happy and sometimes that means taking drastic steps. Now, we have an agreement, don't we? You'll find yourself a suitable husband. After all, you have choices,

Soraya. If you haven't found a man by the deadline then your family will find one for you."

All her life, Soraya had tried to stand up to her mother, her successful uncle, and the rest of her family. She had to compete with culture, heritage, wealth, and ambition. And she had always – despite many heated arguments – bowed to her mother's wishes in the end. Soraya stared at the carpet beneath her feet. Her mother was right – she *was* Persian in that she wanted her own man and children, and her own home. But Soraya had seen too much freedom and excitement to relinquish them easily.

For once, Soraya found herself hesitating, considering her mother's words, and wondering whether she could survive without the support of her family and their wealth. Or was she just a spoilt girl without any real character?

The thought was an uncomfortable one.

"You have four months," Anahita said gently.

A moment passed, and then another. Soraya was still staring at the carpet. "No," she said finally.

"What?" Anahita asked, her tone rising. "No?"

"I can't do it."

"You can. You'll find a man, dear, or we'll find one for you."

"No, that is the point," Soraya said urgently. "You can't find one for me. I have to do it for myself. In my own time."

"All right," Anahita said in a freezing tone. "If you're going to be unreasonable, I'll have to be brutal. You've forced me into this. Either you agree or you're on your own. I've done all I can for you. The whole family has. If you think your life is so wonderful, then get out and live it!" She expected Soraya to be shocked, to plead with her and offer reconciliation. But this time her daughter stood rigid in front of her. In her panic, Anahita lost control. "I see! Apparently, you think that you don't need your family or our support."

"I didn't say that."

"You obviously think it!" Anahita roared. "Go on then, get a job, rent an apartment, pay the checks, date a string of handsome men with zero substance. A Useless Guy, a no doer, one of those drop-dead gorgeous model types with chiseled jawlines and silly pouts that look like they've been struck by lightning – extremely handsome but zero substance. Nothing to add to dinner conversations or life itself. Just about useful enough for making a baby – hoping that the child takes after his looks and praying to God it doesn't get his brains. You'll soon see how your city life will be. You won't like it. Oh, you'll soon come running home." She took in a long breath, staring at her daughter. Anahita knew she had won. Soraya would do as she said. But she couldn't resist one last jibe: "You wouldn't last a day out there on your own."

Anahita paused, waiting. She *knew* Soraya would cave in. The challenge would be too much for her. She didn't have the experience or the guts. She was a good girl, an obedient Persian girl. An old-fashioned girl at heart.

Which was why Anahita was left standing with her mouth agape as her daughter walked out.

Four Months Until the Deadline

TWO

"Are you fucking joking?" Dante asked, in his thick Italian-American accent. One hand was holding Soraya's Maltese terrier, Prada, the other hand turning off the hairdryer. "Thrown out?!"

Slumping on a stool, Soraya stared at Dante. He was one of her closest friends. Super gay and the proud owner of a stylish hair salon with additional dog grooming facilities for his most VIP clients in Beverly Hills. Dante had a live-in lover who was idle and impressively stupid but magic in bed (so Dante had told Soraya many times, with details that sounded more like wishful thinking than reality). But Angelo did have an impressive reputation and a not-so-well-hidden flirtation with a career in pornography in his past.

"Your mother was joking."

"She was serious, believe me," Soraya countered. "She just didn't think I would take her seriously."

"So don't."

"You mean go back home as though nothing had happened?" Soraya replied, staggered. "My mother gave me four months to find a husband, otherwise I have to marry someone chosen by my family." She lifted her little dog off the grooming table, getting Dante's full attention. "You think that's something I should take lightly?"

"Your mother," he said coolly "wasn't expecting you to take her up on her threat. I mean, how could she?"

"How could she *what*?"

"Give me the dog back."

"Not until you answer the question," Soraya replied, regaining her seat on the stool. The Maltese snuggled into her jumper as she stroked its head. "You said that my mother wouldn't expect me to take her up on her threat. Why?"

Wrong footed, Dante shrugged. He put down the hairdryer as he heard the sound of his lover's feet in the apartment upstairs.

"I mean—"

"Yeah?"

"that you're great, but—"

"Everything before the but is bullshit," Soraya said. "That's what Jean-Luc told me once."

"Well, he was the expert on bullshit, wasn't he?" Dante responded archly. He paused, taking the stool next to Soraya and pulling a sympathetic face.

"Sorry. Does it still hurt?"

She hesitated. "Damn it, I'm not over him."

"He was no good."

"I know."

"He took advantage of you."

"I know."

"He was a douchebag."

She nodded, then her eyes narrowed. "You really don't think I could survive on my own, do you?"

Flushing, Dante reached for the little dog again, and tried to comb her whiskers. The terrier snarled under its breath. "Well, darling, I mean… you've never had to survive on your own."

"What makes you think I couldn't?"

Even to her own ears, her voice sounded lost. In the time since she had left the family home so dramatically, Soraya had spent one hour in a bar, thirty minutes staring into space, and the last thirty minutes in Dante's salon. And in those short two hours she had felt the first cold draft of panic. She was tempted to turn back. An apology would soon smooth out the argument with her mother. The mere act of returning would be apology enough.

But going back home would mean compliance. It would signal an agreement to abide by her mother's wishes and that stupid deadline. Besides, giving in was what Soraya always did.

"Why couldn't I cope?"

Dante blinked. The Maltese turned round ceremoniously on the grooming table between them, its black eyes moving from Dante to Soraya as the conversation continued.

"You don't have your own home for a start."

"Anya or Niloofar would put me up if I were desperate."

"That's not the same," Dante replied. "If you were really independent, you'd get your own apartment." He folded his arms. "Don't tell me your mother's stopped your allowance?"

"I can manage."

"On what, darling? You're like your little dog – pretty and spoiled, with everything done for you. Without the family money you couldn't even afford to have your claws clipped."

"So, who does your anal glands?"

His eyebrows rose in amusement. "Feisty! I'm beginning to see another side to you, Soraya. But it's only been a couple hours since you left home. Hardly revolutionary yet."

"I can find a job."

"You've had dozens of jobs, Soraya. You get bored, remember? You can't settle – which doesn't matter if you don't have to rely on a regular salary to cover the bills."

"If I found a job I liked."

"Is there one?"

She made an impatient clicking sound with her tongue. "If I found a job I liked, I could rent an apartment and pay my way. I'd be independent."

He smiled, touching her knee. In the years Dante had known Soraya she had proved to be good company, quick-witted, and generous. Unlike most rich girls, she had never been blind to other people's struggles. Before Dante settled down with Angelo, there had been a couple of occasions when he found an envelope stuffed with a generous amount of cash tucked under his phone. Nothing had ever been said, but the money had always arrived when he had been desperate. You didn't forget a friend like that. Even when Soraya spent days talking about the toxic Jean-Luc, even when she had bored him to insanity about her mother and uncle, and even when she had acted like a 19th century Persian princess, he had forgiven her because she was kind. But tough? No way.

"Sweetheart," Dante said carefully "this deadline is crazy, but you could go along with it."

"What?"

"You know so many people, you could easily scratch up some eligible man who your family would like. Then the pressure would be off. Get engaged, please them. And, if you want to dump him later, you can. The point is you'll have done what they wanted and fulfilled the deadline. You'll have shown your family that you're serious."

"Shit, you don't get this at all, do you?" Soraya snapped in disappointment. "This isn't just about the deadline. This is about whether I give in to my family or strike out and try and make a life for myself."

"But you want to get married!"

"To the person I choose!"

"And you think you're going be able to do that living like a normal girl in the middle of LA?"

"Why not?"

"Oh, grow up, darling! Think of the practicalities." He tied a pink bow onto the Maltese's head as she began to growl again. "What about Prada? You could hardly tote her around all day."

Soraya looked longingly at her little dog. "Would you take care of her? Just until I get myself sorted? She loves you and trusts you. She knows you. Please?"

He rolled his eyes. "You know I will. But even with me looking after Prada, you couldn't get by on a normal salary in a tiny apartment with very little money. Your family name gives you status, honey. Without their name and their money, you're just another pretty girl trying to make it in the big city." He turned to Soraya then frowned, surprised by the expression on her face. "What is it?"

"What if I did live like a normal girl?" she asked, her tone steady. "What if I didn't use my family's influence or money? What if I really walked away from everything I am? Spent the time anonymously, without any of the advantages?"

"It's not for you."

"That's what you think. That's what everyone will think. And it's definitely what my family will think. Which is why I have to try and prove you all wrong." Soraya slid off the stool, with the dog watching her. "If I can't hack it, I swear I'll go back home and marry the man they pick for me."

"Soraya."

"Honestly, Dante, I need to do this," she said firmly. "I've *got* to do this."

"But—"

"You're worried I'll fail," she said frankly. "So am I. But what if I don't? What if I succeed? What if I go home in four months' time having proved myself? And having found a man?"

"Fuck me," Dante said, admiringly. "You do that, Soraya, and I will marry you myself."

THREE

"Of course, she'll come back!" Anahita said sharply as her brother poured himself a drink. He flopped into his seat in the drawing room. The argument had been overheard by both the staff and Anahita's parents. Soraya's dramatic exit had been commented on above – and below – stairs. In the basement, the staff were laying bets that Soraya would return by morning. Meanwhile, upstairs her grandparents suggested calling the police.

"Oh, don't be stupid!" Anahita snapped at her mother, Parvaneh. "Soraya will be staying with one of her friends."

"What if she isn't?" Parvaneh asked, looking elegant in a silk dress, with her eyes expertly made up. She was young enough to be mistaken for Anahita's sister. "What if she's walking the streets? Anything could happen to her."

"Maybe we should call her friends."

At once, Anahita turned on her brother, Amir. "Never! That's what she wants – for us all to go running after her. No, let her stew. She'll be back." Her voice was firm, but her mind buzzed like a trapped wasp. What if her adored daughter was indeed walking around the streets, confused and alone? What if she fell into the hands of some disreputable man? What if she was attacked?

"What brought on the whole argument anyway?" Amir asked, loosening his tie. He stared hard at his sister. He adored his niece, and was proud of her, spoiled her, and generally treated her like a daughter. But she was still female, and he couldn't take any woman that seriously.

"Nothing really."

"You're lying."

"You might be a wonderful businessman, Amir Milani," Anahita retorted acidly, "but I know more about family."

He cut her off, wily enough to know that she was hiding the truth.

"Something triggered this. What was it?"

"Nothing." She blushed as she looked away.

"Oh, Anahita..." her mother sighed.

Her father said nothing.

"I didn't do anything!"

"I don't believe you. Was it something you said?" Amir continued relentlessly. "Or something someone said to you?" He stared into his sister's face, reading it like a copy of the Financial Times. "Ah! Someone said something to you."

"Soraya should be married!" Anahita wailed. "I just couldn't stand those women going on about their daughters being settled and doing so well. I just..."

"Yes?" her mother and brother asked in unison.

"I just said that Soraya was engaged."

There was a long pause.

Amir was the first to speak. "And I suppose that once you'd said it, you had to follow through?"

"That was it, yes!" she replied, relieved and sure that he understood. "So, when Soraya came home, I told her she had to settle down and find a man. In four months."

From the far end of the room, Parvaneh laughed. Anahita ignored her and stared urgently at her brother. "I had to push her, otherwise Soraya would never do anything! She might end up unmarried, and then what? All the Persians in the city would be laughing at her."

"And laughing at you."

"What's so wrong about wanting to see my daughter married?" she shrieked. "Every mother wants that!"

"But not every mother gives her daughter four months to find a husband."

Anahita's expression hardened. "Soraya's been looking for a husband all her life. There have been plenty of love affairs, plenty of men, but no husband." She looked over to her own parents. Her mother glanced away, while her father held her gaze. Anahita studied him. "What are you thinking? You think I'm mad? You think I shouldn't have given Soraya a deadline?" she walked over to him; the protest in her voice softening as she sought his advice. "Baba, I want her married. What should I have done?"

He paused then shrugged. "Don't ask me. I arranged your marriage and you got divorced. What would I know?"

Exasperated, Anahita turned to Parvaneh. "What about you?"

"What about me?"

"What do you think I should do?"

Parvaneh glanced at her watch, then stood up. "Serve dinner," she replied deftly. "And stop worrying. Soraya's no fool. She might just surprise us all."

FOUR

Huddled against the side of the entry to the Metro station, Soraya was scrolling through her cell looking for jobs. It was getting late. When a man pushed past and nearly knocked her off balance, Soraya hurriedly moved on and sat down at a table in a Starbucks café around the corner. Outwardly she appeared calm, but her stomach was knotted tighter than a surgical stitch and her hands shook as she tapped the adverts open. Feeling alone and unnerved, she jumped when her cell rang. A familiar voice spoke down the line.

"Making a bid for freedom, hey?"

Soraya smiled to herself. Of course, the first person to hear about the argument would be Mark Tehrani. He was her uncle's closest friend, and the one man Amir could never bully because Mark had his own company and his own money. And his own opinions. He was also someone who Soraya counted as a friend. He might be forty years old to her twenty-nine, but it felt like Mark had always been around in her life, watching her successes, as well as her boyfriend fiascos, and her clashes with her family. Although Mark was married to the reserved, sweet-natured Riley, he had often acted as Soraya's plus one, filling in for a boyfriend or husband at those incessant Persian gatherings. Easy company, he had been a huge support when the digs about Soraya's marital status – or lack of it – hit home. He would lift her out of her dark moods and mock the society matrons who treated any single woman above twenty-five as an outcast.

"Hi, Mark," Soraya sighed. "So, you heard?"

"I admire your bravery," he replied. "You need a go-between?"

"I might. How's my uncle taking it?"

"Amused."

"My mother?"

"Unamused."

Soraya shrugged. "I had to make a stand. You understand, don't you?"

"Of course." Mark replied. "You need anything?"

"No, I've not spent all of last month's allowance. It should last me, if I'm very careful. And I doubt they will remember to cut off my credit cards until the next bill arrives."

"Amir said you walked out with nothing."

She smiled, despite herself. "Yeah, that was stupid. I've only got the clothes I'm wearing. I'll have to buy some things." She was feeling the cold draft of unease as the enormity of what she had done hit home. She was out on her own, with nothing familiar around her. No home comforts, with barely any of her clothes, and certainly no car. Shit. What the hell had she done?

"If you need help, or a shoulder to cry on, just call," Mark said, sincerely. "I've spoken to Riley. We both want you to know that you can stay at one of our properties."

"No, thanks, that would be cheating. I have to do this properly."

"Ok," he said, covering his unease. "But don't get out of your depth, Soraya. I can pass on messages or keep secrets."

"I know, you always do. Thanks, Mark."

"No problem. So, you want me to tell your family anything?"

"Nothing they'd want to hear."

Her bravery was evaporating rapidly. Soraya looked round at the simplicity of the café and the disinterested faces of the people around her. It was only for a short time, she told herself. The four months would pass quickly. And besides, she would be preoccupied. She would need a job. But where? And she would need an apartment and she would have to look after herself. Soraya frowned, daunted at the enormity of her mission. For God's sake, she was a 21st century woman. Surely, she could cook and clean for herself. How difficult was it to make a meal or put some washing in a machine?

The longer she thought about it the more difficult it seemed. Soraya had never had to look after herself. The mundane tasks of life had been undertaken by others, leaving her free to travel and socialize. She could catch a plane anywhere in the world but iron a blouse? Unsettled, Soraya reached into her bag and made two hurried phone calls. Ten minutes later she was relieved to see a tall, blonde, blue-eyed woman walk into the café and glide into the seat next to hers. Anya Petrova, her friend, worked mainly from home but was so rich that she did it as a hobby. She had her own driver, spent three months of every summer in Monaco with her family, was dressed head to toe in designer clothes, and refused to date anyone who drove anything other than a Rolls Royce or a Bentley. Her other criteria in a man included a Titanium American Express credit card (the Black Amex was so last season), a mansion in Bel Air (Beverly Hills was also acceptable), his very own private jet, a yacht, a villa in the South of France, a chalet in Aspen, a fabulous penthouse in New York, membership to all the best clubs in LA, and not a day younger than sixty-five.

In short, Anya lived the life of a princess, with her own car and personalized number plate (she hadn't passed her driving test) and two apartments in Beverly Hills. One was a housewarming present from Daddy, even though she lived in the extended part of the family house in Bel Air five minutes away from Soraya. To round it all off, Anya had a live-in maid, chef, and masseur, as well as the biggest collection of Hermès bags Soraya had ever laid eyes on. Oh, and she loved sex, but rarely with any of the sixty-five year olds.

"So, sweetie," Anya said after a hurried peck on both of Soraya's cheeks. "What's the problem? A man?"

Soraya shrugged and gestured to another young woman who had just walked into the cafe. Slim, pretty, and brunette, Niloofar Stewart was her half-Persian, half-American girlfriend. She pulled out a seat at the table and leaned towards Soraya with a look of intense concern.

"Are you okay, babe? Is there some trouble?"

"If it's a man, you should tell him to fuck off," Anya said in her rich Russian accent. "Never let them get to you, *dahling*. I keep telling you, you call all the shots."

Niloofar was less forthright. She stared sympathetically into Soraya's face. "What's up?"

"My mother's nagging me to get married. You know the drill – 'you're not getting any younger, beauty only lasts so long.' "

Anya laughed outright. "So, what's new?"

"It's just getting too much!" Soraya insisted, skirting round the core of the issue. "God knows, she never pauses for breath. All my family nag me about settling down. And I would if I could. I mean, we all know that my personal life's a failure – hell, I'm a damn failure!"

Niloofar took her hand. "Aw, don't say that. You're a wonderful person and an amazing friend. You've always been there for me when I've been through tough times. Don't worry, I'm sure your mother was just blowing off steam. When you get home, she'll have gotten it out of her system."

Soraya didn't want to tell her she wasn't going home, and even managed a weak smile as Niloofar continued: "I've got something that'll make you laugh. You remember that guy from 1 OAK?"

Soraya nodded. "The boring one who was drinking at the bar alone?"

"Yes, him. Well, we met up last night. We went for dinner, nowhere swanky like Providence, but nice enough. We had sushi in Malibu and the jerk made me admire his gold Amex before making me split the check! For Christ's sake, he's a banker. And it was just a few pieces of sushi, not lobster and caviar!"

"Oh dear"

"He was a banker wanker!" Niloofar laughed, which was what they always called wealthy, good looking, but arrogant and stingy men.

"I guess there won't be a second date?"

"There should never have been a first one," Anya interrupted. "You're not sleeping with him, are you?"

Niloofar pulled a face at her. "I don't sleep with everyone I go out with."

The dig sailed over Anya's head. Soraya wondered how she could steer the conversation back to her current situation without making too much of it. But then again, she had known her friends for years and she knew she could tell them anything. After all, they had shared everything, including all of Niloofar's relationship traumas and Anya's dramas.

Unlike the more cautious Soraya, Anya had no fear. She loved sex and acted like a man when it came to emotional matters. Bedding who she wanted, she would move on without leaving so much as a phone number. Her job – hobby – as a stylist was perfect for a cool society girl and, although her reckless nature was the opposite of Soraya's, her problems with her controlling family were similar. Of such things tight bonds are made. And besides, she made Soraya laugh.

But Niloofar was much gentler. Soraya sighed. Niloofar had no problems with her super rich family. She was free to do pretty much what she wanted, but what she really wanted was the one thing she couldn't get – a steady relationship. Endlessly optimistic, Niloofar would tell Soraya about her terrible love life and, endlessly sympathetic, she would empathize with Soraya's pressures at home. God only knew how many late night and early morning conversations they had shared. It wasn't blood but sympathy that ran through Niloofar's veins. If there was an emotional rock in human form, it was Niloofar Stewart. And Soraya would have given anything to see her happily settled.

Remembering her own disastrous situation, Soraya wondered – not for the first time – where the Perfect Gentlemen were hiding. The men who opened doors for their women; who bought flowers even when there was no special occasion; who called every night to make sure you got home safe; who brought soup when you were sick; who said 'Bless you' when you sneezed; and who loved you unconditionally.

Who are they? And, more importantly, where are they? Soraya wondered helplessly.

"I've left home," she blurted out.

Both girls turned to her and exclaimed in unison, "What?"

"My mother gave me an ultimatum – I have to find a husband in four months, or they'll find someone for me." Anya's expression was incredulous, while Niloofar stared open-mouthed. "We had a real row, and I said I'd find the right man, and then I walked out."

"Well, walk back." Anya said bluntly. "You can't just leave home."

"I'm taking a stand."

"Soraya, how can you manage on your own?"

"I'm not an idiot!" she snapped. "I'll find a job."

"Oh, come on, *dahling*! You know you never keep a job for more than a week or two," Anya replied. "And without a job how could you rent somewhere nice to live? You couldn't live just anywhere. You've got high standards." She paused, her blue eyes steady. "Go home, sweetie."

Without replying, Soraya turned to Niloofar. "Don't you think I could pull it off?"

There was a prolonged pause. "Well, think about it. You'd have to find a job and a home and a man all in four short months. And on your own."

"So, you don't think I can do it?"

Niloofar touched the back of Soraya's hand. "You can stay at my place."

"But what would that prove?" Soraya replied, suddenly determined about her plan of action. "I have to find my own apartment and my own job."

"And your own man – all in a few months?" Anya replied. "Listen, sweetie, you haven't found Mr Right in all these years, what makes you think you can do it in four months? Also, you're used to your family, your home, and their support. You've never had to go it alone—"

"—I can do it!"

"Alone?"

Soraya nodded; her mind made up. Obviously, her family and friends didn't think she had it in her. Maybe she didn't. Soraya paused, shaking off the panic and self-doubt. She was going to prove to everyone that she was up to the challenge. She would manage on her own in LA. Find a job. And a home. And a man.

Even though the thought of it was terrifying.

"Think about it carefully," Anya advised her. "You and your mother are always fighting, and you always make up. She'll be waiting for you now, expecting you to walk in at any moment—"

"—which is why I can't go back!"

"You need your family."

Soraya narrowed her eyes, her irritation with Anya obvious. "I need to find the right man."

"Out on your own?"

"If it has to be like that, yes."

Anya sighed, folding her arms. "It's not your way of living, Soraya."

"I know!"

"You've never had to cope without your family behind you."

"I know!"

"Never had to go it alone," Anya said.

"You're wrong," Niloofar said firmly.

Surprised, Anya's eyebrows rose. "Huh?"

"Soraya won't be on her own."

"How do you make that out, *dahling*?"

"Because she'll have us."

In that instant, Soraya realized there was no going back. She just prayed that the Cupid Index was on the rise again.

FIVE

That night, Soraya stayed at Niloofar's apartment in Beverly Hills. Despite being one of Soraya's richest girlfriends, her place, though comfortable, was cluttered with an odd selection of good furniture and cheap junk. Soraya was staying in the cramped guest bedroom, which had a steel rail pushed up against one wall filled with Niloofar's impressive collection of clothes and the bed was perched on top of a pile of boxes and paperwork. There was no room to move. Niloofar was loving and supportive, but she had never been tidy.

Lying in a borrowed t-shirt, with her makeup still on and her neck strained painfully to one side, Soraya woke up the following morning after some horrible dreams only to realize that she was living in a much worse nightmare. Ducking her head under the covers, she wondered momentarily if she couldn't just sneak back, return to her own room, her own clothes, and her own spacious bathroom, with its deep, inviting bath. The thought was so tempting that Soraya almost gave in. She was reaching for her cell just as Niloofar entered.

"Hey, babe, you're awake!" she said cheerfully, flopping on the side of the bed. She handed Soraya a mug of coffee. "How did you sleep?"

She wanted to say that at one o'clock in the morning she had taken half a sleeping tablet, and the other half two hours later. But she just smiled instead.

"Fine. Thanks for putting me up."

"I heard about an apartment round the corner," Niloofar began, slurping her coffee. "I could arrange for you to look at it?"

Soraya had already decided that Pasadena wasn't for her. It was too depressing, and too far away from everything she knew. Perhaps somewhere closer to town would be better? Even if it was the size of a biscuit tin.

But before she could say another word, her cell rang. Soraya picked up to a voice that demanded: "What the hell are you thinking?"

She rolled her eyes at Niloofar and leaned back against the pillows.

"Hey," Soraya replied, wondering whether she was pleased or horrified to hear from her friend, Vince. Vince, the man with a beautiful penthouse apartment in West Hollywood, who threw the best parties in town and invited the most beautiful people in Los Angeles. Vince De Luca, who knew half of LA's most eligible bachelors.

Soraya had known him all her life. They practically grew up together, spending all their time playing tennis. Vince was an unusual mix of Iranian and Italian. He had grown up from a slightly awkward boy into a very handsome, tall, athletic, charming, and extremely successful man. He had his own real estate agency in Melrose Avenue and a beautiful collection of all the latest cars. He currently drove an Aston Martin James Bond-type car, which sounded more like a Lamborghini when driven. And women were always throwing themselves at him.

Soraya and Vince had briefly dated when they were younger, but nothing came of it. Both of them had decided they were better off as friends, especially as Vince wasn't the type to be tied down to one woman and Soraya wouldn't sleep with him. Besides, Soraya couldn't see her family approving of him as husband material, even though he ticked most of the boxes: well-educated, from a good family, ambitious. Oh, and how could she forget? Rich!

However, Vince wasn't known for being the faithful type. He could have four girlfriends at the same time and still be dissatisfied with the amount of sex. So, what did he do? He went out and looked for more. Over the years, Soraya had become used to being Vince's alibi. It usually went like this: he would call her up and say, "Babe, I need a big favor. Need you to tell the girls I was away last week on some business trip. Thanks. Ciao!"

Hardly listening to what he was saying, Soraya let her thoughts drift. Someone like Vince could never be satisfied in his sex life. He always wanted more. In fact, he had taught Soraya a valuable lesson – never date a Vince.

"Are you listening to me?" Vince asked impatiently.

"Sure, sure," Soraya replied, still letting her thoughts wander.

At age thirty-five it was unlikely Vince would ever settle down and give up the bachelor lifestyle. Last week they had gone to some party at his friend's house, and he was chatting girls up left, right, and center. His most successful pickup line to date was "I'm trying to quit smoking. I've gone a whole week without a cigarette but I'm feeling weak, help me," and for some reason women fell for it. Soraya shuddered. What a jerk! He had left that party with six phone numbers. When he was struggling to 'seal the deal' with a woman he would say, "Wow, you're such an amazing girl, I could marry you someday." And then he would kiss his victim on the forehead. The girl thought she had struck gold, while Soraya knew he'd probably fly her to Napa Valley on his private jet, take her on his yacht someplace romantic, sleep with her, and never call her again.

Knowing she could never change him, Soraya had stopped trying. But, at their last meeting, she had lost patience with him.

"Don't you even think about the girl's feelings?"

"Hey baby, don't stress. It's only sex," Vince had replied.

"How can you say that? Don't you care about getting a disease from one of these random girls you pick up in bars and clubs, not to mention all the dating apps like Raya?" Raya was an elite invite-only dating app for celebrities and the uber rich.

Vince had laughed. "Chill out, Mom. I take precautions."

"That's not the point! You can't keep acting like this, it's not nice. Why can't you just choose one girl and stick with her?"

"Baby, sex is sex. All I care about is getting laid. Doesn't matter who with."

But sex had never been a big deal to Soraya. She would look for other things in a relationship. For her, sex was about getting closer to the person. To her, it was about making love. Her romantic relationships were never about the sex, even when it was mind-blowingly good, but rather because she was looking for kindness, generosity and, most of all, a friend. She would rather break things off than be unfaithful. No, that was not her style.

"You're not listening!" Vince snapped down the line. Soraya finally jerked back into the present.

"I was."

"It's all over town that you've lost your mind. Go home."

"Is that all anyone can say? Go home?"

"It's good advice."

"It stinks," Soraya replied shortly. "And incidentally, the reason I walked out was because my mother gave me precisely four months to find a husband."

"So, marry me."

"Yeah, right." Soraya replied sarcastically. "Anyway, you must know all about what's happened already; otherwise, how would you know I was staying at Niloofar's?"

"News travels, babe," he replied. "Have your family really cut off your allowance?"

She snapped. "I can manage!"

"Like hell, honey!" Vince retorted. "You'll have to go back home. Your uncle will welcome you back. Just say sorry."

"And let them find me a husband?"

"You want me to find you one?"

The thought made Soraya's hairs stand on the back of her neck. "You?"

He laughed down the line. "Suit yourself. Anyway, keep me posted, but I reckon you won't last a week on your own."

"Well, prepared to be surprised, asshole!" she snapped back. "I'm going to show all of you what I'm made of."

When he had stopped laughing, his voice was serious. "Okay, okay. You need a job?"

Her temper faded. "What?"

"Do you need a job?" Vince replied, slightly impatient. "You must, if you insist on doing this the hard way. You have to find work and a place to live. Well, I know someone who needs help."

"You do?"

"Chloe Morgan. She needs a PR assistant at the Beverly Hills Hotel. You'll be perfect for the job. Tell her I sent you and the job's yours."

Suspicious, Soraya frowned. "Is she an ex of yours?"

"We had a fling."

"Vince!"

"Look, you need a job now and she needs help. Never question a gift, babe. I'll text you her details and then you give her a ring. Mwah," he blew an extravagant kiss down the phone. "Ciao for now, bella."

Pre-occupied, Soraya flicked off her cell and shuffled into Niloofar's bathroom, just in time to hear her friend call out a hurried goodbye. After a quick shower and fresh application of makeup, Soraya put on her clothes from the previous day and decided that her first stop would be the shops. She couldn't wear the same clothes twice. She would have to get some new underwear too, and shoes. Oh, and what about her hair? Soraya glanced at the mirror and saw the all too familiar frizzy wave beginning at the temples. Okay, she could borrow Niloofar's straighteners while she was staying with her, but she had to get some of her own.

Walking into Niloofar's room, Soraya spotted the hair straighteners and plugged them in, burning her finger as she tested how hot they were getting. Of course, there was one big problem: Soraya had never straightened her own hair. She usually had it done at the salon. Surely it couldn't be that difficult? She had watched Dante do it hundreds of times and it seemed easy.

Taking a section of hair, Soraya slid it between the irons of the straighteners and held it there, perhaps a little too long. Then she slowly drew the straighteners downwards as she smelled burning. Horrified, she stared at her reflection, at the wiry two inches at her scalp, and the uneven length; it was crinkled all the way down to her collar bone. Jesus! What the hell had she done? Perhaps it might be easier to start at the back.

Soraya extended her arms and the straighteners round the back of her head but panicked when she burned her scalp and knotted a large strand of hair in the metal jaws of the smoldering tongs. When the sickening smell of burning hair returned, she shrieked and yanked the straighteners out, only to rip a clump of hair out of her scalp at the same time. Eyes filling with pain and frustration, Soraya stared at her reflection in horror. Her face was flushed and her hair unevenly rippled, like a beach after the tide had gone out.

She remained valiant. Okay, so the straighteners would need some mastering. Still relatively calm, she pulled her hair back in a ponytail and walked into the kitchen, looking for an iron. Her blouse was creased, hardly fit to go shopping in – not on Rodeo Drive, anyway. Plugging in the iron, Soraya ate some cereal before trying to set up the ironing board. The board wouldn't fold out, so she searched for an even surface to use instead. In a flash of misplaced inspiration, Soraya decided to lay down her blouse on the kitchen worktop and iron it. By pure luck, the iron wasn't too hot. It pressed the material nicely, until Soraya turned the blouse over and saw – to her amazement – that not only did it have a blotchy, black, and grey stain on it, but that she had also managed to burn off the top layer of the worktop.

God, she was fucking useless! Turning off the iron, she tried frantically to repair the damage, but the burn remained – just like the strange, blotchy imprint on her blouse. Close to tears, Soraya stared at the iron, then reluctantly put on her shirt and covered it with her jacket. She was hot with humiliation. How had she reached the age of twenty-nine without being able to do her own hair and iron her own blouse?

She felt desperately drawn to the siren song of home. No one would blame her for giving up. In fact, her uncle and her mother would be delighted to see her walk back in through the door. She could then have a shower in comfort, get dressed, and throw away the shirt she had just ruined. And then she could have her hair done properly at the salon.

Lost, Soraya sat at the kitchen table by the damaged worktop. A simple apology would solve everything. Or would it? No, giving in would be too easy, she decided. Giving in would mean she had handed her future over to her family and let them seize her power. Giving in would mean giving up on the life she craved. Soraya sat in the kitchen, thinking for another ten minutes. She was surprised by the quiet. Having always lived with her family, she was used to a certain amount of noise around her, even if it was only the housekeeper tidying up. She longed for company but resisted. For the first time in her life, she was completely alone.

And it was very, very lonely.

It turned out that Chloe wasn't exactly a gift. It also turned out that Vince's favor wasn't exactly a favor, either. At quarter to three that afternoon, Soraya walked into the reception of the Beverly Hills Hotel. The previous day she had bought herself – on her credit card, naturally – what she considered to be the perfect office outfit. But she felt strange wearing a suit, even though she liked the fact that it made her feel like an executive. Wearing a sassy Hugo Boss jacket along with a trendy knee-length pencil skirt from Maje and brand new Prada shoes, she was feeling pretty confident as she knocked on a door marked CHLOE MORGAN. The job, she believed, was in the bag.

And it was. But it was a bag Soraya would soon want to escape.

"You're Soraya Milani?" Chloe asked, her blue eyes just the wrong side of cold.

"Yes."

"A friend of Vince?" Chloe was implying something unpleasant. Their mutual involvement with Vince De Luca made both women uneasy.

Soraya hesitated, sensing the familiar frisson of sexual jealousy. There was nothing between her and Vince anymore. The stupid woman had no reason to worry about that.

"Vince and I are friends."

"Vince and I are friends," Chloe repeated in a deathly tone. "Close friends, I imagine?"

"No." Soraya lied.

"He said otherwise."

Fuck you, Vince, Soraya thought. Of course, he wouldn't have been able to resist some sexual bragging, even if it wasn't true. And, while Soraya was long over him, it was horribly obvious that Chloe carried a torch that could put the Olympic flame in the shade.

"Honestly, we're just friends," Soraya said lightly. Her smile was ignored.

"We all work hard here. You'll have to buckle down, like everyone else," Chloe said. "Have you met The Director yet?"

"No."

Pausing, Chloe studied Soraya for a long moment. It was long enough for Soraya to feel uncomfortable and start playing with her jewelry. It was clear that Chloe's scrutiny was for a purpose – she was figuring out the unexpected competition. It was clear that Chloe was wrestling with whether to shoo her away or to keep her enemy close and have Vince in her debt.

Chloe stared at Soraya coldly. "All right, I'll hire you."

"Thank you."

"Oh, don't thank me," Chloe replied, "that would imply you're going to enjoy it."

Later that night, worn out mentally and physically, and a little depressed, Soraya staggered back to Niloofar's apartment. Her clothes were creased, her heels rubbed raw from her new shoes, and a coffee stain decorated the front of her blouse. Her confidence had not fared well. Chloe had turned out to be a demanding, authoritative, demeaning, and spiteful woman, who made no effort to help or like her new employee. Soraya was merely an assistant to be pressed into mundane and tedious clerical work: the office lackey used as a communal runner. Public Relations? More like Public Humiliations.

She was four days into her four-month deadline and one day into her job. How would she survive the next few weeks, let alone have the time and energy to meet Mr Wonderful-And-Ready-For-Marriage-Right-Now? It was a lonely, confused, and subdued Soraya who phoned Anya.

Trying hard to put a positive spin on her first day at work, she took the amusing route. "It was Vince's idea."

"*Dahling*!"

"Yeah… anyway, I could just about stand having a shitty job as the badly paid PR assistant at The Beverly Hills Hotel if I didn't have to put up with Chloe. She is the boss from hell. She's a total bitch. Oh my god, I swear she's the nastiest human being on the planet – after Jean-Luc obviously. She's the same age as me but looks so much older. She's got a really terrible bob hairstyle and dresses like an old-fashioned grandmother. I mean she must buy her clothes from some random flea market."

"Ouch," Anya said, clicking her tongue.

"Maybe for antique pieces, but clothes? Please, that's just pathetic! You'd think she'd have picked up some fashion sense given her job. Not only does she dress badly, but she also acts like she's got something stuck up her ass – probably the paycheck from her last job!"

Anya laughed. "And she's one of Vince's exes?"

"Can't see what he saw in her," Soraya said, still making light of her depressing day. "The bitch really has it in for me. I think she's still got a thing for Vince. That must be it, otherwise she wouldn't be so nasty. I made coffee for her about a hundred times – and I know it was just to give me the run around. She didn't even drink it."

"Tomorrow will be better."

"And she puts on the air conditioning even when it's 60 degrees out, like today. She's not human! I bet she sleeps upside down, hanging from a beam somewhere," Soraya paused, before continuing. "I must say, though, knowing Chloe for even just a day will have improved my tennis a lot. I can now pretend the ball is her head and I know that I will be able to drive through with so much more aggression than before. It will be much cheaper than therapy. Boy, Vince must have really screwed around with this woman for her to be so angry."

Anya laughed again. "You don't have to do this, sweetie. Go home."

"Why is that everybody's answer?" Soraya fumed. She still tried to sound positive even though she was irritated that Anya appeared to side with her family. "I can't stay with Niloofar any longer, so I'm viewing two apartments tonight. One's in the Fashion District, and the other in Brentwood."

"Brentwood? Not cheap. I thought you were economizing?"

"It's a one-bed so it's not too bad. Anyway, I can pay the rent out of my savings. Well, for a little while, at least." Soraya paused. To be honest, she had very little money put aside, and having no family backup or allowance brought home to her just how hard it was to get by alone in LA. As for the price of food, why had no one told her that avocados cost two bucks each? And bread, who knew bread was more than the Metro fare into town? "Anyway, if I get the apartment, I'll have a little housewarming and we can have a few drinks."

"Sounds good, sweetie," Anya replied, "You seeing anyone yet?"

Soraya's eyebrows rose.

"I only left home a few days ago! I've already got a job and by tonight I might have an apartment. How in God's name could I have got a man too?"

"Just checking, *dahling*," Anya said coolly. "Just checking."

SIX

Not wanting to view the apartments alone, Soraya asked Dante to come with her. He met her on the street outside the apartment in Fashion District, which was rated as one of the most dangerous neighborhoods in downtown Los Angeles in 2020. Prada, Soraya's dog, was tucked under one arm, with a Hermès bandana tied at a jaunty angle, while Dante had a huge scarf wrapped around his neck three times. Dante's jeans were tucked into heavy combat boots, and a cashmere woolly beanie was pulled down over his forehead.

"Fashion District," he said by way of greeting. Soraya picked up her little dog and cuddled Prada. "Oh my God, not Fashion District!"

Soraya looked around very quickly, the area was about 100 blocks long and full of quaint little retail shops, lots of fabric shops, cafés, wholesale vendors, and warehouses. The place looked like a strange kind of outdoor market that she had never come across before, everything looked cheap and dirty.

"I told you not to bring her. I said I'd call round later and see her at the salon." Soraya looked around. "Dogs aren't allowed here."

"Are you sure humans are?" Dante looked horrified. "Fuck, babe, this place is for aliens."

"You have to hide her," Soraya said, trying to conceal Prada under her jacket and failing. Finally, she tucked the little Maltese under Dante's scarf. The dog snuffled in satisfaction as she settled into the warmth.

"I'm not going in!" Dante wailed. "We might never get out again."

"It's not that bad!"

"It's worse," Dante replied. "Norman Bates wouldn't live here. Why don't you just—"

"—If you say, 'go home,' I'll hit you!" Soraya hurried him up the steps towards the forbidding doorway. "It might be nice inside. Come on!"

A moment later, a grumpy-looking middle-aged woman wearing a long, velvet skirt and a creased lace jacket showed them into the apartment. It was small, smelly, with mold in the corners and damp stains on the walls. She pushed past several packing boxes. "Sorry about the mess," she told them.

"The last tenant had to leave suddenly."

"He's probably under the floorboards," Dante whispered. Soraya gave him a bleak look as the landlady continued her tour.

"We don't allow animals," the lady said firmly. Soraya noticed Prada's black nose peeking out from under the twists of Dante's scarf. Gesturing frantically to him, Soraya looked back at the landlady innocently.

"I don't like dogs myself. They stink and make a mess all over the place. We had a problem with fleas once. After that, no dogs. Can't stand them. Damn things should be banned."

Prada's nose disappeared at once, a soft whining noise emanating from under Dante's jacket.

Hearing it, the landlady turned. "What was that?"

Soraya glanced over to Dante.

"He has a bad chest. Asthma," Soraya replied. Dante picked up his cue and wheezed. "Which means that you must have damp here. I'm sorry, but the apartment won't do." Seeing Prada's nose poke out again, Soraya hurriedly adjusted Dante's scarf; his enthusiastic wheezing drowning out the little dog's whines. "Thank you, anyway."

Back on the street, Dante paused and took a long, hard look at Soraya. "Where next? Downtown?"

"Brentwood."

"Are you sure? You don't fancy Skid Row maybe?"

"Stop whining."

"I'm not whining; it's asthma."

In silence, they caught an Uber to Brentwood – Dante paid for once – and finally stopped outside the apartment. Wrinkling his nose, Dante looked hard at the neat block, then cast a glance at the entrance.

"You'd be living in a one-bed you said?"

"You can't judge until you see it," Soraya told him, although her heart was sinking fast as she walked up to the entrance and rang the landlord's bell. After a moment, a young woman opened the door. She was visibly pregnant. Dante (who was allergic to children, born or unborn) made an excuse to stay outside with the dog.

"Please come in," the woman said, stepping back to let Soraya enter.

"I'm Jenny." Her heavy blond hair was tucked behind her ears and there was a thick wedding band on her left hand. "The apartment is on the fifth floor just next to ours".

They took the tiny elevator up to the fifth floor and entered a narrow hallway. Jenny went to fetch the keys to the apartment. As Soraya waited outside, she noticed an older man sitting in a room to the left. Jenny hurriedly closed the door and showed Soraya to the apartment next door. Although her first impression hadn't been good, Soraya was amazed to find herself shown into a brightly decorated and welcoming – if small – one-bedroom apartment. Not quite the ten-bedroom palatial homes she was used to in Bel Air, but it could be worse. Soraya had checked the prices of many one-bedroom apartments but LA properties were just crazy expensive. A one-bedroom apartment in a decent area where you don't have to worry about being murdered in your sleep were at a premium, with prices to match. She even looked in neighborhoods further away, like Venice Beach, but then she'd be spending four hours a day commuting in the traffic. Also, Ubers were so cheap in LA she wouldn't even need to drive to work from Brentwood. All in all, it was a good compromise.

Smiling, Jenny looked round. "I wanted it to be cheery, and it does get the light in the afternoon." Her tone was fragile, her hands clasped over her stomach.

"Have many people seen it?"

"No, you're the first," she replied, fiddling with her hair.

Soraya suddenly realized the woman was close to tears. "Are you okay?"

"I'm fine" Jenny replied. "It's just that things have been difficult. My husband was killed in a car accident recently."

"God, I'm so sorry," Soraya replied, glancing down as Jenny touched her stomach again.

"The baby's due in three months."

"And you're on your own?"

"My father's staying with me this week," Jenny replied. "He thinks I need a man around. But you know what men are like. They don't really know what to say." She paused, struggling to sound lighthearted. "I've never had to rent out this apartment. It used to be my art studio. I paint in my free time, so I hope I'm getting it right. The rent includes the electricity and gas".

Soraya smiled: "I've never rented a place before either. I don't suppose either of us really knows what we're doing."

Visibly relaxing, Jenny prayed that the young woman standing in front of her would take the apartment. She had dreaded it being occupied by some hard-faced professional or some city type. Meanwhile, Soraya was wondering how it felt having to rent out your art studio because you were widowed, pregnant, and clearly in desperate need of money. She knew that if Dante had been with her he would have dragged her out, telling her that she didn't need any more problems. Anya would have said the same. Only Niloofar would understand why, of all places, this tiny little apartment was going to be her temporary home.

"I'll take it."

"Great!" Jenny replied, before frowning. "I suppose I should ask for references?" She shook her head. "No, I like you; I know you're okay. Can you sign up for three months? And give me one month's deposit?"

Why not? Soraya thought. She had enough of her savings to pay for a month's rent in advance. After that, she would pay Jenny the remainder either out of her allowance, or from the fantastic job she still had to secure, as working for Chloe certainly didn't meet that criteria. Soraya wasn't sure exactly what was going to happen. She only knew one thing – that she had a base. It wasn't home. It wasn't grand. But it was a snug, temporary little place that would bear witness to the most incredible four months of her life.

SEVEN

Anahita paced nervously around Amir's study. Like the rest of the house, it was decorated with neutral colors, and styled by The Archers. The place looked expensive yet modest. She played frantically with her hair, fiddling with her rings and bracelets. She looked almost frightened with worry, whereas Amir was very composed.

"It's been five days! I can't believe we haven't heard from her." Anahita said, turning back to her brother, Amir.

"Are you sure she didn't leave a message at your office?"

"Why would Soraya leave a message at my office? She'd call my cell, like she always does."

"But maybe she didn't want to talk to you directly."

"She didn't call you either."

"We had a fight."

"Well, there you are."

"What's that supposed to mean?"

"She's okay," Amir said emphatically, watching as his sister's head shot up. Her hair was immaculately blow-dried, her skin glowing from another facial. In the three days since Soraya left home, Anahita had kept the Hotel Bel-Air Spa afloat with her constant massages in a futile attempt to work the worry out of her.

"Have you seen her?"

"No, but Mark's talked to her."

"Mark! Why can she talk to him but not us?"

"Because she didn't have an argument with him," Amir responded in a clear and even tone, albeit crinkled a little at the edge with mild irritation. "Stop stressing, Anahita. I've got someone watching out for Soraya."

"Spying on her?"

"Not exactly." Amir replied, "Just keeping an eye on her. See that she doesn't get into any trouble."

"So, where is she?"

"She's doing okay."

"Where?"

Immune to Anahita's questioning, Amir had decided that his niece had – for once – impressed him. To walk out of her home, without her allowance, and determined to make her own way was pretty remarkable and unexpected, but all the more impressive for that. Of course, being a woman, she would fail and have to return, and her family would end up finding her a husband. But this little rebellion amused him. Not that he would tell his interfering sister how he felt or keep her up to speed on Soraya's secret activities. He was entitled to know where and what his niece was doing, but Anahita deserved to be kept in the dark.

"You have to tell me. I'm her mother!"

"All you need to know is that she's safe. I've given instructions that I will only get involved if or when Soraya gets in trouble."

"Like when she's murdered!"

"I'd definitely be told about that," he replied sarcastically. Then he turned back to his sister and, in a soothing tone, said, "Let Soraya have her freedom. Let her have a try. It's only for a few months. No harm will come to her, I promise you. If there's trouble, I'll be told."

"Has she got a place to live?"

"I don't know," Amir lied.

"Has she got a job?"

"I don't know."

"Has she met a man?"

"I don't know." Amir picked up his copy of the Financial Times and disappeared behind it. He could hear his sister take in an exasperated breath. A moment later, she slipped on her Yves Saint Laurent shoes and left the room. Breathing out, Amir dropped the paper onto his lap and thought of Mark Tehrani. He had known Mark for over twenty years. And although Mark was ten years younger at forty, Amir considered him to be one of the wisest, most gifted, and most reliable men he had ever met. Independently wealthy, Mark had worked with Amir on a few occasions, but had never been employed by him. Although rich, the half-American, half-Iranian Mark was by no means in the same league as Amir. But, while not as financially prosperous, he was more emotionally blessed, with his previously happy private life a marked contrast to Amir's public marriage of convenience.

Marriage to his childhood sweetheart, Riley, had been blissful until the unexpected death of their only child from meningitis. From then on, the marriage had been frail. Neither were unfaithful, and they remained loving and caring, but the ghost of a dead child had managed what life and temptation had not and driven a wedge between them. Their love swiftly became muffled and too weak to fight for air.

It was natural for Amir to turn to Mark Tehrani when Soraya left home because he knew the two of them would be in touch. Mark had always looked out for Soraya. She had been a frequent guest to their home, becoming close to Riley. But when their child died, Riley had drawn back, and Mark made allowances for his grieving wife. It was Mark who had told Amir not to worry when Soraya left home. He would get someone to watch over her, he said. Someone discreet. Someone trustworthy. Someone who could be relied upon. As usual, he had been true to his word.

A reassured Amir discreetly tracked his niece, and now found himself – to his intense surprise – amused and fascinated over what she would do next.

Anya's face tried not to betray her feelings as she looked around the tiny apartment in Brentwood. Her long-limbed body curled itself into one of the armchairs, her Louboutin's flung across the floor. Known for her bluntness, she was battling between wanting to tell Soraya what she thought of the place and keeping quiet to avoid hurting her feelings. After all, Soraya had invited her, Niloofar, and Dante over for a pre-housewarming. Yet, it seemed more like a house mourning to Anya's eyes.

Sensing the disapproval in her Russian friend, Soraya turned her attention to Niloofar and, after refilling her glass, topped up Dante's. His eyes were puffy from crying over his boyfriend, and his arms were wrapped around Prada. The little terrier stared mournfully up at him.

"I like it here." Niloofar said, looking around approvingly.

"*Dahling*, it stinks," Anya replied. "Too small, too quiet, and too far from Beverly Hills."

Soraya shrugged, "It suits me."

"What's your landlady like?" Niloofar asked, shooting Anya a warning look.

"She's lovely, but she's having a difficult time as she's six months pregnant and her husband was recently killed in a car accident."

"Oh my God," Niloofar said, her hand over her mouth. "Poor woman."

"If you're not careful," Anya murmured, glancing over to Soraya, "she'll end up crying all over you, sweetie. You have your own problems, don't become someone's therapist."

Her words were brutal, and Soraya found her friend's callousness chilling.

"So, how's the job?" Niloofar asked, changing the subject while shovelling several crisps into her mouth.

Soraya shrugged. "Freezing. I work in a cold, damp basement."

"Just like here then; you must feel at home," Anya cut in.

Ignoring her, Soraya continued: "It has no heating, as my stupid boss broke the nozzle. I've had a sore throat since yesterday because of the air conditioning and I get paid almost nothing."

"So, go home."

Infuriated, Soraya continued to blank Anya. Dante drained his glass and refilled it immediately.

"You know, when he was starting out, my uncle once put laxatives in his employer's coffee," Soraya chuckled. "Said he did it to keep him shitting instead of hassling him."

"Did it work?" Niloofar asked, all the women turning as they heard a muffled sob.

Dante was looking at them, his eyes pitiful. "Will he come back?"

In unison the women nodded in his direction, knowing instinctively that he was talking about his boyfriend, Angelo.

"Babe, of course he'll come back." Soraya reassured him. "He always does; you know that. Don't worry."

Sighing, Dante looked down at the dog in his arms while a slightly tipsy Soraya continued her previous train of thought. "Lately, my employer has taken to pulling down the shutters so that no one can peek through the windows. I feel like I'm in prison. It's cold, it's dark, and it's depressing. Half the time I don't know if it's light or dark outside."

"It can't be that bad!"

Soraya emptied her glass, smiling giddily at Niloofar. "But there was one interesting piece of news. One of the hotel guests was offered a complimentary night at the hotel when she spotted a speedy in her hotel room."

"A what?"

"A speedy. It's an industry term we use to describe a mouse. It's also the term Chloe uses for dinner."

"Why, *dahling*?" Anya intoned. "Does she eat mice?"

"Probably raw," Soraya replied, taking another long swig of her wine and wondering, only fleetingly, how bad she was going to feel in the morning. A hangover while living at home was one thing. A hangover when you had to get up early and earn a living was quite another.

Noticing a fleeting smile around Anya's lips, Soraya turned to her. "So, what's new with you?"

"Oh, just work and sex, the usual."

"Who's your latest victim?"

"This gorgeous Russian man I met at a jewelry show. Tall, sophisticated, has his own law firm. Lives in Beverly Grove in a beautiful penthouse. And he drives the latest Rolls Royce – well, his chauffeur drives it. He just blew me away."

"So, do you think this one's a keeper?"

She looked at Soraya with horror. "Sweetie, I'm young and beautiful, why would I want to get tied down in my prime? I can have any man I want, when I want, as often as I want. Why spoil the fun? Incidentally, *dahling*," she continued, smiling, "you'll never guess what just happened to me. Some fat Russian man offered me 10,000 dollars to sleep with him. Isn't that disgusting?"

Soraya flinched. "Yes, it is."

"I'm worth more than that, surely?"

"Ah, and here I was thinking you were upset that he mistook you for an escort," Soraya said jokingly. Inside she found herself judging her friend, something she would never have done before.

"I would never accept a proposal like that, but he could have at least offered me more."

If she was from Earth, Soraya thought, then where the hell was Anya from? Surely, they can't come from the same planet? They were polar opposites. Or maybe they were just from the different sides of the tracks? Anya the rich girl and Soraya – albeit temporarily – the poor friend?

Taking another sip of her wine, Soraya kept her gaze averted. This was something she hadn't expected. Along with all the problems of living alone and supporting herself, Soraya had never anticipated this shift in status. And it unsettled her.

"Well," Soraya said carefully, "I'm more into romance and falling in love. All the stuff you hate, I suppose?"

"No, sweetie," Anya continued smoothly. "I'm just enjoying myself. When I'm ready I'll settle down. But for the time being I'm loving life just the way it is. Anyway, aren't you forgetting the most important thing? You have to find a man."

"Give her time!" Niloofar said, immediately jumping to Soraya's defense.

"But she doesn't have time, sweetie. That's the point. It's nearly the end of the first week and Soraya still hasn't found a man."

Suddenly sober, Soraya glanced over to her friend.

"Where on Earth am I going to find myself a boyfriend so fast? Facebook? Instagram? Raya hasn't come up with the goods. Maybe we should have a girls' night out, hit some trendy club where all the hotties hang out – or resort to calling Vince for his help."

"*Dahling*!"

Getting tipsy, Soraya leaned against Niloofar on the couch.

Dante sighed dramatically at all the man talk. "Why did God create such horrible creatures in the first place?"

"I've been trying to find love since the age of fifteen," Soraya said. "I've had crushes. I thought I was in love once when I was seventeen, but in retrospect it wasn't that exciting. Then I experienced what I thought was true love with that asshole Jean-Luc."

"Jean-Luc." Dante mumbled morosely. Soraya ignored him and carried on.

"Who knows? Maybe it was a Fool's Love, like Fool's Gold. It looks like real gold, feels like real gold, and behaves like real gold, but when you actually try and make something beautiful with it, you find that the illusion crumbles to reveal a rotten core."

Niloofar laughed. "You're getting pissed."

"I know," Soraya agreed. "But why do men have to make our lives more complicated than they already are? Why do we have to deal with assholes as well as work and family pressures? If I knew life was going to be this hard, I'd have never come out of my mother's womb. I would have insisted on staying put."

Niloofar sighed mournfully. "I know what you mean. I'm in an unrequited love trap."

Ah, unrequited love. Soraya had been there at the age of twelve, when she had a crush on one of her tennis coaches. She used to follow him around like a lovesick puppy but, for some inexplicable reason, he never felt the same way.

Soraya blinked blearily at Niloofar, who was also beginning to feel the effects of the wine. "What's going on, babe?"

"I think I love this guy, but I don't think he loves me back," Niloofar said. "I'm going to run away to a convent and become a nun. Is it really better to have loved and to have lost than to have never loved at all?"

Dante watched her intensely. "I'm not so sure. What's so good about having loved someone with all your heart, then losing that happiness. Why is that better than never having felt love at all?"

"But why are you talking about loving someone with all your heart when you've only just met this guy?" Soraya said, her head on one side. "Unless it's love at first sight, which I doubt even exists."

Niloofar shrugged. "Why can't we choose the people we fall in love with? Then we could prevent ourselves from going through all this heartache and rejection."

"If only," Dante murmured quietly to himself. "I mean, why is it that we almost always fall for the wrong guy?"

Soraya raised her eyebrows. "You're asking me? I'm the Professor of Falling in Love with the Wrong Guy."

Refilling her glass after opening another bottle, Niloofar sighed expansively. On the sidelines, Anya watched as she continued talking.

"I'm never going to fall in love again, never ever. Never."

Soraya wondered why it was that whenever women had a bad experience, they would say "I'm never going to fall in love again." Maybe it had a lot to do with them not wanting to get hurt again. Maybe they are protecting themselves by making such silly remarks. Soraya had lost count of the number of times she had said it herself. She was growing more sober even though she was knocking back wine as though it was water. For some reason, the light-hearted conversation with her friends was becoming annoying. What would have previously amused her now sounded like an out-of-tune song. Here she was, in a tiny apartment, alone and out of her depth, and yet her friends were carrying on as though nothing had changed. Which, in their case, was true.

But her life had been turned upside down, Soraya thought. She was feeling very vulnerable, but it seemed as though it was just one more joke. One more piece of gossip.

Patiently, she turned to Niloofar. "I'm sure you'll meet someone else."

"Two years! I've been single for two years!" she wept.

Sighing, Anya leaned towards Niloofar.

"*Dahling*, come out with me. We'll go to some bars and I'll find you another man. Forget this silly boy; he's no good for you. He's clearly not making you feel any better. You don't need that." She turned back to Soraya. "And you can come with us too."

"I can find my own man."

"Hah! You've got a fucking deadline, *dahling*!" Anya snapped, her patience finally giving way. "And what are you doing about it? Nothing! A man won't just walk into your life. You have to find him, or your family will – and that should get you moving if nothing else does."

Irritated, but determined not to take offence, Soraya took in a deep breath. "Did I tell you what they said the other day? Not only have my mother and grandmother nagged me about my roots showing, but they apparently also think I'm letting myself go everywhere! They enrolled me in a 'Personal Improvement Program!' to knock me into shape even before they gave me my wedding deadline. Even though I haven't actually found the groom yet!"

Unable to stop herself, Niloofar laughed.

"The day before I left home, they showed me an itinerary. It consisted of an incredibly expensive monthly laser hair removal treatment." Anya laughed, as Soraya continued: "A block booking for monthly visits to get my eyebrows shaped; regular appointments for manicures and pedicures; as well as facials 'to work on my dull skin.' And they want to sign me up with a personal trainer to tone up my body! Thanks so much! Way to make me feel better about myself!"

"I could get Angelo to do your highlights," Dante perked up. "Your mother said I could."

"My mother!"

He shrugged. "She came into the salon. She told me and Angelo all about you and your romances, you naughty girl!"

Soraya stared at him, baffled. "I don't know what you're talking about."

Slyly, Dante swirled his wine around his glass, giving her a sideways look.

"What do you mean? Stop being so coy. I heard from your mother and grandmother that you have all these men flying in from London and New York."

"It's news to me."

Confused, Dante put down his glass. "You mean to tell me you have no idea what I'm talking about?"

"No, no idea."

"Your family said there were all these gorgeous men, flying in from all round the world to meet you."

"My God! What men?"

"But your mother said there was only one man who was special to you."

"What!"

"And that we would soon hear of a proposal. You can tell us, Soraya. You can trust us. My little princess is getting married at last! Bambina!" He cupped Soraya's face like she was a puppy and shook it affectionately. "You can tell us. You can tell."

"There's nothing to tell! She made it all up! I don't know what my mother – or my grandmother – are up to. No one's getting married."

"Confess, my little princess. Confess!" He was still cupping her face.

"What the hell are you talking about?"

"Your husband to be. And there will be one very soon, I think." Dante wiggled his finger at her. "But first they have to be interviewed by your uncle, I hear, eh? He is evaluating them first, eh? And I hear a million-dollar dowry as well!"

"Jesus!" Niloofar exclaimed. Anya burst out laughing as they all stared at Soraya.

It was obvious from her face that she hadn't heard about the dowry. One million dollars. Was that really the way to get the right husband? Stunned, Soraya knew that it would bring all sorts of suitors out of the woodwork. Her mind blurred at what she had just heard. Her mother had been talking about all these suitors, but she didn't realize that there was a price on her body. Also, why the rush? Why this sudden hurried activity? What the hell had precipitated it? What had someone said or done?

The clouds in her mind parted as Soraya suddenly realized what must have happened. Her mother had made up a proposal story to impress Persian society. The rushed deadline had been put into motion to save her mother's humiliation! That was why a man had to be found so quickly. Some poor, unsuspecting guy flown in to fulfil Anahita's reckless prediction. And her uncle was in on it too, offering her up on a plate, with a million-dollar price tag!

Simmering with anger, Soraya glanced at her friends. So, her mother had been talking to Dante, had she? And Dante had been talking about her behind her back. How long had her private affairs been common knowledge? And why hadn't Dante mentioned it before?

"You never said you'd been talking to my mother."

"She just came into the salon."

"But you didn't tell me."

"I'm telling you now, bambina!" he almost screeched.

"Couldn't you have called me?" Soraya persisted. "I mean, if we hadn't all met up tonight, when would you have told me?"

"*Dahling*," Anya drawled. "Stop being paranoid."

"Paranoid?" Soraya shot back. "He's talking behind my back and he doesn't tell me, and you think that's paranoid?" She turned back to Dante. "You're my friend, Dante. I listen to you going on and on about Angelo. You could show some interest in what's happening to me."

He was on his feet in a second.

"Show some interest? I'm looking after your dog!" he hissed. "That's cruel, Soraya."

"I'm sorry."

"We went apartment hunting together!"

"I know, I know. I said I was sorry." Soraya wondered if she had overreacted. "It's just hard hearing that you'd been talking to my mother."

"Have you ever tried silencing your mother? I can't put my fucking hand over her mouth, bambina!" He sat down again in a fluster. "So, who is this man?"

Soraya sighed, draining her glass. "I swear there's no man. No fiancé. No proposal."

Dante's eyes widened. "Nothing!"

"Nothing. But there will be."

"You have someone in mind?" Niloofar asked, intrigued.

"No. Not yet." Soraya's voice hardened. "But I'll tell you one thing – I will choose the man I marry."

"It's not the choosing that's hard," Niloofar said prophetically, "it's the finding and keeping that sucks."

Three Months Until the Deadline

EIGHT

On the first day of the second month of her deadline, Soraya staggered home after a particularly bad day with Chloe at the office. Hurrying into her apartment, she noticed Jenny's apartment door was slightly open. She peeked through and noticed her landlady sitting quietly at the kitchen window. There was an air of sadness about her. She initially went to duck out of sight. Then, remorseful, she gently knocked on the door. Smiling, Jenny waved, gestured for Soraya to come in, and began making her a coffee. Her conversation was light-hearted and good natured, but when she sat down Soraya could see how swollen her ankles were already. She wondered how she was managing to cope with facing the imminent birth alone.

"Have they given you a date?"

She nodded. "The 31st."

Oh my God, Soraya thought, the same date as her deadline. How weird was it to have two women, living next door to each other, under pressure to deliver on the same day?

"Have you got a name for the baby?"

Jenny paused, fighting her emotions. "My husband wanted Adam if it's a boy – after him – or Fleur if it's a girl."

"Pretty," Soraya remarked. She paused for a moment. "Is your mother going to help you out?"

"No, my parents are divorced, and my mother remarried," Jenny explained, passing Soraya some cake. "She lives in Europe now."

"But surely she'd want to be with you."

"We don't get on."

"Yeah, that happens in families."

"But I like having you around," Jenny volunteered sincerely. "I like hearing your music and seeing your friends calling by. I did want to ask you something, though."

"Sure, go ahead."

"What are you actually doing here?"

Wrong-footed, Soraya paused for a long moment. "I'm a working girl, living in LA."

"But you come from money," Jenny said evenly. "That much is obvious. I was wondering if you'd had to leave home for some reason?"

Not wanting to get drawn into the subject of the deadline and the inevitable questions about how long she would be staying, Soraya sighed.

"Let's just say I've had a falling out with my family."

"Family," Jenny said simply. "Well, I hope that whatever the problem is you're able to resolve it."

And Soraya realized then that her problem was solvable, not like Jenny's. Nothing could bring back her husband or stop the birth of her child. How simple and downright silly Soraya's problem would seem to her.

But then, Jenny, feeling that she might have said too much, brightened up.

"You want to have a bite to eat with me?"

"Can I take a raincheck on that? I don't feel much like company tonight. Had a hell of a day." Smiling, Soraya made her excuses and left. As she walked across next door, Jenny waved, but behind the smile was something Soraya couldn't quite grasp and didn't fully understand.

After an early night, her alarm went off, jolting her awake at seven o'clock. For a moment, Soraya lay in bed thinking how much she would love to call in sick. She even allowed herself to daydream about bumping into a handsome, eligible man in the pasta aisle of Whole Foods. But the fantasy didn't gel, and her mind turned back to her list of exes, hoping against hope that there might be someone she still cared about. It was only when Soraya thought of Jean-Luc that she jerked awake, forcing herself out of bed one limb at a time – first her right leg, then her right arm, and then, eventually, her whole body.

Yawning, she dragged herself to the bathroom. She washed her face, brushed her teeth, and finally got dressed, shivering throughout. Putting her hand against the window, she frowned. It was freezing. There was no way in hell she was going to tolerate the air conditioning in the office on a day like this.

Slipping into her one and only pair of warm boots, she told herself she'd change into her shoes when she got into work. If it wasn't too cold. It got so chilly in the basement she could feel the cold in her bones. It was an unusually cold winter for LA. It must be climate change. Smiling, Soraya imagined rocking up to work in a fur coat. Chloe would be too stupid to understand it was a fake, and she would probably throw red paint all over it.

Tying back her hair, Soraya glanced ruefully at the unused straighteners she had bought. What a waste of money. She could have bought food instead. Opening her wallet, she checked her cash and frowned. If she stopped at Ralphs on the way home from work, she could pick up something a little less expensive for dinner. Preferably something she could microwave. Soraya hadn't mentioned it to her friends, but along with the hair straighteners, the iron, and the ticket that had jammed in the machine at the train station, the oven had turned on her too. Soraya had inadvertently set the timer for 7am, instead of 7pm, and gone for a nap. By 9.15, the apartment smelled of burnt chicken. She had snapped awake, running into the hallway holding a black carcass that emanated grey smoke. If Jenny had noticed, she was too polite to comment. For her supper that night, Soraya had a peanut butter and banana sandwich.

But there were only so many peanut butter sandwiches a woman could eat, and cereal lost its appeal after eating it every evening for weeks. In the end, Soraya decided she would conquer the everyday objects people took for granted. Gradually, she worked out the technical properties of the oven. A day later, flushed with success, she decided to hang a picture on the wall. After looking around she had found the electric drill under the kitchen sink. Curious, she stared at it, and wondered. She even plugged it in. But some god was looking out for her – before she plunged the drill into the wall, Mark Tehrani called round.

He was the only person in whom Soraya confided her many slip ups. As he entered, she was standing with the drill in her hand.

"There are easier ways to kill yourself," he said lightly, glancing at the wall. "What are you about to do?"

"Drill a hole."

"There?" he had asked, pointing to the wall.

"Yes, why not?"

Patiently, he took the drill out of her hand. "Because there's likely to be a water pipe there." He sighed, "Please don't drill into the walls. If you have any DIY that needs doing, ask me."

"But I want to be independent."

"Independent? Or electrocuted?"

Her thoughts returning to the present, Soraya said goodbye to him, leaving him with the drill poised, and headed out to go to work. On the street, it was so chilly the car windows were almost covered in ice. Soraya thought longingly of her own Mercedes. If she were still living at home, she could be snug in the driver's seat now with the heater turned up to the max. Public transport – once one of her few means of showing defiance – had lost its allure now that it had become routine. She made a mental note to finally start up that new Uber account.

Half an hour later, Soraya was standing in the marketing and sales office while Chloe bored everyone to death about a new account. Soraya took notes patiently and nodded politely to a good-looking man who was watching her across the boardroom. Her mind wandered to the inevitable: Was he married? Was he successful? Was he available?

Jesus, Soraya thought, as she walked back down to the basement office fifteen minutes later. She was obsessed. But then again, who wouldn't be with a deadline and a dowry on their head? Praying that Chloe had opened the shutters to let in some daylight, Soraya entered the office. It was pitch black, no lights were on, the shutters closed from the day before. Flicking on a light and grateful that her boss was going to be out of the office for a while, Soraya sat down and spent the morning preparing some PR for cookery manuals. But the silence didn't last, as Chloe walked in an hour later.

Soraya tried a smile. "Is there anything I can help you with?"

She was blanked for her trouble. Soraya asked her three more times and Chloe ignored her all three times.

Finally, she spoke.

"Did you talk to The Director?"

"Who?"

"Little Miss Innocent," she said meanly. "At the meeting, did you talk to The Director?"

"No, I don't know who he is."

"Well, when you do know, don't bother him. He doesn't want to have his time wasted by temporary staff. Even little girls running around in short skirts." She paused, picking up her bag. "I have to go out again. There's a list of things I want done, so get on with it." Pointing to her desk she narrowed her eyes at Soraya, her tone venomous. "I can't believe you're a friend of Vince's. Vince, of all people," she sneered. She walked out, leaving Soraya sitting with her mouth hanging open.

Fucking cheek! Soraya stared into the air as Chloe's feet tapped away up the stairs. She should have retaliated and told her what she thought. After all, she should be the one to be surprised that Vince would touch the likes of Chloe. Although, knowing Vince, it would only have been for sex. But perhaps Chloe didn't know that. Perhaps she thought – could she be that stupid? – that he was a one-woman man? That she could charm her way back into his bed?

Taking in a deep breath, Soraya pulled her notepad towards her. She hated the job. Worse still, she resented her family for putting a price on her head. But every time she missed home, every time she felt lonely in her miniature little apartment, every time she longed to see her mother or uncle, all she had to do was remember what they had done to her and then all homesickness evaporated. As though no man would marry her without being paid! What an insult!

Soraya's anger gave way to a sudden flush of reason. But who could blame them? All her relationships had been failures. Perhaps selling her off was the only way?

"Oh, grow up!" Soraya told herself, turning back to her notepad.

She would find a man in three months. It was possible, but only if she concentrated and put her mind to it.

Half an hour later, The Director came down into the basement and unexpectedly took the seat next to Soraya. He was far too good-looking to be in this job. That chiseled jawline! The dark, slicked back hair; those piercing blue eyes. Damn, he smelled good. What was that fragrance? Allure by Chanel? Remembering what Chloe had said, Soraya ignored him and kept working. The last thing she needed was more grief from her boss. Chloe would never believe that she hadn't encouraged the top man. After all, he was quite handsome. But the wedding band was off-putting. She didn't get involved with married men – it was a no-go area. They were complicated, they never left their wives, and the women always wound up hurt.

Hoping that The Director was waiting for Chloe, Soraya pretended to be intensely involved in her work.

"Hi there," he said nonchalantly.

She guessed she had to say something back. "Hi."

"Working hard?" he said with a gorgeous smile.

"Uh huh," Soraya muttered.

"Are you enjoying your job?"

Soraya realized he wasn't going anywhere anytime soon. She was stuck. Somebody save me, please! She thought. Phone ring now!

But the phone didn't ring. Instead, Chloe walked in. She entered, paused, and stared at Soraya and The Director. Her eyes flickered and she switched her attention to the other office assistant, Madison, who handed her some messages. Relaxing, Soraya breathed a sigh of relief as she watched Chloe and The Director move into another office.

Having seen the exchange, Madison walked over, curious. "Hey, what was all that about?"

"Thanks for rescuing me!"

She smiled slyly. "You know The Director likes you right?"

"No! Anyway, he's married!"

"I saw the way he was checking you out just now."

"He wasn't."

"He was!" Madison laughed. "What are you going to do about it?"

Soraya stared at her colleague. "Nothing. He's married and that's that. I don't want more complications in my life."

"You know that he's Chloe's property, right?"

"Huh?"

"I caught them fucking in the stationery cupboard once. I mean, we all know that Chloe's sex mad, but she's also got The Director as randy as a bull," Madison went on casually. "I'd watch my step if I were you. Just get on with your work and keep out of The Director's way. Well out of the way."

Jesus, what would Madison have to say if she knew what was really going on? It would be office gossip in no time – unless Vince had already filled Chloe in, and everyone knew about the fucking deadline! Calm down, Soraya told herself, just keep calm. But when The Director began sending her emails later, Soraya realized that Madison was right about him liking her. Why else would he email? Just to be friends? Hardly.

As Soraya was leaving work, The Director – The Married Director – came over and winked at her.

"We're all having some drinks later. Will you join us? It should be a fun night."

"I'll have to see." Soraya said evasively, "I'm going out with a friend."

"Well, try to come even if it's just for one drink. It's at the hotel bar."

Typical. Damn typical. He was handsome, had a good job, and just happened to be married! Just her luck, Soraya thought. She picked up her bag and heading out to catch her train. He was off limits. And if that wasn't enough, he was also Chloe's bit on the side. God, she was a busy girl, Soraya thought sarcastically. What with Vince and The Director, it was a miracle she found time to be a bitch. But it did explain Chloe's antagonism towards her.

Walking down the street, Soraya cast her mind back to the deadline and the damn dowry. Talk about East meets West. Here she was in the middle of LA, being bid for like a racehorse. The pressure! It was all getting too much. Making her grand gesture had been dramatic, but here she was, one month down the line, tired, frustrated and beginning to panic. It wasn't brave, or even funny; in fact, it was starting to look rather pathetic.

Just as Soraya was about to enter the Metro station, her cell rang. It was The Director. Should she pick up or not? Did she need any more complications in her life? To pick up or not to pick up? Oh, what the hell, Soraya thought recklessly, I'll pick up.

Before she could say anything, he spoke. "Hey you, where are you? Had second thoughts about meeting your friend? Want to join me? It's quite fun, and harmless. All the guys from work are here."

It was work, Soraya thought, and she wasn't doing anything else, so why not?

After a frosty reception, where she had to ignore Madison's smirks and Chloe's glacial stare, Soraya regretted her decision. Ten minutes later, she left The Director's group in the bar and sat separately in the lounge, drinking vodka on ice. But it wasn't long before The Director joined her, sliding into the adjacent seat. He then casually put his arm around her. Soraya was too surprised to react. Instead, she pretended she hadn't noticed. After all, Chloe was her direct boss, but The Director was the bosses' boss. He could have her fired, and God knows she needed to keep her job. Apparently requiring no response or interaction, The Director talked easily. Then, out of the blue, he leaned in and kissed her.

Horrified, Soraya pulled back. "What the hell!"

"I'm sorry. I don't know what I was thinking," he whispered. "I got carried away in the moment. You're amazing."

"And you're married!"

"I know. It's just I've never met anyone like you. You're incredible."

"And you're still married!" she practically shouted. "I'm sorry but I can't do this, I should go."

With that Soraya walked away and got into the first cab at the stand outside the hotel. Director or not, he was married. What she needed was a husband, not a fucking migraine.

But after a restless night in the apartment feeling cold and hungry, Soraya arrived at the office the next morning and was immediately accosted by Madison who was desperate to be briefed on the night before.

"No fucking way!" she yelled. "He did that?"

"Shhh! Keep your voice down," Soraya said anxiously. "I don't want the entire workplace knowing what happened."

"Oops, sorry. So, what are you going to do?"

"Nothing, of course. I'm going to keep my head low and avoid him."

Fascinated, Madison pushed her. "Has he tried calling you since?"

"He sent me a message this morning apologizing, but I didn't reply."

"He's so got the hots for you!"

"Stop it, Madison. Nothing is ever going to happen. Anyway, I'll talk to you at lunch."

Returning to her desk, Soraya tried to get stuck into her work, but it just wasn't happening. She couldn't concentrate. Two hours later, a handwritten letter had been placed on Soraya's desk. It was from The Director.

Soraya,

In all the forty-two years of being in this world, never in my life have I felt more alive! It's never been like this with my wife. I don't want to leave these feelings unexplored forever, otherwise I'll regret not opening up my heart to you. I know I'm asking for a lot, but please would you consider taking this chance with me?

Soraya sighed. She didn't believe it was the first time he'd sent such a 'beautiful' and 'touching' letter, but she needed this job and had to play the game. She emailed him back straight away:

To: director@bhh.com

I'm very touched by your heartfelt letter, but I can't be the person or the reason to break up a marriage. Had the circumstances been different, I might have taken this chance with you, but I couldn't live with the guilt of exploring a relationship with a man who's already involved. It's not in my nature to embark on a journey that's already very complicated. I need to start on a fresh page. I hope you understand where I am coming from. I simply couldn't cope with the pressure.

She looked incredulously around the office. Jesus, what a set up. It didn't take a genius to work out that The Director made a play for every new employee. No wonder Chloe was so antsy, having to keep tabs on her lover and her job.

There were many things Soraya wasn't sure about, but one thing was certain. She never got involved with anyone who wore a wedding ring. She wouldn't be able to live with herself if she broke up a marriage. Her conscience would have eaten her up alive.

NINE

Amir sat on the comfortable couch in Ralph Lauren, trying on casual jackets while Mark Tehrani scrolled through his emails on his cell. Suddenly Amir flung off his jacket.

"Fucking hell! She's driving me out of my mind!"

Mark looked up. "Who?"

"My damn sister. Day in and day out, night in and night out – all I hear is 'Soraya.' Where is she? What is she doing? Has she found a man?" He rolled his eyes, leaning towards Mark. "So, has she found a husband yet?"

"My latest information is that she hasn't."

Amir looked at him slyly. "Any message for me?"

"She said she loves you."

"She's fucking killing me!" he roared, then lowered his tone. "But no husband?"

"No husband."

"You see!" Amir replied, with not a little triumph. "And the deadline is drawing nearer every day. I told you, Mark – in the end, her family will have to find the right man for her." He picked up the navy jacket again and admired himself in it. His paunch may have been growing and his temples getting greyer, but he had a great complexion for a man of his age.

"You got anyone in mind?"

"Anahita wants to put someone forward."

"Soraya won't listen to anything her mother says."

"She won't know it's coming from her mother!" Amir replied. "Anahita's arranged it so that this young man – Brian – will be introduced via her cousin, Kam."

"You think it will work?"

"It has to! There's only so much I can take of this," Amir barked. "I got married, had kids. It was easy. I don't recall it being a big deal. But with Soraya? Now it's a big deal."

Mark shrugged. "Any others in the running?"

"There's her ex, Jean-Luc. He's not a frontrunner, but a possibility.

There's Richard Parker who we all adore, and well… we all liked Michael. But let's face it, he's just too young to want to settle down."

"You have a list?" Mark was taken aback.

"Of course, someone has to be thinking clearly."

Mark sat back on the couch to try and digest what was happening. He had wondered if Amir was really serious about the deadline, but now he was sure he was deadly serious.

"Amir, just out of curiosity, why are you all so concerned about Soraya's personal life? Because you want her to be happy?"

"She's my favorite niece!"

"She's your only niece," Mark replied, smiling wryly. "And don't change the subject. Are you concerned about her happiness, or because you're following tradition?"

"You're half Iranian yourself!"

"Half," Mark agreed. "But my mom was American, and I married an American girl."

Amir was still looking at himself in the mirror.

"Look, it's got a lot to do with being Iranian, but it's not just that. The family really think it's about time Soraya stopped changing boyfriends and settled down."

"And you don't think she'll find the right man on her own?"

"Well, she hasn't so far, has she?"

"She's still young."

"Almost thirty soon!" Amir replied, turning to his friend. "You and I both know how things work. She needs to be settled with a family. It's the way things are. Besides," he added ruefully, "Anahita's driving me out of my fucking mind over all this."

"But pressuring Soraya only drove her out of the house," Mark reminded him. "You should admire the stand she's taken."

"I'd admire her getting married a lot more," Amir replied. "You know women. They need to be told what to do. And Soraya is the same. This act of defiance will soon lose its charm."

"But look at it from her point of view. You're making her sound like a commodity. As though you're giving her away to the highest bidder," Mark said carefully. "What makes you think that offering such a large dowry will attract the right man? It might attract the wrong type. A man who's only interested in Soraya for her money."

Piqued, Amir took off the jacket and sat down next to his oldest friend. "I want the best for Soraya. She can be very stubborn, and she always picks unsuitable men."

"And offering a million-dollar dowry will bring Prince Charming?"

"It might."

"But only if you approve of him?"

"Of course."

"So, Soraya might end up marrying someone her family approves of regardless of her happiness? But then again, what if she chooses to be with someone she loves, and you disapprove of them? That would also make her unhappy. This is a no-win situation."

Mark paused. He had to be careful not to antagonize Amir. They were close and had been for fifteen years, probably because Mark had his own successful business and family life. He was no threat to Amir, so he could speak his mind. But, on the subject of Soraya, he could see that emotions were running high. It didn't take a mastermind to work out how much Amir's sister was hassling him. He knew what Anahita's reckless lie had set in motion, and he could easily imagine the pressure that Persian society was putting on the whole family because of the phantom proposal. But that didn't mean that he approved of the deadline or the dowry bait.

Having known Soraya since she was nineteen years old, Mark had seen her insecurities, as well as her fights with her overbearing mother and her well-meaning but difficult uncle. Her determination to live as an independent woman was admirable, but he knew only too well that Persian girls found it hard to shake off their heritage, and that Soraya had been longing to marry since he had known her. Thinking back, Mark remembered a painful dinner he had with the family a couple of years earlier.

The evening had gone well, until Anahita suddenly turned to Soraya and asked whether there were any nice men at work.

"Not really," she had replied unenthusiastically.

"Well, we have someone in mind for you," her mother announced. Mark hardly dared look at Soraya.

"Yes, he's very nice," her grandmother chimed in.

"He works for me. Michael. I just employed him," Amir said.

Soraya frowned skeptically. "And what's wrong with him?"

Anahita laid down her knife and fork, smiling coolly. "Nothing's wrong with him darling – he's tall, good looking, and earns a good salary."

"But, Mother, your idea of good looking and mine are two totally different things. I really don't want to be set up again. It's starting to get tragic."

"You haven't even given him a chance."

"Mother please, I'll find my own guy."

"Like the last one you found?" Anahita countered. She was getting into her stride and forgetting that Mark was there. "Why do you always go for the weird ones? Why can't you just find a nice guy?"

"What do you mean 'weird'?"

"Well, if I remember correctly, the last one looked gay."

Soraya's voice rose. "Oh! Come on! Hans was a lovely person. Okay, so he was slightly metrosexual, but he wasn't a bad person."

"What's metrosexual?" Amir asked.

"It's a guy who's in touch with his feminine side and really looks after himself."

Her uncle rolled his eyes. It's official, Soraya thought, he's never going to take me seriously now!

"You either pick the ones who have no money," Anahita went on, "or they're dumb. Or completely strange."

Mark felt uncomfortable about the family focusing their attention on Soraya's woeful taste in men. He'd always had a soft spot for her. They have always had a way of poking fun at each other without it being taken offensively. And they could talk to each other, which is more than he could do with Riley since his son's death.

"Look, I don't see what the big deal is here," Soraya soldiered on. "Hans was nice, but it just didn't work out. What's wrong with the other guys I went out with?"

"Where do we start?" Amir said mockingly.

Trying to soothe the waters, her grandmother chimed in: "We only say these things because we love you."

Here we go, Mark thought; here comes the emotional guilt card.

"And I don't want you to make the same mistakes I made," Anahita warned, patting her immaculate hair. "I want you to have a good future and to be able to give your kids everything. And yes, some of it does have to do with our culture. We're Iranian at the end of the day, even though you were brought up here."

Though he remained sensibly mute, Mark was only too aware of the pressure Soraya was under. After all, he had seen it for himself at the Persian functions they had all attended – the mothers looking at Soraya oddly because she was on her own. But he was surprised to see how much Amir cared about society's opinion. Anahita, yes, but Amir? It had given Mark another insight into his friend's character: a flaw he had never suspected before.

His thoughts returning to the present, Mark realized that, although Amir loved his niece, he regarded all women as foolish sub-humans who had to be controlled. In Amir's eyes he was doing the best for Soraya because she had no father to guide her. The dowry was his way of saying, "Look what I can offer you. A lovely wife and money too. Look what a catch Soraya is."

But Mark could see that this set-up was demeaning. She didn't want to be seen as a good catch or as a possession, but as a woman. No wonder she walked out, Mark thought. No wonder she wanted to prove a point. But could she hold out? Could Soraya really live without her family's support and find a man in a matter of months?

One month down, less than three to go.

"Is she dating anyone?" Amir asked, walking to the counter to pay for the jacket.

"No, not yet."

"She will be soon. When her cousin Kam passes on Brian's email address, that'll set the ball in motion."

Mark frowned. "You don't think Soraya will suspect her mother's hand in this? Or yours?"

"Why should she? She adores Kam, they've always been close. The introduction will seem natural coming from him," Amir reassured his friend. "Soraya will never suspect us."

"God help you if she ever finds out," Mark said wryly. "She's not the same girl who left home. It's not been long, but you'd be surprised how much Soraya's changed."

Amir turned to look at him. "You make an excellent go-between, Mark," he said slowly. "Very few men have the ability to remain detached like you."

TEN

From: Brian1993@yahoo.com

Hi Soraya,

You don't know me but your cousin, Kam, suggested I reach out to you. He has been very persistent for good reason and speaks very highly of you. So (awkwardness aside), hello, my name is Brian. I'm 28, I live in San Francisco, and I'm a corporate lawyer, but I visit LA every few weeks. I enjoy travelling, reading, eating out, sports, and belly-dancing. Just kidding about the last one! But I remain open to it one day. I think I'd look good in a belly-dancing outfit! I hope this finds you well and look forward to hearing from you.

Brian

Soraya read the email again. It was an introduction from Kam, which meant it was safe. Untouched by her mother's or uncle's hand. Worth looking into. She liked the fact that Brian had a sense of humor. She took a look at the attached pictures. The first photo was blurry but the second one was much clearer. Okay, so he passed the test in the looks' category, and he seemed to be funny. Maybe she would email him back, but not for a day or so at least.

That afternoon, Chloe lost some information on the computer and all hell broke loose. Her screams were so piercing they could be heard in the outer office.

Soraya glanced at Madison. "Jesus."

"Oh, you've seen nothing yet," Madison grinned. Chloe suddenly emerged and walked over to Soraya's desk. In one swift movement, she slammed down her fist.

"You!" she hissed. "This is all your fault."

"I haven't touched your computer!"

"Shut up! I should never have hired you, but I did, as a favor to a friend. But you're a damn idiot! You just laze around doing nothing."

"Hey!"

"Don't interrupt!" Chloe snapped, bending down towards Soraya. "You think I don't know what's going on?"

She turned to Madison and jerked her head to the door to indicate that she should leave, which she did, hurriedly. Then Chloe turned back to Soraya. She was blazing, her eyes sharp, and her voice thin with spite, with all the pent-up malice of the previous ten days pouring out of her.

"So, the poor little rich girl decided to play at real life for a few months."

Damn Vince and his big mouth, Soraya thought bitterly.

"Why? Because her family wants her to marry a rich man they choose. And are even prepared to pay some fool a million fucking dollars for the privilege!"

"What the hell!"

Soraya was silenced at once.

"And you think you can do better on your own? Stupid bitch!" Chloe's voice was thick with rage. "Vince asked me to help you out, and I am. But I don't have to like it. Once your self-imposed exile is over, girl, you're out of here." She turned to go, then turned back. "Oh, and don't bother thinking you can leave and get another job for the next few weeks. I won't give you a reference. And believe me, employers out there won't give you the time of day."

"Why are you talking to me like this?" Soraya snapped back. "I haven't done anything to you."

"You've irritated me," Chloe replied, "The way you look, talk, dress. You think you're a fucking princess, and you've even tried to get your claws into The Director."

"That's not true!"

"He's off limits to you, girl. He's married."

"But not to you!" Soraya spat back. "I don't want him, or Vince. Because that's what this is all about, isn't it? Your jealousy."

Chloe's face turned puce with rage. "Jealous of you? Do me a favor!"

"Liar!" Soraya retorted. She knew she should shut up and keep her job. She needed it. But, on the other hand, she was damned if she was going to let Chloe walk all over her. She was tired, short on patience, and rapidly learning to stand up for herself. "You've been jealous from the moment I walked in."

"How dare you! Your family's world might revolve around you but in the real world you're nobody. No skills, no particular talents, just one more working girl among thousands."

Soraya's hands were clenched tight. "You can't talk to me like this!"

"Oh, but I can. Because I'm paying your salary, which is paying for your apartment. You need this job. That's the way life goes, sweetheart. Normal working girls have to put up with a lot of shit every day." She looked Soraya up and down. "Keep away from The Director."

"He flirted with me!"

"Hah!" Chloe snapped. "Nothing is ever your fault, is it? It's all 'poor me, poor little me.' Well, if I were you, I'd get home as fast as my feet could carry me. You want to know why? Because you're not special enough to strike out on your own. You need a family to tell you what to do, what to think and who to marry." She smiled coldly. "Poor Soraya, I'm afraid that when your deadline is up you may well have discovered just how useless you are."

"Really? You think so?"

Noticing the warning tone in her voice, Chloe should have backed off, but was too stupid to see that she had overplayed her hand. She continued imperiously.

"You should be grateful you have a job."

"And how do you keep yours, Chloe? You're nothing but a whore, putting it about. Even sleeping with The Director and screwing him in the stationery cupboard."

Chloe reeled back. "You're fired!"

"No, I'm not." Soraya replied, her voice low. "Fire me, Chloe, and I'll tell Vince all about you. And you don't want that, do you? I'll tell him not to touch you with a ten-foot pole. That you're sleeping with The Director and every other man in the building." She stared into her employer's ashen face. "I'll say that I read a note from your doctor saying you have an STI."

"You bitch!"

"It takes one to know one!" Soraya replied. "Now get off my back, Chloe, or I swear you'll be the one who comes off worse."

Triumphant, Soraya stared after her boss as she swept out of the room. Rage choked her, along with another, unwelcome, emotion: doubt. Chloe had bluntly stated what her friends had been too kind to point out: she was going to fail. Staring down at her desk, Soraya clenched her trembling hands. She felt humiliated and vulnerable, but oddly focused. Chloe's contempt had shaken her but not scared her. And then Soraya realized something – that the more people expected her to fail, the more determined she was to succeed.

She would get to know Brian, and she would, even in her straightened circumstances, have a little gathering for her housewarming at the weekend. She couldn't afford a big splashy party, but she would invite her friends to celebrate with her. And she would make sure she included Richard, a long-time admirer, plus new-on-the-scene Brian, and Jean-Luc, the man who had broken her heart more times than she could count.

Time was marching on. Soraya's happiness was at stake, as well as her pride. It was time people respected her. Her family and the likes of Vince and Chloe obviously thought she was just a spoilt rich bitch – and maybe they had been right. After all, she had been indulged all her life. But not anymore. That afternoon, looking up at a blue LA sky, Soraya made herself a promise – however hard it got, she was going to succeed.

And then she began to type.

To: Brian1993@yahoo.com

It's interesting to say the least!

So, tell me more about your belly dancing. This I have to see. Do you have a pretty outfit? Now, a little about me: I'm 29, live in Brentwood, work in PR, I speak 4.5 languages (the 0.5 being Russian as I only took that up this year), I have been playing tennis since I was four, took up skiing a few years ago, and my mother thinks I need to go to rehab for my Instagram and text addiction!

How's life treating you in San Francisco?

S.

The first shot had been fired. The Cupid Index was back on the rise.

ELEVEN

Having just washed her hair, Anya was sitting on the side of her bed as she picked up her cell and called Soraya.

"Oh *dahling*, I'm so happy to hear your voice," she said when Soraya picked up. "I haven't heard from you in two days."

"I've been busy with my job."

"Are there any nice men for me there?"

Despite herself, Soraya smiled. "Anya, I haven't had sex since my last boyfriend. That's about a year now! If anyone should be feeling horny it should be me, not you. Now forget about men and concentrate!"

"Okay sweetie, calm down."

"Hang on a minute." Soraya reached for her laptop. "I just want to see if this guy has emailed me."

Anya laughed. "And you tell me that I'm the one who spends all my time thinking about men!"

"This is different. This one could be a potential husband, not a lover."

"Okay, point taken."

Excited, Soraya checked her emails. There was one from Brian. Slowly, she read it to Anya over the phone.

From: Brian1993@yahoo.com

Just got back from a conference in New York where I was meeting and partying with our clients. Good to be back in San Fran. The weather here is wonderful, and everyone is out. I'm quite lucky as I live within walking distance from my office so I'm immune to traffic. I like to hang out with friends on weekends and check out new restaurants and lounges. I enjoy surfing, running, hiking, and power yoga with a little Pilates fusion – yes, this is all wonderfully "California." I actually just started playing tennis again after stopping at the tender age of twelve to become a fish in the water with water polo and surfing. I only speak 2.75 languages, so I'm concerned about our back-up means of communication in case English and the others don't work out. I suppose we could always try our hand at mime!

Anya sniffed down the phone line. "How old is he, *dahling*?

"This is a guy my cousin knows. He's called Brian Zachary, he's American, and he's around my age."

"Too young. What does he do?"

"Lawyer."

"Is he rich?"

"How should I know?"

"Well, *dahling*, if he's poor why are you interested?" she said point blank.

"Because he seems nice! Anyway, you and I never see eye to eye when it comes to men." Soraya changed the subject deftly. "It's my housewarming on Saturday".

"I'll take you out!"

"No, I'm having some friends round to the apartment."

"The apartment?" Anya said disdainfully. "*Dahling*, we have to go to a club. Oh, I'm sorry. You can't afford it, can you? It must be terrible having no money."

The barb struck home. Anya's candor was beginning to rankle. Soraya wondered if she had always been the same way, or if she was only just noticing it. Had she ever been as callous and unfeeling?

"I can't take you all to a club," Soraya replied patiently, "so I want my friends to come here. Come on, Anya, enter into the spirit of the thing."

"But what if I don't agree with it?"

Soraya stiffened. "What exactly don't you agree with? Coming to the apartment? Or my being here at all?"

"You know what I think."

"You've made it pretty clear, Anya, but we're close friends. I would have thought that counted for something. Can't you support me? Every time I want to talk about the job or the apartment you change the subject."

"It's boring, *dahling*."

"Boring?" Soraya retorted. "I'm struggling here."

"So, go home and stop struggling." She replied, "You'll never catch a man being so serious about life, sweetie."

Holding her temper, Soraya ignored the comment. "Everyone's coming here around eight on Saturday. Is that okay with you?"

"If I must," Anya said, sighing with resignation. "If I must."

After ending the phone call, Soraya answered Brian's email.

To: Brian1993@yahoo.com

I'm not too familiar with San Francisco. I was there a few years ago. So, what other girly activities do you participate in other than yoga and Pilates? And which 2.75 languages? I took up Russian 4 months ago, which I believe I already told you. It's so hard but it really gets the brain ticking, and some of my closest friends are Russian so I get to practice with them. Do you travel to Europe for work? Don't suppose you're on Insta?

Almost immediately, Brian replied.

From: Brian1993@yahoo.com

Ha, yes! Yoga is the extent of my girlie-ness, although some people believe the idea of getting a good workout and finding "inner peace" with all female counterparts to be genius. But seriously, it's a great way to balance the stress of the working day and I actually enjoy the practice.

I speak Farsi, French, and Spanish. I used to be much better at French, having spent a few summers in Montpelier with my cousins when I was younger. I picked up a little Spanish from our maid and from travelling a bit around the country with friends, but I soon realized I needed a little more training in Argentina last month as no one spoke a word of English! My work takes me up and down the East Coast for client cases. And, like I said, I come to LA often. This coming weekend, in fact.

Ah yes, I am on Instagram. I avoided it for a long time but that's hard to maintain when everyone uses it. Shall we follow each other?

Aww! How cute is he? Soraya thought. The office was quiet. Chloe was out for the day, and Madison was smoking in the backyard. Her third cigarette in an hour. Thankful that she was alone, Soraya called Niloofar, who let the phone ring seven times before picking up.

"Hello?"

"Hey you! How are you?" Soraya said cheerfully. "How's your man?"

"Hey, honey! I'm good thanks. My man's good. Great actually."

"I thought you might be busy with him. I've left a few messages."

"Well, yeah, I was going to reply, but you know how things go. You get so busy. Actually, we're looking for a place together."

Stunned, Soraya winced. Oh no, so soon? Please don't get hurt again.

"But you said it was unrequited love?"

"Not so unrequited now," Niloofar said, laughing.

"But you've only been dating for, like, a few months!"

"I know, babe, but I have to move out of home as my dad wants to refurbish the house, and I'm tired of schlepping from my place to his all the time."

"I hear you. Whatever makes you happy."

"He makes me happy," Niloofar said. "He's so sweet. And I want to be with him so much."

God. Soraya should have felt excited for her friend, but instead she was bruised, seeing how quickly Niloofar had moved on with her life. The closeness she had enjoyed with Anya, Dante, and Niloofar seemed a distant memory. Was she becoming an outsider so soon? Had the clique excluded her? Not deliberately, but edging her out in subtle ways? Certainly, all the support that had been promised at first had evaporated. The phone calls had dropped off; the visits decreased. Their attitude spoke louder than words – what the hell are you doing?

"The reason I rang, babe," Soraya said, "is because I'm having some friends round on Saturday for a little housewarming. Can you come?"

"Try and stop me! Oh, but my man's away so I can't bring him." She said suddenly, remembering. "Is it just us girls?"

"Er, no."

"Soraya!" she said happily, "Have you met someone?"

"Maybe… Look, I'm serious about finding Mr Right, so I've started making some moves. I've invited Richard."

"He's always adored you." Niloofar said. There was relief in her voice. "His family are rich aristocrats, and he's an anesthetist."

Richard was a tall, lanky, awkward man; the type you'd usually find solo sipping a gin and tonic in the corner of the room or chatting with his mom.

"And his mother's very pushy!"

"Only because Richard's been unlucky in love. Mrs Parker just wants to see him settle down with someone nice. Like you, babe."

"Yeah, but I don't feel that way about him. Oh, and I've invited Jean-Luc."

"Are you crazy!" Niloofar said anxiously. "He's not good for you."

"I know," Soraya agreed, "but he was the big love of my life and having him there with this new guy around as well might help put things in perspective."

"What new guy?"

"He's called Brian Zachary. But before you get all excited, don't." Soraya warned Niloofar. "I always have my hopes up prior to meeting someone and end up disappointed."

"It doesn't always have to be disappointing."

Soraya wondered how Niloofar could say that after she had been through so many love crises. The triumph of hope over experience?

"So, you'll come to my little party? Around eight?"

"Can't stop me, babe!"

With a thumping heart, Soraya then emailed Brian.

To: Brian1993@yahoo.com

How lucky was your email? You said you're over here this weekend, and it's my housewarming on Saturday! Would you like to come to my place and hang out with my friends? It's not a big do. Just casual. Last year, I had a big party, courtesy of my mother. God knows, the arrangements took weeks and the restaurant had only allocated me a certain number of seats, and of course everyone wanted to come with girlfriends and friends, etc. Nightmare! It wasn't a wedding where everyone is required to bring a date. I only wanted to have all my good

friends there and it was chaos! I just drank myself into oblivion on the night and didn't worry who sat where! This will not be like that!

Anyway, let me know if you can make it.

S

The reply was immediate.

From: Brian1993@yahoo.com

Sounds great. Where and what time? Can't wait to meet you.

Brian

TWELVE

Amir looked at Mark Tehrani and narrowed his eyes as he considered what he had just been told. So, Soraya had made contact with Brian Zachary, had she? And he was coming to her housewarming party on Saturday. This was good. Another thought immediately followed as Amir remembered the conversation he'd had with his sister that morning.

"My baby's housewarming and she doesn't want to see me!" Anahita had wept. Her own mother disappeared into another room out of the way.

"If you want to see Soraya so much, ring her up and apologize."

"Me apologize?" Anahita snarled. "She walked out! It's Soraya who should apologize to me!" Her expression hardened. "So, what have you heard?"

"About what?"

"About Soraya! What else?"

"She's still working at her job."

"She is?"

"And she's paying the rent on her apartment."

Anahita had made a snorting sound. "I don't suppose she's keeping it tidy. Or eating well. And it's so cold; how do you know if that ghastly apartment is heated?"

"It's not ghastly."

Immediately her head spun round in his direction. "How do you know? Have you seen it?"

"I've been told. I explained before that Mark Tehrani has arranged for someone to watch out for Soraya."

"And report back to you?"

"No, they're reporting back to the United Nations."

She threw up her hands in exasperation. "Oh, you're impossible! Soraya is impossible! This whole family is impossible!"

Watching Mark put down the morning paper, Amir's thoughts returned to the present. He considered what he had been told about Soraya's progress. Not for the first time, he looked at Mark and wondered why he couldn't have been single. Amir couldn't have wanted anyone better than his friend for his niece. There would be an eleven-year age gap, but what was that in reality? Nothing. Mark didn't look older than thirty-five, he took care of himself, was handsome, smart, socially adept, and rich. And married. Off The List, Amir thought regretfully.

"So, Soraya's having a housewarming party?"

Nodding, Mark looked up. "Apparently only a few friends. She's invited Brian, as I said, and Richard Parker."

"I've always liked Richard." Amir said approvingly. "What do you think of him?"

Tactful as ever, Mark fudged the question. "Well, he's not got a lot of spirit."

"Soraya has spirit."

"Which is why she would be better with a stronger man."

"Like?"

Mark shrugged. "I haven't got anyone in mind. Have you?"

"There's always Jean-Luc," Amir said thoughtfully. "The asshole."

"Come on, Amir, you like him really. And he's an asshole your niece is very fond of." Mark paused. "Besides, you said he was still on The List."

"On and off."

Amused, Mark thought back to the night of the infamous Interview. Everyone in their immediate circle had known that Amir always took potential suitors aside and gave them a working over or, as it was euphemistically called, The Interview. When it became clear that Soraya had been in love with the gallant, attractive, and financially stable Frenchman, Amir had 'interviewed' Jean-Luc.

They had been at a party and Amir, spotting his prey, had dived in.

"So, Jean-Luc, how's business?" Amir Milani always went straight to business.

"It's not the best of times I have to be honest."

"Yes, I understand, everyone is suffering these days."

"Yes, it's tough."

"And what are your intentions with Soraya?"

Goddamn! Mark had thought. Amir is blunt. Jean-Luc is going to run straight out of the restaurant in a cold sweat. How could he ask him such a direct question?

"Er, what do you mean?" Jean-Luc said, trying to buy time for himself. Panic was detectable in his voice, which went as high as a schoolgirl's.

"I mean," Amir continued, "are you going to marry her or are you going to continue messing her about?"

Overhearing this, Anahita turned in Jean-Luc's direction.

Realizing he had been cornered, Jean-Luc shifted slightly in his seat. He needed to get to the ATM to buy more time, quick.

"Well, you know that I care for and respect your niece very much," he said, then paused.

"Yes?" Amir waited for more.

"But, you know, I'm not sure I am ready to settle down just yet. But when I am it will be with Soraya, no doubt. I love Soraya with all my heart, and I only want the best for her. Perhaps, in a few months' time I will be ready? There is no doubt in my mind that she is the one for me!"

Mark remembered with amusement how this had cut no ice with Amir.

"You do realize she has other suitors?"

Floundering, Jean-Luc blundered on. "Well, no I didn't know and obviously I would be very devastated if she got married. But do you want me to marry her when I am not ready and give her a hard time?"

"No, I would want you to marry her, love her, and respect her," Amir had replied evenly. "But if you can't promise to do that then I wouldn't want you to marry her at all."

Jean-Luc's accent became more and more pronounced as he grew more flustered.

"I do love her, I just don't want to hurt her like I have done in the past, for which I am very sorry about. I want to be absolutely sure that I can give her everything that she deserves in this life; I do not want to disappoint her again."

"Hah!"

Even from the sidelines, Mark winced. He knew what a jerk Jean-Luc had been with Soraya in the past, but watching the merciless grilling was painful. Like watching David and Goliath, except David had forgotten his sling and there was no stone in sight.

Amir was relentless. "Well, just think about it, Jean-Luc. You know we all think of you as family and you two get on so well. It would be a shame to throw it all away for the sake of a few more years of partying. You won't find another girl like Soraya. She's truly one of a kind."

"I know, and I would be an idiot to not marry her." Jean-Luc looked down at his plate and rummaged in his pasta. Still no sign of a sling. "But I'm scared that I will hurt Soraya again if I rush into something too quickly."

Without even looking in Amir's direction, Mark was able to read his friend's thoughts. Jean-Luc was out of the running – for now, at least.

Soraya had never loved anyone else as much as Jean-Luc. Boyfriends had come and gone. Some were liked by the family, some loathed, but no one had made the same impact. The Frenchman was always in the background.

Mark glanced over to Amir. "Does Soraya still love Jean-Luc?"

"He had his chance!"

"But does she still love him?"

"No, no!" Amir replied, waving his hand irritably. "Soraya thinks she does but, if a man who she liked came along and put a ring on her finger, Jean-Luc would be forgotten soon enough. Women always want the one they can't have."

"Women want the man they love."

"Do they? You married for love, Mark," Amir said. "But you were one of the lucky ones. Love never lasted long with Anahita. As for Soraya, a good stable marriage is what all women need. Love is a bonus."

Unaware that her every movement was being watched and reported back, Soraya was thinking about how she wanted to look her best for her housewarming. She had mentioned her cash flow problem to Dante, hoping he would offer his or Angelo's services, which he did. Not long after, Soraya found herself in the salon with her Maltese terrier, Prada, on her lap, and Dante sitting in the seat beside her while Angelo stared at her hair.

"Fuck!" he said in his strong Italian accent, picking up a strand and pulling a face. "What did you do with your hair?"

Flushing, Soraya waved her hand at him. "I tried to straighten it myself."

"What with? A corkscrew?"

"Soooooo," Dante interrupted, "I want all the gossip. Who are you going to marry? Angelo tells me your mother's been telling everyone—"

"—Damn it!" Soraya snapped. "Look, I don't know what she's been saying but it's all nonsense. I'm not marrying anyone."

"The deadline's off?"

"Unfortunately, the deadline is still on. I just haven't met anyone yet," Soraya shot back. "Honestly, it's enough to make me lose all interest in my love life."

"You've lost interest in men? Honey, maybe you should try it with a girl. What do you think?"

"I think you should shut up." She smiled to herself, wondering what she would do without Dante.

Super stylish, always dressed head to toe in black, and often found wearing a slim-fit pair of Prada trousers, black pointy shoes by Dolce and Gabbana, and a black Alexander McQueen shirt. He was one of her essential and eternal bastions; a friend she simply couldn't live without. And in the familiar surroundings of the salon, she felt comfortable for the first time since she had left home.

"Why do some men never grow up?" Soraya asked wistfully. "It seems that after a certain age – and I think that's about twenty-one – they just stop maturing. They may be in a body of a thirty-something year old, but their maturity levels haven't changed since they were twenty-one." She winced as Angelo tugged a knot out of her hair. "So why do some girls go for older men?"

"Money, bambina."

She blew out her cheeks. "Anya rarely dates a man a day under sixty-five unless he's exceptionally loaded and an aristocrat of some sort. I've met a few of the guys she's had relationships with. One had a belly and spat whenever he spoke, but took her to the best restaurants, bought her the latest Manolo Blahnik's, took her on fancy holidays, and maybe he was even good in bed."

"My, my! Tell me more."

"Another of her lovers was some kind of lord with bad teeth, but he managed to satisfy her in other ways – sexually, maybe; financially, probably. Personally, I'm starting to think that younger guys have less baggage and are less phobic about commitment."

"Unless they are Jean-Luc."

She nodded. "Jean-Luc is your typical Class A asshole. Arrogant, mean, and likes to play infinite mind games. I don't know how I put up with him. He would phone when he pleased, see me on his time schedule, take me out to the places he liked, and kept me hidden in order to leave his options open in case a prettier girl came along." Amazed, Soraya looked over to Dante, her expression incredulous. "I must have been crazy!"

"You said it."

"Is it the challenge that keeps us on our toes, or do we just like being treated like shit?"

Pausing, Soraya's mind ran on – the hair dryers humming around her, a coffee materializing on the table in front of her. Yes, why had she allowed it? Why had she allowed some handsome jerk to walk all over her and treat her as if she was some kind of object? She knew that every teenage girl went through a phase of being attracted to assholes, but surely that phase had long passed by late teens or early twenties?

Obviously not with her.

Annoyed with herself and uncomfortable with her memories, Soraya changed the subject. "I'm meeting up with a new guy."

Dante was all attention. "You are?"

"He's younger than me."

"Are you feeling motherhood again?"

She frowned. "What do you mean by that?"

"If you want to mother someone, why don't you buy yourself another puppy!"

"Very funny. He might turn out to be The One."

"Maybe." Dante replied, shrugging. "You think he will take your mind off Jean-Luc? Who we all know you still think about, bambina. Your first love."

"Dante!"

"But a first love never lasts forever. It will always remain as your first love and nothing more."

"Who died and made you Dr Phil?"

He shrugged. "Me. Myself. Experience, suffering, growing up, and being a people person."

"Okay, keep still!" Angelo snapped suddenly, jerking Soraya's head round. Dante leaned closer.

"So, this little housewarming party you invited us to. Who else is coming?"

"Anya and Niloofar."

"Any more blind dates? Any potential husbands?"

"Richard Parker's coming. He's the son of a family friend. I've known him for a long time, but we just don't click. Then there's this Iranian guy from San Francisco – Brian Zachary – who I've just started emailing and—"

"And?"

"Jean-Luc."

"Silly girl!" Dante said, glancing at Angelo and rolling his eyes. "Silly, silly girl."

As Angelo continued putting bleach on her hair and pressing each foil packet with the comb to seal it, Soraya started to zone out. Did she really need a man in her life to make her happy? Jerking her head upright, Angelo tutted several times. Soraya watched through the mirror as he talked to Dante. The warmth of the salon was making her drowsy and, as she surveyed the other clients, she wondered how many were truly happy. How many were settled in relationships? How many were still looking?

She was about to doze off when Dante leant towards her: "So, are you excited about meeting this Brian?"

"I suppose I am."

Was she? Soraya stared at herself in the mirror, staring at the tin foil and the black towel around her shoulders. For a moment, she didn't see herself as she was, but as she longed to be – getting herself pretty for someone special. Making herself beautiful for a man. Perhaps Brian? Perhaps, on Saturday, she might even look at the charming Richard and fall in love? Perhaps, she would find The One by the deadline and take him home? And then all of Persian society could get off her back and take her family with them.

"Oh dear," Dante said, seeing how quiet she had become and sensing a real sadness. "Perhaps inviting Jean-Luc on Saturday was not the right thing to do?"

"I still care about him," She said, almost ashamed.

He tapped her shoulder sympathetically. "I know, bambina, I know. Perhaps it will be too much for you to see him again?"

"No," Soraya said firmly. "I might still love him, but he won't commit, so I have to look elsewhere. Besides, it will do him good to see other men take an interest in me."

In that instant, her cell buzzed. It was a text message from Niloofar.

Hey, you'll never guess what. Saw Jean-Luc at 1 OAK on sat. He's got a new gf. – Don't worry tho, she's nowhere near as pretty as you.

Soraya felt sick to her stomach. Asshole. I hope his penis falls off and she breaks his heart. So much for all that bullshit about not wanting to be in a relationship. She texted back:

Hey babe, hate Jean-Luc, hope his dick falls off and she leaves him.

Within seconds Niloofar replied:

Haha, believe in karma, babe, something bad will happen to him.

And it couldn't come soon enough, Soraya thought angrily. It couldn't come soon enough.

THIRTEEN

A locked door is no bar to women on the scent of gossip.

"Anahita! Darling! Where have you been? Tell us the news – how's dear Soraya and all her plans for the wedding?"

Sitting back comfortably on a massage chair at the spa, Anahita's face was covered with cream, which was drying rapidly into a white crust. On her left sat a manicurist, filing her nails, and at the base of the bed another woman was giving her a pedicure. Immobilized and unable to escape, Anahita's eyes rolled over in the direction of the voice to see Mona Sattari entering the room along with another notable Persian gossipmonger, Ariana Amanpour.

"I heard about Soraya. You must be so excited!" Mona said.

Anahita could feel her face burning under her mask; her mouth settling into a fixed grin.

"Wonderful."

"What, dear?" Ariana asked, bending down to Anahita. "I can't hear you clearly."

"W-on-der-ful," was all Anahita could manage. Mona moved round to the other side of the bed, staring hard at Anahita's feet.

"We all knew your daughter would find someone eventually."

Anahita groaned.

"So, what does he do?"

Pointing to her face mask, Anahita rolled her eyes to imply that she couldn't talk. But, if she hoped the women would back off, she was in for a surprise. Seeing their prey vulnerable and going nowhere, they bombarded her with questions.

"Is it true about the dowry?"

"Is it true that he's Iranian?"

"I heard he was a divorcee?"

"Is it true he's over fifty?"

"I heard he was staying here?"

"I heard he's richer than Amir?"

"I heard he's a first cousin?"

Stunned, Anahita made a strangled sound in her throat. Mona snapped at the manicurist, "Be careful! Can't you see you're hurting her?"

A persistent Ariana turned back to Anahita. "So, when do we get to meet Soraya's new man?"

Anahita's eyes rolled again.

"This weekend?"

She made a guttural sound in her throat.

"Next week?"

Another moan came from the petite figure.

Taking Anahita's squeaks for pain, the shrill Ariana snapped at the beautician, "Don't be so clumsy! You're not shoeing a horse!"

"Of course, we all know it will be a big wedding," Mona smiled, glancing down at Anahita's toes thoughtfully. "It'll be the marriage of the year."

Anahita could feel herself shrivel further under the rapidly drying mask. If those society harpies found out Soraya had left home and there was no man, no fiancé, and no wedding, she would be a laughingstock, who would never be allowed to forget her foolishness. Even her money and status wouldn't save her from the lie she had set in motion, which now looked like it was going to swallow her whole.

"She can't talk," Mona said finally, her disappointment obvious. "I'll call you later, Anahita." She tapped her on the shoulder lightly. "Can't wait to hear all the news, darling."

"None of us can!" Ariana chimed in, as they left the secluded lounge area.

The manicurist looked at Anahita expectantly. "Your daughter's getting married?"

"Oh, shut up!" Anahita barked, her face mask cracking, sending flecks of white powder everywhere.

That Saturday, Soraya woke up and stretched, remembering that it was her housewarming and the end of the second month. How had it passed so quickly? Two months down, two to go, and she was still no nearer to finding her man. Stretching, she sat up in the small bed, staring out of the window. She could hear the comforting sound of Jenny moving around next door, with her radio playing softly. If she had been at her mother's home, Soraya would have stayed in bed until noon, then gone to visit friends before being taken out for a sumptuous dinner. But, oddly, she was missing the luxuries of her old life less and less. She was also noticing a change in herself. Though she loathed her job, she had experienced the satisfaction of standing up to Chloe and getting the upper hand, albeit making a vicious enemy in the process. Soraya might find the cramped appeal of the apartment limited and shopping, cooking, cleaning, and general day-to-day chores were tedious (who knew the lid of a wheelie bin could break two fingernails if it fell down unexpectedly?) but, for the first time ever, she was in charge of her life. And that felt good.

By the time the evening came around, Soraya had made the apartment pretty with flowers and candles. She had been forced to buy a cheap dress from Melrose and sharpen it up with some not-so-expensive jewelry. But, after a bit of a struggle, the final effect had pleased Soraya and she wondered how grudgingly impressed her mother would be with her ingenuity.

Excited, Soraya stood by the door of the apartment and waited for her guests to arrive. One by one they ascended the elevator to her cozy little apartment: Richard with his little brother, then Angelo and Dante, followed by Anya and Niloofar, and, finally, Jean-Luc. He was tall with an athletic build, wavy dirty-blond hair, and green eyes (Soraya's grandmother always told her to steer clear of green-eyed men but did she listen?). As usual, Jean-Luc was immaculately dressed in tight jeans, a crisp white shirt, dark blazer, and trendy Prada high-top sneakers. Even from a distance, Soraya could smell his aftershave. Sneezing, she smiled as she remembered how he could suddenly decide to be so charming, and she'd always be too powerless to resist.

Despite her mouth drying and her heart going into arrhythmia, Soraya was deliberately offhand with him. It was one thing to be cool when hidden in the dark depths of a nightclub, but far more difficult in the confines of a one-bedroom apartment.

Luckily, Anya was soon monopolizing the Frenchman and, when a handsome dark-haired man came strolling through the door, Soraya hurried over.

"Brian?"

He nodded, smiling nervously. Brian was preppy looking, wearing a washed-out blue polo, khakis, and boat shoes. Average height and build, curly brown hair, and green eyes, yikes! She liked him on sight, even though he was a little shorter than her in her high heels and he lacked the presence of the other men. But he had taken a flight to meet her, so the least Soraya could do was to make him feel comfortable. Weaving Brian in between the talking guests, she led him to Niloofar and introduced them, beckoning Richard over to meet the stranger. To Soraya's surprise, the night was going very smoothly, and everyone was getting on well.

Well, it was before Jean-Luc began checking out Richard and giving her circumspect looks.

"Who is this guy?"

Soraya was all cool and indifferent. "Oh, Richard? He's a friend."

"Why is he flirting with you?"

"I'm a free agent, and he's just being friendly."

Ha! She thought, so Jean-Luc is jealous. Good!

"I don't like him," he said sulkily.

"What's he done to you?"

"I just don't like him," he repeated.

Soraya ignored him and continued her conversation with her friends. As the evening progressed, both herself and her guests were getting tipsy. A bunch of them decided to go to 1 OAK.

Seeing Soraya's shocked face, Anya whispered to her, "This is on me, *dahling*; don't worry about the money. I know how embarrassing it is for you being broke and feeling out of place."

In that instant, Soraya wanted to tell Anya exactly where to put her money. So that was what really mattered, was it? Her mother had been right. Being poor made you an object of pity, if not derision. From having been almost equals (Anya's father was only a millionaire, while Soraya's uncle Amir was a billionaire on the Forbes 400 richest list), in just two weeks, Soraya had been downgraded in Anya's eyes to a minion. She'd lost her status as well as her home.

But, not wanting to spoil a good evening, Soraya allowed Anya to help and, along with Brian, Angelo, Dante, Jean-Luc, and Niloofar, they all moved on to the nightclub. Richard left early, pleading an early start the next day. Still stung by Anya's patronizing words and feeling withdrawn, Soraya was caught off guard when Jean-Luc slid into the seat next to her, blocking Brian.

"So," Jean-Luc said.

"So what?" Soraya replied.

"Are you going to kiss me?"

"What?"

"Well?" he continued.

She looked at him with outright astonishment. "Jean-Luc, why are you even talking about kissing?"

"I don't know," he said feigning shyness.

"It's over. I'm not going back there." Her voice was low. "I mean, given our history and your commitment issues, I'm hardly likely to let you hurt me again."

Folding her arms, Soraya leaned back in her seat, wondering why she didn't move away from Jean-Luc. Brian was sitting next to Anya and Niloofar, but he kept gazing over to her. She wondered how she would have felt if she had made the trip from LA to San Francisco to find him flirting with an old flame.

"This isn't on," Soraya said bluntly, leaning away from Jean-Luc.

"I know I have hurt you and I was horrible to you, but I don't want to hurt you again."

She paused, shaking her head and smiling at Brian. The attraction between her and Jean-Luc was as potent as ever. She felt the same thrill whenever she looked at him. But he was an asshole. He couldn't commit and he wouldn't marry her. And, only a few feet away, was a nice guy who just might.

"I'm not getting involved with you again," she told Jean-Luc shakily. "It's taken me a long time to get you out of my system. Getting over you almost killed me, and I can't go through that again. I just can't."

His expression was genuinely contrite.

"I'm so sorry that I hurt you. I didn't mean it. I know I was bad and that you deserve better. But I still love you, ma chérie."

She felt the words like a punch.

"But I still cannot commit. I am scared. So, what do we do?"

A long moment passed. Soraya turned away from him and looked at the floor. The stakes were high. This was her life, her self-esteem, her choice of who to love. Who she wanted. Who wanted her. Who deserved her. It wasn't just the deadline; it was much, much more.

"Maybe we should just be friends."

"Ah."

"After all, you chewed me like a piece of gum and spat me out every time you were done with me."

"Oh, come on, I know I was bad but not that bad." He tried to lighten the atmosphere. "I don't know what my problem is! I always thought that by my age I'd be married with kids. I'm nearly thirty-four and it's time to settle down."

"But not with me."

"Not yet."

She smiled wistfully. "I see."

"You have to be patient."

"And, while I'm being patient, Jean-Luc, what happens if another girl comes along and you like her better than me?"

He shrugged. "None of us know what's in the future."

She shook her head. "No, we don't. But I now know what I don't want my future to be." Soraya rose from her seat, walked across the floor, and sat down next to Brian.

She could see the confusion, followed by irritation, on Jean-Luc's face. She watched him get up and privately willed him to come to her. Come over here and tell Brian that I'm yours, that he hasn't got a chance. We have so much chemistry; the only thing holding you back is giving up your bachelor lifestyle. But you can. And, if you really love me, you will. Make the move. Please, make the move.

Slowly, Jean-Luc walked over to Soraya. He looked down at Brian and then at her. Then he smiled before taking Soraya's hand and kissing it.

"Happy housewarming," he said simply. "I wish you a very, very happy housewarming."

FOURTEEN

Angry with herself for letting Jean-Luc affect her so much, Soraya picked up her cell as it rang next to her in bed. She was hoping it was him, but it was Niloofar's voice on the line.

"You okay?"

"Yes, I'm okay. Thanks for asking."

"Jean-Luc was a jerk last night."

"I know."

"You should forget him. Honestly, he's no good, and he messes up your head every time you see him."

Sighing, Soraya leaned back against the pillows. It was Sunday, thank God. No work and no Chloe. Unsettled, she remembered her old life and what she would usually be doing – going to play tennis at the Country Club or having lunch with the family. She quickly put those memories aside. It was only because she was upset that she longed for home, for the comfort of familiarity, and for the safety of being surrounded by loved ones.

"Men suck at communicating their thoughts and feelings," Niloofar said. "Why is it so damn hard for them to open up and tell us what's on their tiny little minds? We're not asking them to do it every single hour of the day. It would just be nice if they could communicate with us once in a while."

"Trouble?"

"Yep," Niloofar agreed. "Don't they know that a lack of communication is the main reason most relationships break down?"

"Turbulence in paradise?"

"No communication in paradise," Niloofar replied.

"I used to try to communicate my feelings to Jean-Luc, but he would just look at me blankly."

"Statistics prove that women are more empathetic than men."

"Do they have to clam up like a clam during hibernation season in Clamville?" Soraya fumed. "Are we really supposed to be Freud, solving every missing piece of the emotional jigsaw puzzle of our relationships?"

"And then there are the issues in the bedroom," Niloofar said, dryly. "Hey, guys, what about me? What about what I want? What about my fun and pleasure?"

"Men," Soraya said perceptively, "only have two means of communication – all out or all in. I mean, honestly, it's not going to make them any less of a man to show some emotion, or even ask us what we're feeling and what we want. It might even rescue a relationship."

"Hey, babe," Niloofar said sadly, "I don't think this relationship of mine is going to work out long term."

"Be positive" Soraya replied gently. "Give it some more time."

"Unrequited love that you thought was requited and then turns out to really be unrequited is a bitch."

"So is not getting over your first love."

"And he snores so loud!" Niloofar said, ignoring Soraya's comment. "Babe, it's deafening!"

"Jean-Luc used to snore too. I know that love can make you blind, but can it make you go deaf too?" Soraya tried to sound light-hearted, even though she was desperate to talk about how she really felt. How Jean-Luc's actions had hurt her. How she felt vulnerable, raw, and rejected.

"Niloofar."

"Of course, I could be wrong; it could work out."

"Niloofar."

"But then again, it might not."

"Listen to me, please!" Soraya implored. "Almost two months of the deadline have gone and I'm no nearer to finding Mr Right than I was when I started. I know who Mr Never-Could-Be-Right-In-A-Million-Years is, so that's something. But I've got to concentrate now. I've got to stop fooling around."

Niloofar snapped out of her own preoccupations to focus on Soraya. "Okay, babe, okay. So, what do you think of Brian?"

"It's too early to tell. We talked until the early hours last night."

The memory was fresh in Soraya's mind. After everyone left the party, Brian stayed behind. He and Soraya had chatted about life, his surfing, his roommate, his roommate's dog, her passion for tennis, his travels, and her love for Prada. The conversation was pretty easygoing, just like in their emails. After a few more shots, they shared a little kiss. Soraya felt it was too early to tell whether he was The One. Her feelings were all over the place and Jean-Luc wasn't helping with his constant hot and cold behavior. And this deadline was stressing her out. How could she choose the man she was going to marry in the space of a few short months? Was that even possible?

"Wow!"

"No, we just talked. Well, we had a little kiss." Soraya paused. "He's sweet, but he's… Anyway, I'm seeing him tomorrow, so I might have a better idea then.

"What about Richard?"

"Oh, you know Richard's always around," Soraya said fondly. "My uncle would love me to marry him. His parents would love me to marry him. It's just me who's not so keen."

Niloofar paused down the line. "You really set yourself up, you know."

"What?"

"Well, giving yourself this pressure. Leaving home and running around trying to find a fiancé. Honestly, babe, everyone thinks you've gone over the top."

"Everyone?" Soraya countered, her tone icy cold. "So, everyone's talking about me, are they?"

"People in our circles don't act like this."

"What do they act like, Niloofar? Let themselves be married off rather than take their lives into their own hands? Is it wrong of me to leave home? Am I embarrassing my friends?"

"Well, actually yes you are, kinda."

Stunned, Soraya took in a breath before Niloofar hastily added: "I mean, you… you're rich; you don't have to act like this. It's not what people like us do." She was mortally embarrassed, not wanting to hurt Soraya. "Look," she stumbled on, "I reckon you should give Brian a chance."

"I'm going to give him a chance," Soraya said quietly.

"He might surprise you. I really liked him. He seemed like a nice guy, babe."

Soraya's voice was low. "Don't nice guys finish last?"

"Who said that?"

"Probably the asshole who came in first."

❧

Soraya was on her way out of her apartment block when she saw Mark hanging around by the entrance. It was hardly a coincidence, but it was always nice to see a friendly face in this neighborhood. Mark Tehrani looked happy to see her. That morning, he had received the latest on her movements and was relieved that she seemed to be coping well with her new life. In fact, he was impressed by her stand. He knew that Amir was impressed too but would die rather than admit it. The girl they had all thought was just a pretty doll had turned out to have some real spirit about her.

Mark liked the change in Soraya. He had seen the effect of her parents' divorce and watched her difficult adolescence as her uncle took over the role of surrogate father. For a while, he had even wondered if Soraya would go off the rails and become just another drug-addled offspring of the seriously rich. But she had surprised him, and he admired her stab at independence.

"Hi," Soraya said, smiling as she approached him. "How are you?"

"Good. I've just seen a client in this part of town,' Mark replied, "and so I thought I'd drop by to see you at the same time. Any DIY need doing?"

"You just don't trust me with that drill, do you?" she teased him.

"Only if it's unplugged," Mark replied, smiling. "So, how are you getting on?"

"I'm halfway through the deadline. My friends are all embarrassed by me and I've ended up blackmailing my boss, but otherwise I'd say I was coping," Soraya shrugged. "But no closer to finding my soulmate."

"Perhaps you're looking in the wrong place?"

She glanced over to him; her head tilted to one side. "Why are you married?" she joked. "All the good men belong to someone else."

"All the good men are older," he replied, teasing her. "Your uncle's worried about you. Your mother is too."

"Are they okay?"

"Same as ever."

"That bad, hey?" Soraya joked as they walked along.

She had always got on well with Mark, as she found him smart and easy company. But that morning, under the bright sunlight, he looked different. He was confident, urbane, and handsome. God, Soraya thought, almost blushing. Stop looking at every man as a potential candidate! This is Mark Tehrani! And he is married. Very married.

"I'm seeing someone new. A guy called Brian Zachary."

"Do you like him?"

"Maybe." Soraya paused, glancing down the street. "You know why I did it, don't you?"

"Did what?"

"Left home. I had to. I had to try life out here on my own. I don't really like it, Mark, to be honest. I felt this frisson of achievement the other day, but it didn't last. Then something bad happened and I wanted to run home, like a hurt kid. I don't suppose I'm very tough really. I'm not exactly streetwise."

"Don't sell yourself short, Soraya," he said kindly. "Most girls in your position wouldn't have the nerve to do what you did."

"Maybe not. But I just can't let my family find me a husband!" she said, knowing that Mark would understand. "I can't! Anya thinks I should give in and let them arrange a wedding for me. Even Niloofar's losing patience. But I can't. If I mess up my life, so be it. But at least it will be me messing it up. I don't want my family or anyone else messing it up for me!"

He laughed, shaking his head. "Do you really think you can find the love of your life in four months?"

"Two months and two days," she said. "Remember, nearly half the deadline has already passed."

"Okay, I'll ask you again. Do you really think you can find the love of your life in just over two months?"

"If I'm supposed to," Soraya said seriously. "If there's a God up there, or Fate, or Luck – call it what you will. If I'm supposed to find the right man, then I will. Something will bring him to me."

Her conviction surprised him. "How will you know it's him?"

"They say that when you meet the right person, you know instinctively. "Didn't you?"

His mouth dried. "What?"

"When you met your wife? Didn't you know?"

"Yes," he said honestly. "When I met her, I felt like she was The One."

"Then so will I," Soraya replied. "So will I."

Summoned to Amir's office in Beverly Hills, Brian waited nervously for half an hour, during which time he drank too much coffee and went to the restroom three times. He had seen Soraya on two more occasions since her housewarming and had grown to like her. There was a certain attraction between them, but he worried that she was not over her previous boyfriend, the oleaginous Jean-Luc, and was not ready to commit to a new relationship. Then there was the question of her family. Brian observed the opulent surroundings in Amir's building. They were impressively wealthy. Could he compete? Certainly, their contacts would be invaluable to a young lawyer, but would they want to impinge on his work? Take him over? Would that matter? Or would the advantages of a pretty wife with influential contacts outweigh the disadvantages?

Amir's secretary roused Brian from his thoughts and showed him up to the office. Smiling, Amir gestured for him to sit down, then took a seat next to him.

"So, Brian, are you enjoying your time here in LA?"

"Oh yes, it's been a great four days so far, I absolutely love it here."

"So, how's work going these days?"

Brian shifted in his seat. "To be honest it's been pretty slow. A lot of my friends have lost their jobs these past few months and our firm has been cutting back on costs."

Amir nodded. "Yes, it's tough everywhere. Do you think you'll be working as a lawyer for a while?"

"I'm not sure actually," Brian admitted. He wondered where the conversation was going. "I was thinking of going into property, but the market has really slowed in California. I was also considering going into the development side of things with a few friends, but we might have to put that on hold for now."

His face betraying nothing, Amir stepped up the pressure. By his reckoning, a man who couldn't withstand The Interview wasn't worthy of his niece.

"So, Brian, where did you study?"

"I went to UCLA."

Uh-oh! Amir thought. Strike One. In his eyes, if it wasn't Harvard or any of the other Ivy Leagues, the man was a dope. Richard went to Yale and studied law.

"Do you speak any foreign languages?"

"I can speak a little French and Spanish."

"Do you know Soraya speaks five languages. Pretty impressive, no?"

"Very." Brian replied, looking a little embarrassed.

"What's your current salary?"

Shocked, Brian faltered. "I'd say it's pretty good. I get by."

"Hmm. And what are your hours like?"

"Pretty long," he said, shifting in his seat again and wondering where the conservation was going. "I do twelve to fourteen-hour days mostly."

"Do you live by yourself in a house that you own?"

"No, I live with two roommates."

Uh-oh! Strike Two.

"What do they do?"

"One's also lawyer and the other is a schoolteacher."

Amir sighed, the sound punching into the air like a curse.

"I see. And do you plan on living with them for much longer?"

"Well, I'm quite happy for the time being but would love to get my own place at some point."

"What are your views on drugs?"

"I'm totally against them," Brian lied, beads of sweat building up around his forehead.

"Do you drink or smoke?"

"I drink a little."

"What car do you drive?"

"An SUV."

Strike Three. Amir continued to look unimpressed. He was expecting Brian to drive a Mercedes or something a little more sophisticated.

"Do you have a five-year plan?"

"Er..." Brian hesitated, "I plan to buy my own place in the next year or two and make partner at the firm."

Not the right answer.

"Do you think you'll make a good husband and father?"

Brian was openly sweating now. "I believe so."

"And why is that?"

"My parents have always emphasized the importance of being a devoted husband and father."

"How many kids do you want?"

"Two. A boy and a girl. If I have a girl, she will probably get away with murder. I don't think I could ever be a strict dad."

"Do you have any criminal offences?"

Stunned, Brian stared at Amir, his voice wavering. "Not unless you call getting a speeding ticket a criminal offence."

"Do you support any American Football teams?"

"I don't really follow American Football. I prefer to surf."

Strike Four! Amir lived and breathed NFL, and Brian – although he didn't know it yet – was perilously close to being shown the door.

"So, Brian, you and Soraya seem to be getting on well. She seems to like you. What do you think?"

"Er, well, er," he stuttered. "Soraya is indeed a lovely girl."

"And how would you feel about moving to Los Angeles?"

"To be honest I haven't given it any thought."

"You don't plan on marrying my niece then?"

Oh shit! Brian thought. Marriage? So soon after meeting the girl? Heart pumping, he stared goggle eyed at Amir. Had he really just asked if he was planning to marry Soraya? Fucking hell. Brian felt like a truck had hit him.

His hesitation was all the answer Amir needed.

"Well, it was nice chatting to you," he said, walking back behind his desk. He gestured to his secretary to show Brian out.

Blissfully unaware of what had been happening that afternoon, Soraya came home from work and waved to Jenny who was on her way out. Soraya felt excited at the prospect of seeing Brian for drinks that night. He was being very attentive and there was a little bit of attraction between them. Could this be it? Okay, so she hadn't been swept off her feet, but he was attractive, had a good profession, and was very likeable. She recalled what she had said to Mark Tehrani earlier: "If I'm supposed to find the right man, I will. Something will bring him to me."

Was this it? Had Fate brought Brian Zachary?

That night, Brian took Soraya out for drinks, and then dinner. Gradually, they both relaxed, and during the meal Soraya put a flirtatious hand on his knee. In response, Brian smiled and put his hand on her knee and kissed her on the cheek. Excited, Soraya continued flirting with him throughout the course of the dinner and then drinks at the bar. Before they knew it, it was 3am.

Leaving the restaurant, they walked towards Sunset Boulevard. As Soraya snuggled into her coat to keep warm, Brian put his arms around her and kissed her on the lips like it was the most natural thing to do.

"When did you first realize you wanted to kiss me?" he asked.

"Just now. What about you?"

"When I first saw you."

"It takes me a while to realize whether or not I like someone and I guess it all fell into place today."

Soon they were kissing again. Having been badly hurt and still in love with Jean-Luc, Soraya hadn't felt sparks in a long time. But with Brian it felt right and comfortable. Most importantly, he was a great kisser. They kissed like teenagers till they were so tired they could barely keep their eyes open. Still chatting, Brian finally walked Soraya home before returning to his hotel.

Jean-Luc who? She thought, laughing to herself. Had she finally found her Romeo?

The following morning a very hesitant Jenny knocked on Soraya's door. She waited, then knocked again. A moment later a sleepy face peered at the door.

"Oh, hi."

"Sorry, were you asleep?"

"It's Saturday. I was having a lie in. Are you okay?" Soraya asked, waking up and staring at the heavily pregnant woman in front of her. "Is it the baby?"

"No, no. The baby's fine," Jenny replied, pulling her bathrobe around her and shrugging. "Sorry I woke you."

"Hey! Don't walk off, come in, come in." Soraya opened the door and made coffee for both of them.

She could tell that Jenny was agitated and uncomfortable about disturbing her. But her landlady had never made a nuisance of herself, so if she had come to Soraya's door early on a Saturday morning there had to be a good reason.

"You need some help?"

"I've started to go to an antenatal clinic on Saturdays," Jenny began, "with a woman who lives nearby. But she just rang and said she couldn't make it."

"Yes?"

"I'm sorry but I just don't want to go alone." Jenny smiled, embarrassed. "Oh gosh! I don't know what I was thinking. I shouldn't have disturbed you."

"You want me to come with you?"

"I do everything else myself. But the antenatal clinic is something my husband should be doing with me. Since he died… well, I just don't feel able to go on my own."

"What was he like?" Soraya asked, surprised as the words left her mouth.

But Jenny looked relieved to talk about him.

"He was everything. When I woke in the morning, it was a good day because he was there. When I was afraid, or upset, he was there. When I made plans, they were never for me – they were for us. Our life was joined, shared. What we had when we were single was nothing compared to what we had when we were together." She looked at Soraya earnestly. "Never settle for second best in love. I might have only had my husband for a few years, but what we had was more than most people get in a lifetime." She paused, taking in a breath. "Would you mind coming to the antenatal clinic with me?

"Do I have to do anything?" Soraya asked, her eyes widening at the thought of a room full of pregnant women, all puffing away.

After all, what did she know about babies? Or pregnancies? When she had asked her mother about it, Anahita had said: "You tell the doctor, 'knock me out and wake me up when the hairdresser arrives.' " So much for child rearing tips.

Jenny stared at her imploringly. "We just do breathing exercises."

"All of us?"

"No, just the pregnant women," Jenny replied, laughing.

"Do I have to wear special clothes?"

"What for?"

Soraya blinked. "I mean, it's casual, right?"

"You try being anything else when you're heavily pregnant."

And so, on that chilly cold winter morning, Soraya drove Jenny to the antenatal clinic, parking the battered Audi outside what looked like a temporary extension. Smiling encouragement that she didn't feel, Soraya walked with Jenny to a large room and stopped dead. Twenty women in various stages of pregnancy were sitting on mats on the floor; the hum of conversation interrupted by grunting as they moved awkwardly around. Two months previously, Soraya would have made a run for it immediately, but she walked straight in as Jenny registered, albeit with surreptitious glances at the swollen bellies surrounding her.

Womb city.

Dear God, so this was pregnancy.

"How far along, dear?" a woman asked, as Soraya sat down on a floor mat.

She looked up, confused. "I'm sorry, excuse me?"

"How far along are you?"

"I've just come with Jenny," she explained.

"For moral support?"

"Yes," Soraya agreed, smiling. "Moral support."

"Ah, so this is your first time?"

And the last, Soraya thought, nodding. "Yes, my first time."

"You're hardly showing."

Showing what? Soraya wondered, baffled. "I came casual," she said, by way of explanation, the woman nodding.

"It's good to be comfortable."

"Sometimes, although I was living it up last night."

The woman frowned. "Drinking?"

"It's not a night out without it!" Soraya went on blithely.

"Recreational drugs?"

"Not anymore." Soraya went on. "I was with this man I'd just met. We didn't get to bed until after 3am."

"I see," the woman said, her tone turning frosty. "Do you go out a lot?"

"As often as I can."

"Do you think that's good for you?"

Soraya frowned. "I can do what I like. I mean, I have no one else to consider."

"But that's not strictly true, is it?" the woman persisted. "You have the responsibility of another life."

"Really?" Soraya said after a moment's hesitation. "But she's just my landlord."

Rolling her eyes, Jenny moved over and looked at the nurse. "She's not the pregnant one, I am."

As the red-faced woman walked off, Soraya and Jenny burst out laughing. A moment of complete understanding passed between them – an unexpected bonding which caught both of them by surprise.

Returning to the apartment later, Soraya phoned Brian, eager to tell him about what had happened. When he didn't pick up, she left an affectionate message, then continued with her day. But Brian didn't phone that evening either and, in the morning, Soraya found no message on her cell as she hurried to work. Casting a quick look at her messages midmorning, she was relieved to see that he had finally texted and had asked her to meet him for lunch. At one o'clock – and aware that she had one hour, and one hour precisely – Soraya hurried to the lunch spot near the hotel and slid into a seat beside Brian in the restaurant.

But, for some reason, he wasn't being his usual attentive self. Perhaps he was tired? Soraya thought. Or maybe he felt embarrassed? She tried being talkative and friendly but wasn't getting anything back from him. After a hurried and uncommunicative lunch, Brian went back to his hotel and she returned to work – just in time to bump into Chloe.

"Where have you been?" she snapped, her eyes glinting.

"Lunch. I only took an hour."

"Did you make my phone calls before lunch?"

"Not all of them."

She was glowing with fury. "Can't you do anything right? I only have to ask Madison to do something once, and she does it. With you, I have to repeat everything."

Uneasy after her lunch date, Soraya bit her tongue and went back to work, knowing that for all Chloe's bluster she had the upper hand. But what the hell was happening with Brian? As the afternoon wore on, Soraya repeatedly checked her phone. There were no calls or texts. What had gone wrong? Why did guys act all into you one day and not the next? Why was it so hard to meet a guy who behaved the same way two days in a row?

Finally, at around four o'clock, Brian sent a message:

Want to meet up tonight?

Relieved, Soraya texted back, suggesting they watch a film at her place.

But that night Brian couldn't have been more distant. Soraya wondered if what had happened before had just been a dream. Embarrassed, and not knowing him well enough to say anything, Soraya sat in awkward silence until Brian had to go back to the hotel and pack his things.

As he was about to leave, he gave her a mediocre hug and simply said, "I guess this is goodbye."

"I guess it is," she said coldly. Then she closed the door behind him and jumped straight into bed, pulling the covers over her head.

What the hell was that all about? Hadn't they been getting on well? How could something that seemed so promising fall apart so fast? She had actually thought, although it embarrassed her to remember it, that Brian Zachary might be The One. She had been excited about the possibility and attracted to him. And then the brush off. What was the point of him coming all that way to see her if he didn't want anything serious? Or was it her? Was it something she had said or done? Was there something wrong with her?

Soraya heard Jenny's footsteps moving around next door. She thought about how Jenny had been widowed and was carrying her dead husband's child. God, Soraya thought, what must that feel like? To lose someone you loved? Someone you were married to? How much did that hurt and tear your life apart? From what Jenny had said about her husband, they'd had a special bond. And here she was, moping around after a guy she had only known for a few days.

But as much as Soraya tried to lift herself out of her mood, it stuck. The unfamiliar surroundings of the apartment, the strange noises from the neighbors, and the somber, thumping pipes overhead all contributed to her feeling of failure. She felt disheartened and terribly alone. Jean-Luc had rejected her and now Brian had left. Even a million-dollar dowry couldn't buy her a husband. Angry with herself, she wondered how she could possibly have thought she could succeed. Maybe everyone was right. Maybe she was just some spoilt rich princess, mollycoddled in an indulgent, cocooned world. Maybe she didn't have the guts to make it on her own, or the wit to find Mr Right. Or, if she found him, the skill to keep him. Would her dramatic show of defiance turn out to be as effective as a toddler's tantrum?

Yet the alternative was unthinkable. To give in to her family and to marry a man she didn't love. To make a promise and have children with someone she didn't care about - what kind of life was that? Oh, it would fulfil her family's hopes and desires, and make her secure but, after the wedding, what then? Her life stretching out before her, day after day, without love? Surely love was the balm of life? The gel that lubricated the hard times; the oil that softened fears, illness, ageing, and disappointment. Surely without love there was only a half-life? And if she settled for that – if she made that choice – there was no escape.

Of course, she still had Richard, who Amir had liked since forever. Richard Parker, who was nice, well-educated, funny, smart, wealthy, and handsome. He could give her a great life Soraya thought, but then she recalled that it had taken him four years to remember her name. And he had no desire to have children. Second best, she thought, remembering Jenny's words. No, second best wasn't enough.

Soraya's thoughts turned back to Brian Zachary. Just what exactly had happened there? She hadn't heard from him, and knew that, if she left it, she never would again. Confused, Soraya continued to brood. What had gone on? And why no explanation? Her confusion intensified. She felt foolish. So much for all her big talk. Her friends would be smirking now after this debacle. Not exactly Mr Right, but Mr Right Off. Surely Brian owed her some sort of an explanation? She would talk to him and ask for an answer; he owed her that much.

Nervous, Soraya dialed Brian's cell number and it rang a few times until he picked up.

"Hello?"

"Hi Brian, it's Soraya."

"Hey, what's up?"

"I haven't heard from you since you left the other night."

"Err, well, um," he stammered. "Sorry, I should have called. I'm going back home today."

"Without saying goodbye?"

"I would have called but, um, what have you been up to?"

She tried to sound light-hearted and talked about trivia. "I've spent a lot of time thinking about how I'd love to get another puppy when I'm more settled. A Maltese would be so cute. What do you think of the name Chanel?"

"How about Diane von Fürstenberg?"

"A bit long don't you think?"

"You can't name a dog Chanel!"

"Why not? I think it's cute. Anyway, I also got another piercing in my ear," she went on, wondering why she was talking about such dopey things. "I now have five piercings in total."

"Wow, is your mum okay with it?"

"She doesn't know yet. She knows about the three in my ears and the belly button piercing. I'm still not sure about getting a tattoo. I was supposed to get one with my cousin, but he chickened out."

"Ha."

"My mother suggested I get a semi-permanent one on my ankle, but I don't like those. I hear they're no good." What the hell was she going on about? She sounded like an airhead. "But if I decide to have kids someday then I can't exactly forbid them from getting a tattoo if I have one."

There was a long pause.

"I've dated some girls who have tattoos," Brian said finally. "Some regret them, others don't. My rebellious side has always wanted a big artistic one on my shoulder, but my mother would be upset, so it's not worth it."

Soraya laughed, but the conversation was stilted, and she was wondering how she was going to get to the bit about him making a run for it.

Taking in a breath, she asked: "Brian, why did you leave so quickly the other night? It was quite the brush off." She blushed as she said it. "I thought we were getting on well."

His embarrassment was obvious, even over the phone.

"I guess it was a bit hard to find things in common to talk about, what with the difference in cultures, work, and life views. Mostly my fault, as my life is quite monotonous compared to yours."

"But we're both Iranian, so culturally we're the same. We both work, we both love sports, and we're both very social. I'm not quite following you here."

"I meant more San Fran v LA. I guess it was just harder for us, or maybe me to relate to how I live my life here. My work-life balance is completely different to being on vacation in LA."

Was he mad? Soraya wondered, not understanding a word.

"But a lot of my cousins are in San Francisco and we get on just fine."

Brian took in a deep breath. "What I am trying to say is that I found it much harder relating to you with all the negative things happening in my life."

"I don't understand."

"Well, back home I've been watching my friends and colleagues lose their jobs, and I'm trying to save my own ass. Meanwhile you're thinking of names for an imaginary puppy. I think it's funny and cute – a break from reality – but I honestly can't relate to that."

Surely, she had just been trying to be cheerful and talk about light-hearted things? Why was he taking it all so seriously?

"Our worlds are so different," he continued. "I don't know what else to say."

"Well, I think you're jumping to some pretty damning conclusions," Soraya replied, hurt. "What you don't know is that I left home two months ago and struck out on my own. The apartment you saw at my housewarming is rented. I took a lousy job and I'm trying to be independent."

She didn't mention the deadline.

"Oh, come on, Soraya," Brian said, his tone soft, the words hard. "You're just playing at it."

"What the fuck?"

"Your family's loaded. You can make a big deal about walking out, but you can go home anytime and straight back to a life of indulgence. You say you've got a job? Well done, but you don't have to rely on it."

"That's just the point, I do!"

He was impatient, quickly brushing her words aside: "It's just another rich girl trick, isn't it? What did your family do that was so bad? Not let you have a new car? Cut back on your vacations? Take away your Platinum card?"

"You asshole!"

"Look, Soraya, everyone knows you're on the hunt for a husband. Your uncle's put up a million-dollar dowry to secure a marriage for you. Be grateful that you have a lucky life, but please, please, don't try and pretend that you're a normal girl. It's an insult to everyone who lives in the real world."

Shaken, she snapped back. "So why did you come all this way, Brian? Was it for me? Or the dowry?"

"If we'd been more compatible, it might have worked."

Soraya winced. What painful, insulting accusations! All she wanted to do was to get off the phone. His words had scalded her. Was that what everyone really thought? That she had no life and that all she did was shop or socialize? Rejected and insulted, she tried, valiantly, to save face.

"Well, it was nice talking to you, Brian, but I have to go and think about more puppy names, you know. It's very important."

The sarcasm was lost on him.

"Okay, well bye."

Stunned, Soraya put down the phone and immediately wrote an email to Brian on her laptop. She went over what she had just written several times. She didn't care if she never heard from him again, she just needed to strike back.

To: Brian1993@yahoo.com

Subject: Different Worlds

Having reflected over your comments you're right, we are indeed from different worlds, I'm from Earth and you're from Mars! I guess aliens and humans don't really gel. Hope you succeed in finding the perfect alienette (bearing in mind the work/life balance, of course).

That'll do, Soraya thought. She had said all that was needed. Clear, concise, and straight to the point, if not a little childish. Feeling vaguely triumphant, she called Niloofar.

"Hey, babe, did I wake you?"

"No, honey, I'm just working on my website. Are you okay?" She asked.

"How's your love life going?"

"Not bad, well not good. In fact, we've broken up. Not for good, I think, I hope."

"Oh, babe."

"But I've got something funny to tell you."

"What's happened this time?"

"Remember David, my ex from a year ago?"

"Yeah."

"We had sex."

Soraya paused, trying to work up some enthusiasm for the story. "Okay?"

"He was being so sweet and so we just ended up sleeping together. And then he fell asleep. I left his place at 5am and, as there weren't any cabs, I had to call him and go back to his. So, I went back, crawled into his miniature bed, and he pulled all the covers off of me and I lay there practically naked and cold."

"God."

"Yes, I woke up the next morning with his arm plastered over my face and he was snoring like a beast. I couldn't help laughing. I couldn't understand how I allowed myself to get into this situation. I mean awkward would best describe the sex. The entire thing was just a flop." She sighed, laughing again. "Honestly, I don't know why I bothered."

Soraya shook her head. "You'll meet someone else."

"Yeah, right. But I can kiss my friendship with David goodbye. I don't think I could ever look him in the eyes after last night. Honestly, he had his hand over my face and didn't even ask me if I had enough space on the bed. I was practically sleeping on the floor!"

"Are you busy tonight?"

"Uh huh. Anya and I are going to 1 OAK. I mean, we would have asked you to join us but it's so expensive there and we know you're on a budget." She hurried on. "Anya said that you were insulted when she offered to pay before."

"I wasn't insulted. It was just the way she said it," Soraya explained. Usually, she was the first person people asked out – the leader of the pack. But now she was feeling more like the runt of the litter. "What about tomorrow?"

"Off to Cabo!"

"Cabo?"

"You know Anya's been seeing someone? Well, he's taking her away and she invited me along for a few days; he's flying us over there on his jet." Niloofar paused. "You want to come? I'm sure there's space, I could talk to Anya."

"Or maybe I could work my passage?" Soraya asked sarcastically. "Do your laundry on the trip?"

"You sound a bit rattled. Are you okay?"

"Well, not so good," Soraya said tentatively. "You remember Brian?"

"I liked him!"

"Yeah, so did I."

"Did?"

"He blew me off! We had a date and he just blew me off. So, I decided to call him tonight and ask him why he hasn't been in touch. And you know what he told me?"

Niloofar tensed on the other end of the line. She had genuinely liked Brian when she had met him at Soraya's housewarming party and had hoped her friend might finally have found Mr Right and get everything back on track.

"What did he say, babe?"

"That we're from different cultures and we have nothing in common because I only care about trivial things, while his friends are getting fired and he's trying to save his own tail! What's wrong with me? Why do guys meet me and then run away? How on earth am I going to make the deadline now? No wonder I choose the wrong guys. At least the wrong guys don't run a mile – apart from Jean-Luc, that is."

"Slow down!" Niloofar pleaded. "Brian didn't understand, that's all. Didn't you explain about how you were living?"

"He said it was just a joke!"

"Oh, shit."

"That it was some rich bitch ploy just to piss off my parents!" Soraya paused. "He sounded like he thought I was an ass. Maybe I am. Maybe I came over that way. I was just talking about dog names because it was a light-hearted topic, but he made me out to be so shallow. Or perhaps that was the way I made myself out to be."

"You're not shallow."

"He said that everyone knew I was looking for a husband and that my uncle had put up a dowry."

Niloofar took in a breath. Of course, everyone knew that Soraya was searching for a man and about the million. But to have a virtual stranger point it out was cruel.

"Brian's not a nice person. You're better off without him."

Soraya wasn't listening.

"He made out that I do nothing with my life and that I don't care about friends and colleagues losing their jobs."

"Forget about what he said, he was an asshole," Niloofar replied, point blank.

"But to hear those things… it was really upsetting."

"He wasn't the guy for you."

Soraya nodded dumbly. "Well, I guess my family were right about one thing. I have to go out with someone from the same background, otherwise it just won't work."

Choosing her next words carefully, Niloofar continued.

"Look, babe, unless you can earn enough to support yourself, you're going to have to be realistic."

"I am supporting myself!"

"On your savings!" Niloofar replied, her tone softening again. "You know how much I care about you, but you have to open your eyes. Look at your closet, for example, or your car, or the holidays you go on, or your jewelry, or the restaurants you eat in. You might be making a stand now, but you come from real money, Soraya, and that makes you one of the lucky ones. Besides, you know that you could go home any time and be welcomed back. Whether you like it or not, that's a safety net."

Soraya was silent on the other end of the phone line.

"What you're doing is great; honestly, I admire you. But you can't pretend that you haven't got advantages in life that most people don't have. Brian is an asshole, but he's right – to an outsider looking in, you're lucky and you don't have anything to complain about."

Soraya paused. "You're saying I should do what my family wants?"

"I'm saying that many people haven't got family or money or any kind of support to fall back on. They stay in shitty jobs for decades because they have no choice. They never have the money to live well and it's really hard financially at the moment for a lot of people. Brian is right – people are losing their jobs, their families, and their lifestyles. They're struggling."

"I can't help where I came from."

"No, you can't. Neither can I. Both of us are lucky, but we have to appreciate it," Niloofar said gently. "Brian wasn't the right man for you, but someone will be."

"I've only got two months left to find him."

"And what if you don't?"

"I have to."

"Why?"

"You know why!" Soraya countered. "I have two months to find a husband or one will be found for me."

"Are you sure there's only two choices?"

"Huh?"

"Well, there is a third one."

"Which is?"

"Stop looking."

Soraya stared ahead pensively. "Yeah, I could… Maybe there isn't another man for me. Maybe I was just in love once, with Jean-Luc, and that's it."

"You can't believe that!"

"Why not? I loved him completely; I still love him."

"He treated you so badly, you can't still have feelings for him." Niloofar added: "But you can't help it, can you? None of us can. That's the bitch thing about love – it's out of control. Your head says one thing, your heart – or, more accurately, your body – says another."

Relaxing, Soraya felt the old closeness between them and the comfort she was desperate for. "No one's ever come close to Jean-Luc."

"Have you let them?"

"God, yes. I've prayed someone would make me forget him, but it never lasts. I thought Brian might do it, I even managed to put Jean-Luc out of my mind when I was with him but then he went. Just like that! Thanks, but no thanks. There was a connection between us, I know it. I felt it and he did. But it wasn't enough. I wasn't enough."

She looked around the apartment, hearing noises overhead. A moment later, she heard the television being turned on and the sound of an advert filtering down through the ceiling. Niloofar was right – they were from a different, privileged world. But, as the days passed, Soraya's homesickness had diminished, and she had found herself looking back at her other life with critical eyes. Whatever Brian thought, people's struggles weren't lost on her. She saw their hardship on the Metro – the beaten down faces of women struggling with kids, or middle-aged men, waxy with disappointment and fatigue. It hadn't escaped her notice how many people had turned to the Los Angeles Times' jobs page. And she never passed a homeless person on the street without reaching into her purse for change. She saw it.

But, previously, she hadn't felt it. Previously, she had travelled in her Mercedes, removed from the streets and the general public. She had gone to restaurants and clubs and never once worried whether she had enough money to fund her extravagance. Shopping had never been curtailed by thrift, by the anxiety of a limit on a credit card, or by agonizing over whether she could afford to take a taxi instead of the last Metro home. Vacations had been provided without saving up for tickets, without begging for time off work, without last-minute, cheap purchases at the markets. She had sailed above the clutter of most people's lives, untouched by financial struggle. And so, maybe, her small attempt at independence would seem farcical to some.

Lost between two worlds, her home and her new life, Soraya felt baffled and lonely. Her determination was faltering, with the harsh reality of Brian's words hitting home and undermining her confidence.

"Listen, babe," Niloofar said, cutting into her thoughts. "I have to get back to work. Relax, your life will work out. Honestly, it will. Just stop pushing and let it happen."

A moment later, her cell rang again. Soraya picked up, expecting to hear Niloofar's voice. But it was someone else entirely.

"So, are you married yet, ma chérie?"

Why had Jean-Luc called now? Especially when she felt so low? Her voice faltered. "No, I'm not married."

"What happened to Brian?"

"He's going back to San Francisco."

"No chemistry?"

"He bored me," Soraya lied, her heart thumping. Why didn't she just put the phone down? But she was lonely and homesick, and Jean-Luc had been in her life for so long. And she had never stopped wanting him. "You know me, I get bored quickly."

"So how come you don't get bored with me?

Because you might be the closest I will ever get to love, Soraya thought. But she didn't say the words. Instead, she laughed. "Probably because I never know what to expect with you. I guess your unpredictability keeps my mind stimulated; however crazy that might sound. If you were always the same, I'd have been bored a long time ago."

"Oh, yes?"

Suddenly Soraya got carried away by the moment.

"You know me so well. You understand me. You were the first person in my life who made me feel comfortable in my own skin. You loved me for being me and you accepted me with all my faults. And, most importantly, you never once tried to change me."

There was a long pause down the line.

"I'm speechless! That's sweet," he sighed. "Do you want to come round? I'll make you something to eat. We could talk."

"No," she said firmly.

"Not even for an hour?"

"Not even for an hour."

"What do you mean Brian Zachary's gone back home?" Anahita shouted, fiddling with her earrings and pushing the maid out of the way as she hurried after Amir. "I thought you said Soraya was getting on with him."

"She was."

"But?"

"It's over."

"You spoke to him, didn't you? You interviewed him!" Anahita stood on the landing as she watched her brother walk down the stairs. "You had to spoil it, didn't you?"

"He was a moron."

"He was eligible."

"And what makes a man eligible to you?" Amir countered sarcastically. "Having a pulse? You worry more about your lie being found out than you do about your daughter's future."

Anahita followed Amir down the stairs. As they entered his study, she slammed the door closed behind her and faced him.

"Don't be so judgmental! You want to see her married as much as I do."

"But I didn't set this whole deadline into motion by shouting my mouth off," Amir countered. "I haven't got Los Angeles, Laguna Beach, and Santa Barbara all holding their breath for some phantom wedding."

"Bring him back!"

"What!"

"Brian! Bring him back!" Anahita roared.

"They aren't compatible."

"They're getting married, not becoming friends!" She replied curtly, throwing her earrings across the room. "If you can't get him back, find Richard."

"Apparently, he's been seeing Soraya too, but nothing's developed between them. Nothing ever has, in all the time they have known each other."

"His parents are very fond of Soraya. It would be a good match."

"It's a lost cause."

"Fine. What about that Texan your cousin was talking about?"

Amir turned to look at his sister, exasperated. "He's over sixty!"

"Then he won't be running after other women, will he?" Anahita answered smartly. "I'll have a little think and work out how I can get them together."

Amir had shadows under his eyes from travelling, worrying, and his sister's constant nagging. He was losing what was left of his limited patience.

"Just leave it."

"Just leave it, he says!" Anahita retorted. "Soraya's happiness is at stake."

"This is your reputation at stake, you mean!" Amir snapped.

Anahita put up her hands to prevent him saying any more. "We have to be practical here. Zachary was a washout. Perhaps, the Texan might be better."

Amir wasn't listening. Instead, he was thinking about another means of raising the marital stakes. "What if I raise the dowry to two million?"

Silence fell between them.

"I don't know why I'm worried," Anahita said, with a sudden and unnerving calm. "After all, in two months Soraya will come home and we can then get this finalized."

"If she comes home."

Slowly, Anahita turned to her brother. "What has she said to you?"

"Nothing! I haven't talked to her."

"So why did you say if she comes home?"

"I was thinking aloud."

"But something must have prompted you to say it."

Infuriated, Amir sighed. "I just said it."

"You never 'just' say things. You always have a reason."

"Well, I didn't ask for this!" Amir replied. He then sighed with relief as Mark Tehrani walked in. Glaring at her brother, Anahita left the study.

Mark raised his eyebrows. "Problems?"

"This farce with Soraya. What's happening now? It's taking up more time than my fucking business."

"She went out last night."

"All night?"

"Yes."

"With whom?"

"I'm not sure."

Amir narrowed his eyes, sniffing out the lie at once. "Tell me straight."

"Tell you what?"

"Don't mess around, Mark! Tell me where my niece was last night." Amir replied, his tone dropping. "But first – can I take it standing up, or will I need to sit down?"

"Sitting down might be good," Mark replied, choosing his next words carefully. "Soraya spent the night with Jean-Luc."

Both men heard the howl of anguish from outside the door, and then the dull thud of Anahita hitting the floor.

Two Months Until the Deadline

FIFTEEN

Soraya woke up with a blinding headache. She rolled over, wondering how her head had turned into a drum beating every second without fail. She reached out to flick on the light, but it wasn't there. Oh God! She jerked upright. I'm in Jean-Luc's bed! Shit! Did we? Didn't we? Oh, no. Mortified, Soraya quietly got out of bed to go to the bathroom, only to realize she was still slightly drunk. Bleary eyed, she walked into the doorframe on her way to the bathroom and then examined herself in the mirror. Her makeup was smudged, and she'd slept with her contact lenses in. No wonder her eyes looked so red. Leaning against the bathroom sink, she thought back to the night before.

She remembered arriving at Jean-Luc's apartment and being let in. She remembered him being kind and chatty, and then kissing her. She didn't really remember the rest. No, wait a minute, it was all coming back to her! They had some wine and she had cried a little. He held her, then kissed her. He had wanted to take all her clothes off. She had refused. He insisted. She gave in and they had sex. Shit!

Wincing, Soraya walked back into the bedroom to find Jean-Luc awake.

"Hello," he said cutely. "Do you realize that you left me naked on the bed while you slipped under the duvet?"

"No, we were both really drunk, remember?" Soraya said in a half-serious, half-jokey way as she got dressed. In all honesty, she had known what was going to happen as soon as she decided to come to his apartment.

"Where are you going?"

"I need to get back home," Soraya said hurriedly. "I'm still trying to get my head around what happened last night."

"You can stay. I'll go get us some croissants and orange juice."

Impatient, Soraya shook her head. "Thanks, but I really need to leave. What time is it?"

"Seven o'clock. What's the rush?"

"I have to get to work."

"Work! Don't be crazy, you don't have to work, Soraya."

"I do. I have to earn money for the rent."

He laughed. "No one believes this little escapade of yours."

She stopped dressing and turned to him. "Don't they?"

"No, everyone knows that you'll do what your family say in the end." He replied, smiling at her. "Don't mess up your cozy life, ma chérie. That would be too funny."

Angry, Soraya snatched up her coat. "Funny!"

"Hilarious."

"No," she said, gesturing to him and to the bedroom, "This is funny. This is hilarious. I must have been mad last night. You, of all people! What is the matter with me? I break up with someone and turn to you."

"Because you love me."

"Maybe I do," Soraya said, disappointed in herself. "Maybe I do love you. Maybe I always will. But I've just realized something – I don't like you. I might love you, but I don't like you. Or what you stand for." She moved to the door, then turned. "And don't laugh at me, Jean-Luc! I'm not a fool, or a child. You should remember that."

"Perhaps, when you stop acting like one, I will."

After hurrying home and getting changed, Soraya made it to work with just minutes to spare. Chloe looked disappointed as she walked in the door. Surprised, Soraya glanced over to Madison.

"You've ruined her day," Madison told her. "She was desperate for you to be late. She's in a real mood. Watch your back."

"Anything in particular?"

"Fight with The Director, I think," Madison said in a low voice. "I could hear them shouting through the office door. She has that look too."

"What look?"

"The I-haven't-had-sex-for-days look, and that's bad. Chloe's a bitch normally but, when she's frustrated, she's impossible."

Taking the hint, Soraya got to work, and was just about to call a client when the phone rang.

"Hi, baby."

"Oh my God, Vince!" Soraya instantly realized that news had travelled, and he probably knew about Jean-Luc. He was his close friend and they shared everything.

"How's the deadline?"

"I'm into the third month."

"Oops. And no man in sight?" Vince teased her. "I hear there's this guy staying at the same hotel as your cousins in Malibu who we all think you should meet."

"Don't you start trying to matchmake as well!"

"I'm just sorry it didn't work out with Brian."

Dropping her voice, Soraya hissed down the phone. "How did you know about that?"

"Ah, friends talk."

"And you're friendly with Jean-Luc."

Vince was smiling on the other end of the line, amused by the whole deadline and dowry business. He had known the family for years but had never expected Soraya to end up being raffled off. As for Jean-Luc, Vince knew that the Frenchman cared about Soraya, but whether that love could ever be turned into a commitment was anyone's guess. Despite Jean-Luc's womanizing, he had always had a real affection for Soraya, and he liked her uncle. Indeed, he had told Vince that if he were going to settle down it would be with Soraya. But, if he was ever asked when, the answer was always the same: not yet, if ever.

Vince could hardly blame Jean-Luc. Giving up the bachelor lifestyle to be tied into a controlling Persian marriage was never going to be that appealing, even for a million dollars.

"Of course," Vince continued casually, "there's always that Persian guy coming to LA from Texas. You should meet him. He's not exactly fit but, hey, he's rich. I've met him and he's okay. I could introduce you."

"You know something?" Soraya snapped. "I can't do this anymore. I'm not some sort of toy you can just pass around to see who wants to purchase me!"

"Hey, babe. We're your friends, we're just trying to help."

"Help someone else."

But there was no stopping him. "Is it true that your uncle has doubled the dowry to two million?"

"What?"

"You didn't know? You're really not talking to him then?"

"I'm not talking to anyone in the family."

"God," Vince went on. "Why don't we get married, Soraya, and split the cash? That's providing I get past The Interview! Do you think I'd pass?"

"It depends," Soraya said coolly, playing along. "What's your bank balance like?"

"Well, it will be a lot better after a two-million dollar deposit!"

Despite herself, she laughed. "Sounds promising! And how many languages do you speak?"

"Five."

"Five? I didn't know you spoke five languages. Uncle will be impressed!"

"Excellent! How shall we spend the money? Because I don't want to blow it all on our honeymoon!"

"Seriously, which five languages?"

"Well, there's English, broken Italian, and broken Farsi, Klingon, and Double Dutch."

"I don't think you're going to get to the second part of The Interview."

"What else does he ask?" Vince pressed her.

"Well, do you have a five-year plan?"

"Sure. I was thinking that Year One would come before Year Two and go on numerically all the way up to Five."

"Ha-ha!" Soraya said sarcastically.

"Are you serious? Does your uncle really ask those questions?"

"Yes. Every time."

"Did he interview Brian?"

"I don't know, I suppose so. Like I said, my family and I aren't talking at the moment."

"I can't believe your mother hasn't been on the phone."

"She doesn't know where I'm living. And she won't find out, because you don't know either," Soraya replied smartly.

"Seriously, when are you going home?"

She hedged the question. "I'm not sure."

"You should pack it in."

"No, Vince. And, when every one of my friends says that, it just makes me more determined to stick it out."

He paused for a moment. "You should call home."

And in that moment she realized what he was doing.

"You're talking to my mother, aren't you?"

"She misses you."

"Stop spying on me!" Soraya cried out. "Is everything I say being reported back?"

"Stop hiding yourself," Vince said, changing tack. "I miss our tennis games. Why can't we meet up?"

"Because I have no time. I have a job – thanks to you – and I'm busy."

"Looking for Mr Right?"

"Yeah, still looking."

"You know, I'd love to meet your uncle one day," Vince said quietly. "It takes a lot to scare me off, babe."

"Really?"

"Hey, I still talk to you, don't I? Even though you've gone downmarket."

Soraya smiled to herself. After all, it wasn't Vince's fault that he couldn't resist gossip. If Niloofar or Anya had been in her shoes, Soraya would have been talking about their situation. It was human nature. She was Vince's ally, they went back years, and shared mutual friends. How could she not expect him to be interested? Had she really thought when she left home that no one would notice? That no one would wonder what she was up to? Hardly. Persian society ran on gossip and, much as she might resent it, Soraya was playing right into their hands by setting herself up as a vulnerable target ready to be knocked down.

The days were passing quickly. How many pairs of eyes were watching her countdown to the deadline? How many people – people who Soraya counted as friends – were reporting back to her family? How strong was their grip, even from a distance?

"We have to play tennis soon," Vince told her.

"We will," she said cautiously. "I promise."

"Okay, but I don't want you wearing that bra with a mind of its own when we play next. The one that almost accidentally gives way when I'm just about to serve."

Soraya flirted back, keen to let Vince think she wasn't upset by anything that had happened. The last thing she wanted was for him to tell Jean-Luc she regretted last night. Or worse, that she wanted to get back with him. And, if Vince was passing on news to her mother, she wanted it to be her version, rather than someone else's.

"I'll just wear my tiny little skirt and flash my panties while you're serving!"

"Okay, that's it! Bring it on," Vince countered, laughing. "I'll have to wear my Wonderpants boxer shorts, the ones that uplift and enhance as they support!"

"Soraya!"

Slamming down the phone, she turned to find Chloe watching her. Her expression was triumphant, almost crowing, as she beckoned for Soraya to enter her office. Without glancing in Madison's direction, Soraya walked into her boss's room and stood in front of the desk as Chloe studied her.

"I want a word with you. I've had a complaint."

"From?"

"A client. And don't interrupt when I'm talking!" The office grew chilly as the rain fell outside. "I don't like people complaining about my staff. Remember, I took you on as a favor to Vince, who I've spoken to this morning." She let the implication hang. Soraya was unnerved by this news. "You know that I would never have hired you except as a favor to him?"

"You've made that obvious."

"I want you to clear out the storeroom."

"What?"

"The storeroom across the landing." There was faint amusement in Chloe's tone.

The storeroom was used for rubbish, old furniture, boxes of files, and records. It was dirty and cramped, and Soraya knew exactly why Chloe was making her clear it out. Her clothes would be ruined. It was the most menial job Chloe could find and it was her way of putting Soraya in her place. There was nothing Soraya could do about it. She had won the war, but the battles were ongoing. Chloe couldn't fire her, but she could still make her life miserable.

"I want the place cleared out, cleaned, and everything put back in order by the end of the day," Chloe said, smugly. "You do know how to clear up, don't you?"

Holding the bottle of hairspray at arm's length, Dante sprayed the woman's hair, then ruffled it a little to add volume. Damn it, he wondered, why did the richest people have the worst hair? He picked up a comb to brush the back. These Persian ladies intimidated him. Smiling at his client, he held up a mirror so that she could admire his handiwork.

After he had called for his assistant to get the woman's coat, he turned away and ran some water into a large sink and swirled it with his hands to check the temperature. He glanced over his shoulder to where Soraya's dog, Prada, was sitting quietly on a chair. As an occasional favor he would wash Prada and groom her. He had previously worked as a dog groomer and so his salon was also kitted out for pampering VIP pooches. He liked to tend to the dogs and their masters at the same time.

"You see her?" Dante said to the snarling fox terrier sitting in his client's lap. "She is goooood. So goooood." With one quick movement he lifted Prada and submerged her up to her belly in warm water.

As Dante washed the Maltese, he let his thoughts drift. He was going out with Angelo that evening. They were, apparently, an item again, although God only knew how long that would last. He toyed with the idea of cancelling the dinner in a show of indifference. But then he realized that Angelo would easily find someone else to share his sushi. Unsettled, Dante continued to shampoo the dog, then rinsed her before slipping her into a special drying cabinet. He watched as the warm air blew.

"Hi Dante."

He turned, relieved to see Soraya enter.

"Bambina! Give me a hug! Give me a proper hug! What's this? It's not a hug!" She hugged him properly, and Dante squeezed her so hard her eyeballs bulged.

"Dante, you're hurting me."

"Come, sit down." He flinched at the sight of her filthy clothes. "My God, what happened to you?"

"My boss made me clear out a storage cupboard."

"In your own clothes?" Dante winced, touching his stomach. "Ah, I have a tummy ache; I should not have had all of that pasta. Do you have anything in your portable medicine cabinet?"

Soraya reached into her handbag, rummaging madly. "What kind of stomachache? Cramps? Bloating? Acid indigestion? I need to know in order to give you the right medication."

"Something for nausea."

"This is what you need; it's a life-saver. Here, take two!"

"Grazie mille bambina."

Soraya sat down, crossing her legs and watching as Dante took the tablets. "I need to talk."

"So, talk."

"Vince is gossiping with Jean-Luc and my mother."

"I haven't seen her!" he cried, pretending to be frightened. "Honestly, I haven't spoken to Anahita for days!"

"Everyone else seems to be." Soraya changed tack and looked around. On the wall was a large glossy photograph of Angelo, big enough to make sure no one could miss it. "Were you happy before you met your boyfriend or when you met him?"

"I was happy before. A relationship doesn't make you happy. Another person can't make you happy. Only you can make you happy. But sometimes people are happier as one. I never thought that it would last this long. Up and down, up and down…" He put his head on one side, his expression more than a little curious. "So how are all your dates going?"

"Don't ask."

"What about the Iranian guy from San Francisco?"

"Oh, Brian didn't work out."

"No one else in the pipeline?"

"Vince said something about a Texan."

"My God, another American!"

"No, he's Iranian, living in Texas."

"Better," Dante said, burping.

"How's Angelo?"

"Breaking my fucking heart," Dante snapped. "On, off, on, off. He's got me on a string, and he knows it. Sometimes I think I'll just throw him out for good, but then where would I be? Oh, I don't want to talk about it!" He turned away then turned back. "All the things I've bought for that man, all the holidays. I pay him a billionaire's salary to do the odd cut and color. Half the time I can't afford it, but I've never held back. I've given him everything. And what do I get in return? Heartache. I don't want to talk about it!" Dante shrugged. "God knows, I don't want to bore anyone with my troubles, and I try to keep them to myself, but Angelo's..."

"Angelo?"

"I don't want to talk about it!"

After checking on Prada, Dante turned back to Soraya, smiling. All thoughts of Angelo were temporarily forgotten as he reached behind the counter.

"Bambina, I've brought these amazing jeans over from Italy, what do you think?"

He showed Soraya a pair of jeans that looked like any other. "I think you'd have to be very skinny to wear them."

"But you are skinny, darling!"

"I'm not skinny!"

"Will you try them for me?"

She shrugged. "What size are they?"

"Twenty-seven waist. I have them in six different colors. They only cost about 1,000 dollars."

"What? 1,000!" she almost yelled. "Are they made of pure cashmere, from rare Nepalese goats that have been handfed organically grown oats and hand-knitted by the President himself? That price is ridiculous!"

He ignored her. "Have you not seen the amazing stitching and silk scarf in the back pocket. Look, even the label on the back is made of super soft handstitched leather." He pointed it out proudly.

"You expect people to pay 1,000 dollars for a tiny scrap of fabric? You're crazy!" She pulled a face, thinking about how much food and how many

Metro tickets she could get for that money. "What are they for anyway? Are you going anywhere special?"

"Listen to you, bambina; you're the one who's usually living it up." He paused, "I heard Niloofar's romance isn't working out. The asshole doesn't deserve her; she's worth more than gold."

"She's better than him and that's a fact," Soraya replied, tying a bow in Prada's hair. "Niloofar is always so optimistic – this is the one, this man's different – and then the affair doesn't work out and she's heartbroken. Not that she would admit it; she just pretends she's okay, but anyone can see she's wrecked inside."

"Not like Anya."

"God no, she'd kick the man in the nuts!" Soraya said wryly. She rolled her eyes. "Not only are my entire family worried that I'm going to be left on the shelf, I also now have my friends trying to set me up all over the place. It's a joke. Even Vince was suggesting people."

Dante clicked his tongue. "You and he were once—"

"—Forget it! Vince is the last man I'd marry." Soraya cuddled Prada and nuzzled the top of her head. "I love you all for trying…"

"But?"

"Back off!" Soraya replied. "Anya has been harassing me to go on a date with this random Lebanese guy for the past month. Then Alina – remember her?"

"I remember."

"Well, she's now in France, happily married and pregnant, but even she's heard about my predicament and is desperately trying to set me up with her cousin who I once had a crush on when I was sixteen!"

Tutting, Dante was mixing the dye for his next client. His salon was always busy and full of rich women who had nothing better to do with their time than to get pampered daily. His clientele was almost entirely female.

"Do I really need a guy to complete me? Maybe I've just been brainwashed into thinking that way. I'm starting to feel like a tennis ball being smacked from one end of the court to the other, from side to side, back and forth across the net, thwack, thwack. Caught in the middle of the longest rally on earth, with no end in sight. Thwack, thwack, on and on it goes. I'm in the middle of a stadium with everyone I know watching and I can't seem to stop. I try calling "out!" but no one is listening – just thwack, thwack."

Dante poured them both a glass of wine and passed one to Soraya. She sipped it half-heartedly, then put a lead on Prada.

"I'll just take her for a little walk," she said, grabbing a couple of poop bags and stuffing them into her pocket.

"Honey, you can't go out! You look like a wreck!"

"I'm not going on a hot date. Anyway, no one will see me. It's dark now. I'll just take Prada round the block and come back. I could do with some fresh air."

"In LA?" he drawled. "Let me know if you find any."

After walking Prada round the block, the little dog decided to turn into a pooping machine. Soraya had already used up two bags and was surprised when Prada looked on the verge of pooping again. Aghast, Soraya looked around to see if anyone was watching. Then, as Prada offloaded for the third time in what felt like five minutes, she realized she had run out of bags. Damn, she would just have to leave it. Luckily, it was dark, so no one could see her. But, as Prada continued pooping, someone walked past. He stopped and watched to see whether Soraya picked the mess up. Praying that the man would walk on, she stood over the dog and the poop, but he didn't move a muscle. Realizing that she couldn't stand there indefinitely, Soraya walked off reluctantly.

"You should pick that up!" the man shouted after her.

"Excuse me?" she said, turning around.

"You should really pick that up!"

"I've run out of bags, unfortunately. Do you have a spare one of anything else I can use."

"Yeah! Use your hands!"

This was turning out to be a shitty day, Soraya thought. First cleaning out the store cupboard, and now being ordered by a stranger to pick up dog shit with her hands.

"It was an accident. I ran out of bags," Soraya said, her temper rising. "Anyway, I don't think it's any of your business. If you're so damn concerned, why don't you pick it up with your hands!"

She walked off.

Of course, the guy was right, but surely he had better things to do with his time than stick his nose where it didn't belong? Guilt nagged at Soraya. Normally she was a good citizen, and always picked up after Prada. She walked back to Dante's salon feeling pissed off. This was not what she needed to end the night.

Moments later, Soraya felt a tap on her shoulder. She turned round to see a police officer standing behind her. Oh shit.

"Excuse me, madam, but that gentleman has made a complaint that you didn't pick up after your dog."

Soraya looked round. The 'gentleman' had gone, and the policeman was the only other person on the street.

"Sorry, officer, but, as I explained to him, I'd used up my last bag just a few minutes ago."

"You know that it's against the law to allow your dog to foul on the streets?"

She felt like a child. Even an evening stroll with her dog led to someone telling her what to do.

"Yes officer, I am very aware of that. And I always pick up after my dog. It just so happened she went three times and I'd already used two bags and didn't have another one." She looked at him, her tone pleading. "I'm really sorry, officer, it won't happen again."

"Well," he said reluctantly. "I'll let you off just this once. Consider this a warning."

Oh my God, she was being cautioned for dog shit. What the hell had happened to her life?

Five minutes later, a very subdued Soraya walked back into Dante's salon. He had turned the sign on the door to CLOSED and was sitting down relaxing with a glass of wine, smiling a warm welcome.

"I just got told off by the police."

His smile faded. "Huh?"

"For not picking up Prada's poop."

Aware that if he laughed there might well be an argument, Dante passed Soraya some wine and encouraged her to sit down.

"Come on," he said, nudging her, "let's get on the computer and look everyone up. I love Instagram – so many bad photoshopped pictures. There's only one thing you can do when you have a day like this one – laugh at people."

Huddled together, they went through their friends. Dante showed Soraya some new photos he had added of Angelo. Soraya searched for Brian's profile and told Dante what he had said to her. They had worked their way through most of their friends, when Soraya noticed that Jean-Luc's sister had recently followed her. Curious, she examined her profile. She had the same profile as her brother, but her big eyes were blue instead of green, and her hair was cut in a sharp crop. She looked kind of mean. Getting on her bad side probably wouldn't be a smart move.

"She's pretty," Soraya remarked.

Dante shrugged. "Better looking than her brother."

"Jean-Luc is handsome!"

"If you say so, bambina."

"I do," Soraya said lightly. "If he was ugly, it would be easier to resist him."

"Resist him?" Dante said, scenting gossip. "You haven't been sleeping with him again, have you?"

"I..."

"After all you said!" Dante went on. "I told you it was a bad idea to invite him to your housewarming party! It just opened old wounds. You're kidding yourself if you think there's a future with Jean-Luc. You want marriage and he's not the type."

Without replying, Soraya scrolled through the pictures on the computer in front of her, and suddenly felt a kick to the stomach.

"Oh my god."

Staring back at her was Jean-Luc's feed. There were no landscapes or arty pictures of coffee and books to break up the usual narcissistic selfies – it was full of pictures of himself posing and showing off. Another body blow swiftly followed – a picture of him playing tonsil tennis with some bimbo.

Dante's eyes were bulging. "Who is she?"

"Jean-Luc's girlfriend, Lisa Kashi," Soraya answered stiffly. "I heard that he was seeing someone, but it wasn't serious. But they must be an item, or they wouldn't be on Facebook kissing. And it's a new photo." She was hardly breathing and felt shaken. "He said it was over."

"I think he lied, bambina." Dante stared at the photograph. "She's so young."

"Nineteen. I can't believe this." Soraya said, close to tears. "He feeds me all this bullshit about how he doesn't want to be in a relationship because he has commitment issues. My God, he even told my family that, when he felt ready, I'd be the first person he'd want to marry! The liar!" Dante leaned back in his chair. Soraya continued, "He was probably just after the dowry. He makes love to me and lets me think I'm special to him, and all the time he's got some fake blonde bimbo warming his bed! So much for karma. So much for trusting him. Oh my fucking god!" she almost screamed. "I'm such an idiot!"

Cautiously, Dante filled up her glass. "She looks cheap."

"I hope she's a gold digger who sucks him dry of every dime he has! Her last boyfriend was this rich Arab about twenty years her senior who also happened to drive the latest Ferrari. Clearly, she's only after his money, and Jean-Luc thinks it's better to date girls in their teens because they won't want to settle down."

"Shhh."

"Don't shush me!" Soraya snapped, as she picked up her cell and called Jean-Luc's number.

"Hello?" he answered in his laziest French drawl.

"I see your taste in women hasn't changed. Still into money grabbing, shallow whores! You're so fucking superficial!" she yelled. Dante tried to take the phone away from her, while Prada growled and yapped behind them.

"Why are you always so hard on me?" Jean-Luc asked.

"You led me on!"

"We're both adults."

"I thought you were a better man."

"Well," he responded coldly, "I hope you find a nicer guy than me."

Soraya shook with anger and disappointment. "What's happened to you? You've changed so much. I don't know who you are anymore. Look at yourself. Your friends are fake; your life is fake! And you know, after seeing the slut you're sleeping with I've lost all respect for you."

"Soraya, calm down."

"Why the hell did you feed me all those lies about wanting to marry me 'when you felt ready'? You were just stringing me along!" She was choking, her words falling over themselves. "Why would you involve my family? What the fuck is wrong with you?"

"I never meant to hurt you."

"Give me a break, Jean-Luc. You'll fill this girl's head with shit for the first few months, take her on shopping sprees, buy her Louboutin's, wine and dine her, take her to Paris to meet your parents, and have mediocre sex with your microscopic dick." Soraya spat. Dante's eyes widened. "Then, within a few months, you'll show your true colors. She'll get fed up with you and your ridiculously low sex drive. You'll turn into the devil that you really are, and history will repeat itself. You'll never change, Jean-Luc. You're sick in the head, just like your friends. Once you're done with them, you move onto the next."

"You're crazy!"

"Yes, crazy for believing you! Crazy for loving you! Well, I'll never care for you again. You don't deserve anything other than a bitch, because you're an asshole! You'll end up old and lonely with a few illegitimate kids here and there – but no family. No one will stick around you long enough and you'll end up having to down a bottle of Viagra each week just to keep up with the children you're trying to date." She paused, crying, and then flung her cell down.

Dante picked it up delicately. "Hello?" he said.

"What?"

"Jean-Luc?" Dante began. "You hurt my friend."

"Fuck off."

"Okay. Your place or mine?"

Despite her own troubled relationship, Niloofar tried to call Soraya as soon as she heard about what had happened. Dante had obviously spread the gossip on the same night while it was still juicy and fresh. But Soraya wasn't picking up her cell, so Niloofar contacted Anya instead.

She was smoking a Russian cigarette and, after a few doses of vodka and Xanax, was feeling mellow when she picked up.

"Hello?"

"Hi, babe, it's Niloofar. Did you hear about Soraya?"

"What is it this time?"

"Jean-Luc has a new girlfriend. She's nineteen."

"Fuck."

"Exactly. And Soraya found out."

"Hah!" Anya replied. "Men like Jean-Luc have to be kicked in the balls every day to get them into line. He always comes back to her, or she always goes back to him, and nothing ever comes of it." She inhaled deeply. "We should talk to her, *dahling*."

"And say what?"

"That she has to find another man. Not Jean-Luc. If she's really serious about this deadline then perhaps we should help her out."

Niloofar frowned. Was this really Anya talking? The same Anya who thought Soraya was an idiot for leaving home? The same Anya who believed Soraya would – eventually – obey her family?

"I thought you wanted her to go home?"

"I do, *dahling*," she replied, "but Soraya has decided to stick to her guns. She really wants to prove that she can live her own life and find her own man. She's crazy, but I admire her."

Pleased that Anya was firmly on Soraya's side, Niloofar continued. "It must really have hurt to find out about Jean-Luc's girlfriend."

"How did Soraya find out?"

"On Facebook."

"Is it that fake blonde with the tattoo on her ankle?" Anya asked, her tone husky. "The one who's always in 1 OAK with those rich Arabs? Lisa Kashi?

"That's the one!"

"She's such a slut, *dahling*! And Jean-Luc is an asshole!"

"I hope he loses his job and his dick falls off," Niloofar fumed.

"What goes around comes around, sweetie," Anya reminded her. "Soraya should have told him what she thought of him."

"She did."

"Bravo! Men like that have to be kept in their place. I've told Soraya to treat them like dirt." She shrugged lazily. "The man is a jerk. He should have at least told Soraya that he was seeing someone else."

Always sympathetic, Niloofar stared ahead and tried putting herself in Soraya's shoes. "I bet she hasn't been able to stop crying since she found out."

Anya was dismissive. "Aww *dahling*, he's not worth it! He has issues and she can do so much better. Let him mess around. Soraya should be jumping with joy that it's some other girl he's pissing on and not her. Anyway, Soraya always said he wasn't so good in bed, so why pine over him?"

"Because she loves him."

"Love?" Anya laughed. "Silly girl."

"Well, I hope his new girlfriend fucks him over," Niloofar said coldly. "It's about time he got a taste of his own medicine!"

"Soraya has to cut Jean-Luc out of her life for good; it needs to be like he never existed."

"You know she slept with him the other night?"

Anya paused for a moment. "Why?"

"She's been feeling down. Things didn't work out with Brian and she felt rejected. I guess she turned to Jean-Luc for comfort."

"Fuck comfort! Mothers are for comfort, men are for sex," Anya sighed, her Russian accent purring. "Jean-Luc doesn't seem to want Soraya to move on. He likes to keep his claws in her. But he never changes. This girl will realize just like the last one did, and she'll leave him. They all do."

"I hope so."

"Don't worry, karma will get him."

"Not if Soraya gets him first."

There was a pause and then they both laughed.

"Perhaps we should get someone to beat him up!" Anya suggested.

"Sounds like a plan, but who?"

"We'll hire someone."

"No, why deprive ourselves of the pleasure? Let's do it ourselves!"

"But seriously, *dahling*," Anya said, sitting upright and stubbing out her cigarette. "We have to try and help Soraya find a man. We could start this weekend. We can go to dinner, then hit a club. Find her a boyfriend there maybe?"

"Why not?" Niloofar said hopefully. "There's so little time left of her deadline. And anyway, Soraya won't mind. She's set me up with guys in the past."

"It's just returning the favor, *dahling*," Anya replied silkily. "Just looking out for our friend."

SIXTEEN

"Tell me this is a joke!" Amir glanced over to Mark, with his glasses half-way down his nose. "My niece had a run in with the police for not picking up her dog shit?" his eyes rolled.

"She usually carries poop bags."

"Poop bags?" Amir frowned. "There are things called 'poop bags'?"

"You've never had a dog, but it's the usual thing. Your dog defecates on the pavement and you use a poop bag to pick it up."

"With your hands?"

"Outside the poop bag, yes."

"That," Amir sniffed, "is disgusting."

"Anyway, Soraya didn't get fined, she was just warned."

"But she still has to use 'poop bags'?"

"Unless she puts a cork up the dog's bum, yes," Mark chuckled. "You are very naïve about some things."

Amir made a low rumbling sound in his chest. "Okay, so what else has she been doing? There are just two months left and no fiancé in sight."

"I know."

"Hah! I told you! In the end, we will have to find my niece a husband."

"Not so fast! She still has time," Mark said with a smile. "A lot can happen in two months."

"Yes, she can get into trouble again for not having enough 'poop bags.' "

Walking out of the office, Mark smiled to himself. When his employee had phoned in early that morning to say he had food poisoning and unable to work, Mark had been irritated. But, now that he'd had time to think about it, Mark decided that he would take over the man's duty that day. How hard could watching Soraya be? Not that he was going to do it surreptitiously. No, he would do it as he usually did – as a friend, dropping by to see how she was. After all, what could be more natural for a go-between?

In truth, Mark was surprised by Soraya's stand. He had expected her to fold pretty quickly. But once the first month had passed, then the second, and now the third had begun, he saw that she was digging her heels in. Far from being the spoilt Persian princess with no steel, she was throwing herself wholeheartedly into the challenge she had set herself. Of course, finding a husband in four months was a damn near impossibility, but the fact that Soraya had picked up the gauntlet was impressive. And Mark had noticed that Amir – for all his indifference and sarcastic comments – was also impressed. The Soraya he thought he knew had been taken over by a more courageous woman. But then, Mark thought, what did her family expect? Her background might be Persian, but Soraya had been raised in the West. Arranged marriages might have been acceptable in Iran, but in LA? Surrounded by women who picked their own partners and married for love, Soraya had been wavering unsteadily between two worlds for too long. The question was, which world would end up claiming her?

Over the previous three years, Mark had often heard the same exchange between Soraya and her uncle:

"Any progress on the husband search?"

"None."

"You need someone you can depend on, Soraya. You need a rock."

"You're my rock, uncle."

"Seriously, you're way too old to be just having fun. You need to find yourself a steady man."

"Okay uncle, whatever you say."

Mark knew that Soraya went along with Amir just to avoid an argument, because she could never win against her uncle. She was always wrong, and he was always right. Mark felt that must have become tiring after a while. How annoying it must be to be ruled by one's family. There were times when Soraya was practically living in the beauty salon, getting all her treatments done for some dinner, or a party, or the Persian New Year. As for Soraya's hobbies... well, her mother didn't think she should be playing competitive tennis. Anahita wasn't interested in any sport and could not relate to her daughter's passion for the game. She wasn't impressed by Soraya's other interests either. All her family were interested in was getting Soraya married.

Their preferred choice, Richard, could leave her for another woman, but even that would be excused. Especially if he had given her a child before he left. Baffled, Mark's thoughts continued as he drove down Sunset Boulevard towards Brentwood. He parked outside Soraya's block and rang the buzzer several times. When there was no answer, he tried her landlord's.

"Hello, can I help you?"

"I'm sorry to disturb you," Mark said lightly, "but I'm a family friend of Soraya's. I thought she lived here."

"She does, in the apartment next door," the woman replied. "But I haven't heard her come in yet. Would you like to come up and wait for her? You can usually hear her when she gets in."

Mark happily accepted her offer. He took the elevator up and was greeted by a heavily pregnant woman, who showed him into the kitchen, made some tea, and sat at the table by the window. Following her lead, he took a seat opposite her.

"Do you mind my asking when the baby's due?"

She smiled warmly, pleased to talk about it. "Just about a month."

"Do you know if it's a boy or a girl?"

"No. I wanted it to be a surprise," Jenny replied. "We both did, my husband and me. We never wanted to know the sex of the baby." She sipped her tea. "My husband was killed a few months ago. I always feel as though I have to say that, to explain why he's not around, you know? Before there are any awkward questions. Not that people want to be awkward. They just ask the normal things and then you have to tell them. It's easier to tell them at the beginning." She paused, pushing her hair away from her forehead. "I'm not making much sense, am I?"

"Perfect sense," Mark replied. "I lost someone very close too. It's difficult, but you always try to make it easier on everyone else. Yes, I know exactly what you mean."

"Did you lose your wife?"

"No, our child."

Her hand went over her mouth. "God, I'm so sorry."

"It's okay," he said quietly. "We've come to terms with it. Well, as much as you can, that is."

She felt an understanding pass between them – a shared empathy she hadn't felt with anyone else. Being pregnant, Jenny had learned to curtail her grief for the sake of the baby. When it was born, she told herself, then I will cry. But not now. Now it might upset the child inside me. Who knew how a mother's distress could travel through the womb? She had willed herself to keep strong. The time would come when she could cry. She smiled at the attractive stranger sitting across her table, wondering who he was and what he was to Soraya. Obviously not a husband, nor a lover – he wasn't the type. A friend? If so, Soraya was a lucky woman. Jenny would have wanted a friend like this man.

"What time does Soraya come home?"

Jenny glanced at the clock. "Around six, usually."

"Do you know her well?"

"Increasingly, lately. She came to the antenatal clinic with me."

He laughed. "Soraya?"

Laughing too, Jenny nodded. "Oh, she got the hang of it in the end. But most of the time, I don't see much of her. She's working, or busy with her friends. All I know is that she's had a falling out with her family. That's it."

Jenny waited, but nothing else was forthcoming. When the elevator made a sound, she gestured to Mark.

"Here she is!" She stuck her head out of the door to the hallway. "You've got a visitor! Come and have coffee with us!"

Surprised to see Mark, Soraya walked into the comfortable kitchen and sat down at the table, smiling. The room was well lit. It was a cold, dark evening, but the interior was warmed by the oven. A delicious smell wafted from the freshly cooked cake that rested on the side table. Soraya felt comfortable and at ease. The kitchen wasn't expensive or equipped with all the latest technology, but it was inviting and drew her in.

"Cake?"

Nodding, Soraya accepted a slice. Mark took another as Jenny made fresh coffee. Watching her, Soraya noticed that, although clearly tired and heavily pregnant, Jenny also seemed radiant and happy to have company.

"It's so nice to have guests. It can get quite lonely."

Soraya glanced up. "Isn't your father here at the moment?"

"No, he had to go home for a while," Jenny replied. "To be honest, I'm relieved. He'll come back when the baby's born."

When she smiled at Mark, Soraya felt a pinch of unexpected jealousy. What the hell? This was Mark Tehrani, her uncle's best friend – the man who had watched her grow up. The man who knew about all her secrets and embarrassments, including her terrible efforts at DIY. The very personable – but very married – Mark Tehrani. Oh, but he had beautiful eyes, Soraya thought. How come she'd never noticed that before? Green eyes, with black lashes. Snap out of it! Soraya told herself, flushing. He's married. Off the list. Out of bounds. Off limits.

"You must like it here," Mark said, turning to Soraya. "This place has a great atmosphere."

"I do, I do," she agreed, looking over to Jenny.

"When my husband was alive, we had so many plans to extend the place, knock down the walls, and join the apartments together. You know, alterations and improvements. But then he died, and they went on hold. Not enough money." She shrugged without self-pity. "What can you do, but make the best of it?"

"Do you come from LA?"

"No. My husband did, but I'm from Boston, so I don't know many people here. I think I've let myself get a little cut off."

"It's difficult to make friends in a city," Mark volunteered. He was perfectly at ease and looked in no hurry to leave. "It took me a while to get used to LA."

"It's not a good place to be pregnant in."

"It's not a good place to be alone in," Mark replied. He turned to Soraya. "And how are you coping?"

"Okay." she said, wondering where the conversation was going. "Still holding down my job."

"I shouldn't keep you two," Jenny said politely. "I'm sure you want to talk privately." Reluctantly, she watched them get up and move next door.

For a long time afterwards, Jenny sat in the kitchen and listened to the murmur of voices from next door. Something about Mark Tehrani had reminded her of her late husband. His calm, good nature was obvious, but there was a strength beneath it that she recognized – and missed.

Meanwhile, Soraya was waiting to find out why Mark Tehrani was visiting her unannounced. But he seemed in no hurry to explain. He just wanted to talk. Before long they were both laughing about embarrassing incidents in their pasts. Like the time when Mark reversed his car into Amir's new Rolls Royce, or when Soraya started clapping before the play was over.

Suddenly Mark turned serious. "She's a nice woman."

"Who is?"

"Your landlady, Jenny. Can't be easy losing a husband and having to bring up a child alone."

"She's incredible. Always very positive."

"Really?" He fell silent for a moment. "She seemed scared to me."

The remark caught Soraya off guard. His perception made her think. True, she had been involved with her own problems, but had she really missed that?

"Scared? Because she's alone?"

"No, because she has no time to grieve before the baby comes," Mark explained. "Everyone needs time to grieve. If you don't, it gets you in the end."

And then Soraya remembered the death of his child. It was the one thing Mark never talked about, even to Amir. They all knew Mark was naturally discreet and kept his own counsel, but there had never been any mention – either deliberate or accidental – of his son's death. It was closed off, untouchable, unreachable – like his marriage. Funny, Soraya thought: Mark was so easygoing and charming that people didn't realize how private he was; how intensely secretive.

"You've only got two months left of the deadline."

"Yep, I know."

"So," Mark said, "you know your family would like to see you. They want you to come home."

"I know."

"They worry about you. Really worry about you."

She frowned. "And you've come here just to tell me that?"

"No," he said firmly. "I don't follow orders from anyone. I came to talk to you because I wanted to." He was very selective about which activities he shared with her family. "They miss you, your uncle and your mother."

She sighed. "They miss bossing me around."

"They don't see it that way. They think you're being stubborn and rebellious."

"Maybe I am," she agreed. "Am I trying to prove a point to my family? And what point might it be? That I have control over my body but nothing else in my life? Is that why I keep going for the wrong guys? Is that why I'm still single and depressed?"

He smiled wryly.

"You're rarely single. For the last couple of years, you've always had a dozen suitors on the go; half of whom appear to be potential fiancés, with various different families flying in from around the world hoping to nod their approval on your forthcoming engagement to their son!" He raised his eyebrows. "As for being depressed, come on! You're young. You can make any mistake you want and learn from it. You could serve a prison sentence for murder and still be out in time to have kids and raise a family."

"Very funny!" Soraya said, her tone dropping. "But I am struggling, Mark."

"But that's a state of mind. Are you struggling? Or embracing a new challenge?"

"So you think I'm 'playing' at this too then?!"

"No! That's not what I am saying. But look at what you have achieved. You have a job, you are paying for an apartment, you are doing things on your own terms."

"I just wish it wasn't so hard. I know I could go home and that would remove some of my problems, but I'd just be encouraging the old ones to resurface. My life is like a gilded cage. If I went home, I would have money, and exotic vacations, and all the designer clothes I could ever want, but I am also controlled all the time. I am told what designer clothes to wear and where it's appropriate for me to vacation. The money is conditional. It allows them to tell me who to go out with, who not to go out with, when to go to the hair salon, when to get my nails done. And it allows them to sell me to the highest bidder."

"Your family wants the best for you."

"Well, maybe their best isn't my best," she countered. "If my family gets their way and I end up marrying a suitor of their choice, I'll go from being financially dependent and controlled by one family to being financially and emotionally controlled by my husband. Isn't that a recipe for disaster?"

"They don't see it that way."

"Besides," Soraya went on, "how is issuing a deadline to find a husband helping me? Oh, and with the added proviso that if I don't find him, they'll pick someone." She leaned back in her seat, folding her arms defensively. "Would you do that to any daughter of yours?"

"I don't have a daughter."

"But if you did?"

He ignored the question.

"Your family don't want you to make the wrong decisions and regret them later in life."

"Well, they will be my problems to deal with and not theirs! I mean, how can they guarantee that I'll be happy living my life the way they want me to live?" She brushed her hair back from her face impatiently. "No wonder I can't have a successful relationship."

He watched her; his expression unreadable as she continued. Obviously, he was bearing the brunt of her frustration.

"You know something? When I go out for dinner, go to a tennis match, or even want to chill out at home, there is always at least one member of my family around. There's no escaping them. I couldn't have a secret relationship even if I wanted one! I feel like I am living on The Truman Show – I'm watched twenty-four hours a day, seven days a week."

Mark felt a twinge of guilt.

"Privacy doesn't exist in my world. My every move is registered. News in this family travels within thirty seconds. If you want something broadcast, tell my mother and it'll make that evening's headlines." She paused, taking in a deep breath. "You know why I moved out? I had to, or I would have lost my damn mind."

"So, has it been better since you've been living on your own?"

She gave him a cold look. "It's been… different."

"And have you found The One?"

"I met an American guy."

"Nice?"

"Not really. Younger than me."

"Ah."

"And there's some Texan who wants to meet me."

"What's he like?"

"Sixty."

"Next."

She smiled. "Of course, my family would be delighted if I married Richard Parker." She paused, looking over to Mark. "What do you think of him?"

"Not exactly a ball of fire."

Laughing, she shook her head. "But he's an anesthetist, Mark! And his family wants the match. These things matter. Surely you've learnt something in all the time you've known us?" They laughed in unison. "No, I haven't met anyone," Soraya sighed.

"You've still got a few weeks left."

"What would you do?"

"About finding a man?" he asked, laughing.

"You know what I mean! What would you do if you were me?"

"You have to follow your heart, Soraya, and do what makes you happy." He glanced towards the next apartment as Jenny's feet moved next door, thinking how thin the walls were here. "Life is so fleeting. Grab it and make the most of it."

SEVENTEEN

It's official, Soraya thought. She was a lost cause. She was now so lost that her friends were making it their mission to find her someone. She had formally become a charity case for the Boyfriend Aid and Relief Foundation, BARF! Seemed so appropriate. Then again, they were just trying to help and, since there was barely any time left, Soraya felt it was wise to let her friends try and find her elusive Mr Right.

Later, when she looked back on it, Soraya viewed the whole comedy of errors like a three-act play, with her playing the starring role – whether she liked it or not.

Act One

Arriving at the restaurant with a strained smile on her face, Soraya saw a man sitting opposite Anya. At first, she thought it was someone she knew but, as Soraya approached the table, Anya stood up and, with a pleased look on her face, whispered into her ear: "*Dahling*, I've found your future husband."

"You what?"

Stunned, Soraya surveyed the small, nerdy, bug-eyed guy, then looked back at Anya in disgust. What was she thinking? Had she completely lost her mind?

But she was in full flow, talking to the frog who would never be a prince. "This is my friend, Soraya, who I've been telling you all about, since I'm no longer available."

Thanks a bunch, Soraya thought, sitting down at the table.

The frog spoke with barely contained smugness and full of the certainty that he'd scored. "Your friend has been telling me all good things about you."

"That's great," Soraya said curtly, shooting Anya a look that could have burned toast.

"What are you two up to after dinner?" he asked.

"Oh, this and that," Soraya said vaguely, glancing down at her wrist. "Dammit, my bracelet is broken! It was a present."

"Oh, that's a shame," the annoying guy said.

As if Soraya cared what he thought! God, she really didn't want to be spending her dinner with him.

"Why don't you two lovely ladies join us later for a drink?"

"I don't think so," Soraya replied abruptly.

"You have other plans?"

"As a matter of fact, yes."

Soraya was in no mood to be nice to one of Anya's cast-offs. She was hungry, her bracelet had just broken, and the last thing she needed was some idiot pestering her over dinner. But it took another half an hour before the frog finally returned to his table.

"What were you thinking?" Soraya asked Anya angrily.

"Oh, come on, *dahling*, he's harmless. And besides, that Iranian from Texas is coming over to LA in the next couple of days."

"He's too old!"

"*Dahling*, stop being so fussy," Anya responded. "I don't know why you don't just get engaged to someone – anyone – and take the pressure off yourself."

"If you tell me beggars can't be choosers, I will hit you."

Anya shrugged indolently. "Okay, okay, I'm sorry. Maybe I'll find you someone nice at 1 OAK later."

"Babe, thanks but you don't have to find me anyone. I'm fine the way I am."

"You know our agreement, *dahling*. I have to find you someone."

It was no good trying to turn her from her cause.

"There's no need for guys; life is so much simpler without them."

Anya casually waved the suggestion aside, her gaze snaking across the restaurant. "Let's just see what happens, sweetie? You never know, you may meet The One tonight, just when you're least expecting it."

God, Soraya thought, this is going to be tough. No one could shake Anya from a course of action when she was set upon it. And besides, men were her specialty. Thankfully, Niloofar arrived to join them for coffee and eagerly agreed to Anya's suggestion that they move on to a nightclub. They had been talking, had they? Soraya began to realize that they had both rallied round to find her a man. Oh God, the humiliation of it all.

Outside 1 OAK it was absolute chaos. People were fighting and pushing just to get in. Soraya and Anya looked at each other, wondering whether it was worth the hassle, even though they were always allowed to skip the queue.

"What do you think, babe?"

She flicked back her blonde hair. "Looks crazy in there. Shall we go and see what it's like, and if it's no good go to Soho House?"

"Sure, why not? I haven't been to Soho House since Halloween."

But when they entered 1 OAK, Soraya looked around and frowned. Damn it, the place was a disaster waiting to happen. There were people lining up on the staircase to get in, while others were trying to get out. The whole place was a fire hazard. After another ten minutes of fighting their way downstairs, they took one look at the place and wanted to leave. Soraya was hardly able to breathe, let alone move.

"This is crazy," she told Anya. "It's way over-capacity and there are no cute guys."

"But, sweetie, I thought you didn't want to meet anyone tonight?"

Soraya pulled a face. "If I'm going to be crushed to death, I'd like to have some pretty people to look at."

"You're right, *dahling*, this place is way too packed, and it smells. It's going to take us another twenty minutes just to get our coats from the cloakroom."

Eagerly, Soraya stepped in. "Don't worry, babe, I'll push to the front. You two go and wait outside."

It was quieter in Soho House, as it was a members-only club. Soraya looked around to see if she could spot anyone she knew. Already tired, she was feeling more than a little conspicuous, like some country bumpkin being trawled around, with her single status as obvious as a neon light flashing DESPERATE DESPERATE DESPERATE over her head. When she couldn't see anyone she knew, the three of them headed straight to the bar where some awkward-looking man started talking to Niloofar.

Ha! Soraya sniggered to herself, now it's her turn to suffer!

A few minutes later, Niloofar managed to pull away, feeling as good-natured and optimistic as ever. "So, anyone you like?"

Soraya shrugged. "We've been here two minutes. Give me a chance."

"What about him?" Anya asked, pointing to a very handsome guy about five feet away from her.

Soraya nodded. "Oh yes, I like him."

A few moments later the cute guy walked in their direction, heading towards the bar. But before he could get any further, Anya grabbed his arm. Embarrassed, Soraya turned the other way and pretended she had no idea what the Russian was about to do. She kept sipping her drink until Anya tapped her on the shoulder.

"Aden," she purred to the man, "this is Soraya."

"Hey, I was just telling your friend that I wanted to meet you."

Wow, Soraya thought, he really was very handsome and had a classy American accent. The family would approve.

She laughed nervously and got straight to the point. "So, Aden, what's your status? Are you single, engaged, married?"

"I'm single with baggage."

"Aren't we all?"

"Want to go out for a cigarette?" he asked.

"I don't smoke but I could use some fresh air," she agreed lightly. "Anya, are you coming?"

"No, *dahling*; I'm fine here with my drink, you two go." She winked at Soraya.

Outside in the cold, Soraya and Aden talked easily, almost too easily. She found out that he had been a student at both USC and UCLA, and was obviously bright. But he was twenty-one! Crap. She would have thought he was in his mid-twenties, at least. Oh well, guess this won't be going anywhere either. What a shame. Then again, what did age matter? The Iranian Texan was sixty. As the night air cooled down rapidly, Soraya realized she could no longer feel her hands, so she suggested they go back inside.

"*Dahling*," Anya called out to her when she spotted them enter, "we're going to go home now."

"What? Both of you?" Soraya asked, looking over to Niloofar.

"Just stay and have fun," Anya said, smiling. "He's lovely, *dahling*."

"You're going to leave me here with a complete stranger?"

Unworried, Anya glanced over to Aden. "You'll look after her, won't you?"

"Of course," he smiled.

Without giving Soraya a moment to respond, Aden grabbed her and started twirling her around, smiling winningly.

"I've just joined a salsa club," he said. "I have a show coming up in a few weeks' time."

She raised her eyebrows. "And I guess you're practicing your moves on me?"

"I need the practice."

Okay, Soraya thought, she would stay and have a dance but then go straight home. There was no way she was getting involved with a toy boy! She had made enough bad choices in her life, and even the looming deadline wasn't going to make her relent. But as they kept dancing, Soraya noticed that he had strong, muscular arms and no hair – just the way she liked it.

Expertly, Aden flung Soraya left and right and spun her around until she got so dizzy she had to sit down, breathless and flushed. I'm too old for this, she thought incredulously. I really need someone my own age.

"Ok, Aden, just one thing here," she said dryly. "I'm not twenty-one, and I'm a little more fragile than you are."

He laughed. And then he kissed Soraya on the lips. Though her head was giddy from the vodka shots and still spinning around from all the dancing, the kiss came as a shock. Maybe it really was time she went home.

"I think I should get a cab now."

"No stay," he insisted.

"It's way past my bedtime."

"Okay, well give me your number before you go, and I'll give you a missed call."

"Okay," she said smiling, as he passed her his cell to enter her number.

He grinned. "Great, let me walk you to a cab."

"That's very gentlemanly."

"I know," he said, and laughed again.

It was only on her way home that reality struck Soraya like a slap. It had been a fun evening, but what the hell was she playing at? A twenty-one-year-old student? Was that the best she could do? Was that the best her friends could come up with? In the whole of LA was there no one more suitable than a kid? Good God, Soraya thought. She let herself into the apartment and tumbled onto her bed. She felt dispirited, tired, and old.

She fleetingly wondered if her family would find out. Soraya knew that Amir had the means to discover what had been going on over the past weeks. He was too possessive to stand back and let her have her way. So maybe they would hear about Aden. Soraya could imagine her mother's face. A student with no job and no money. And only twenty-one. Some catch, hey? How's that for a fiancé, Mom?

Then again, how much of a catch was a sixty-year-old Iranian Texan? Or some creep from San Francisco with no sense of humor? Or Richard, the anesthetist Mommy's boy? Or, God forbid, the bed hopping Jean-Luc? Rolling onto her back, Soraya stared up at the ceiling, bitterly regretting putting her search for The One into her friends' hands. If that evening had been anything to go by, the Cupid Index had crashed and burned.

Act Two

Thanks to Amir's influential connections, Soraya had ready access to a Corporate Box at the STAPLES Center, and – in a misguided attempt at taking Anya's mind off finding her a man – she had suggested they watch a game together that Saturday. Knowing that her mother wouldn't be there and that Amir was in New York for the weekend, Soraya relaxed, certain she wouldn't bump into any of her family. In fact, she was feeling almost cheerful, especially as she was wearing her new leather jacket from Madison in Brentwood. Okay, she had spent virtually all of her leftover savings on the jacket, but she was feeling pretty neat. After all, they weren't going to a club or a party – they were going to a basketball game. What could possibly happen there?

Shit happened.

On arriving at their box, Anya whispered that she had invited some other guests: not only Richard and his mother but some Iranian gynecologist's son.

"I'd like to introduce you to my friend's son, sweetie. I think you'll like him."

Soraya's eyes widened. "Seriously? What's wrong with this one?"

"There's nothing wrong with this one, *dahling*. He's a doctor, he can take care of you."

"Great! The first one bores me to sleep; this one can drug me to sleep. Somebody shoot me now!" Numbly, Soraya nodded to her smiling suitors and slumped in her seat, cursing Anya under her breath.

It was going to be a weird day.

The game went by in a blur. The Lakers were ahead by 10 points. Soraya avoided any eye contact with the doctor's son. Richard was, as usual, looking lamely hopeful. Not for the first time, Soraya would wonder why, and then remembered that, although Richard was American, he was still under his mother's thumb. After two failed engagements, Mrs Parker had decided that her son needed a wife to be found for him ASAP, and that she – and not her uncooperative son – would choose the bride. Soraya looked like a good catch.

Soraya supposed that after having been trapped under Anahita's thumb for years and with Richard equally crushed into submission by his mother, their union did look like a match made in heaven. Of course, it hadn't escaped her attention that it would be good business for the two families to unite. But would a man, even Richard, settle purely for financial gain?

Who was she kidding?

As someone scored, Soraya stole a glance at the Iranian gynecologist's son. He was nice-looking, but deep in conversation with his friend, who he had brought along to the game. So deep, in fact, that Soraya wondered why he had bothered coming at all. He was showing no interest in her.

"He's cute, isn't he?" Anya whispered, nudging Soraya.

"Who's cute?"

"The gynecologist's son."

"Yes, he's okay."

"He's a newly qualified doctor, sweetie."

"Really?"

"*Dahling*," she said softly. "You have to show more passion."

"It seems the only passion he's showing is to his friend." Soraya glanced at Anya. "Are you sure he's not gay?"

"You should invite him to dinner tonight."

"Even if he's gay?"

"Who said he was gay, sweetie? You should get to know him better. And Richard."

"Don't tell me," Soraya said, somewhat displeased, "you've already invited Richard and his parents, and now you want me to invite him as well?" Soraya felt trapped. When was it all going to stop?

"Invite who you like," she said finally, "I won't be there."

"*Dahling*."

"No, I've had it!" Soraya huffed. "If you're so keen on Richard, you marry him. Or let Niloofar bag him. As for the damn Iranian gynecologist's son," her voice dropped, "his parents might not know it, and your radar might have let you down, babe, but he's gay."

Casually, Anya glanced over to him and then glanced back to Soraya.

"Does that mean he's out of the running?"

Act Three

After their failed attempts at finding her a man, Soraya hoped that both Anya and Niloofar would give up soon. But she doubted it. Her only consolation was that her cousin, Kam, was staying in LA for two weeks. It would be cool seeing him, Soraya thought, remembering that she had been invited to another cousin's housewarming party that night. The older members of the family were not invited, which meant that Soraya would be spared a run-in with her mother and her uncle.

The evening would be no problem, Soraya thought, with relief. She would be with her relatives, and even her mother couldn't expect her to marry her cousin.

Getting ready to take a long soak in the bath, Soraya's phone rang. She hesitated before answering.

It was Vince, all full of energy. Suspiciously so. "Hey, what's up? I've heard you're a bit down, babe. Nervous breakdown going to plan?"

"ETA any time now," Soraya replied evenly. "Getting closer all the time."

"Like the deadline. Not long to go now, is there?"

She felt a twinge of irritation but ignored it. "Even you can't shake my good mood, Vince."

"Any more blind dates to tell me about? Found any more teenagers to go out with?"

"Huh?"

"I've heard about your latest."

Soraya sighed. "Who told you?"

"Oh, you know, people talk."

"They sure do."

He laughed down the line. "Is this one over eighteen? Or will I be bailing you out of jail anytime soon?"

"I didn't pursue it."

"Well, I heard you left quickly. I suppose you didn't want to keep him up late with it being a school night!"

"Have you quite finished?" Soraya put down the phone while Vince was still laughing.

Moments later she was lazing in her bath when her phone rang again.

"Hello?"

It could only be her cousin. She was genuinely pleased to hear from him. This was one person she could talk to and laugh with. And trust.

"Hey, Kam, when did you land?"

"About two hours ago. You still in bed?"

"Actually, I'm in the bath. It's Sunday, no work."

He remained unimpressed but having heard all about Soraya's bid for freedom and having – indirectly – introduced her to the very unsuitable Brian, Kam reckoned he owed her. He also felt uneasy about being manipulated by Anahita. But he was family, and Anahita was a tough woman. If Amir couldn't control her, what chance had he got?

"Did you like my text?"

"Hilarious, have D&G shares really dropped since I have been economizing?" Soraya joked.

"Like you wouldn't believe."

"Are you ever going to join Insta, cuz?"

"You must be kidding! I'm not joining Instagram. I don't want to become Cyber Friend Number 543. So, what's new with you?"

"Men trouble."

"Tell me about it! Some guys are just so shallow!" he chuckled. "Fancy meeting up?"

"Whatever. Were you screening my calls earlier?"

"I would never screen your calls. I was in Atlantic City, having a spa treatment!"

"Are you sure you're 100% heterosexual?"

"Ask my girlfriends!" he teased. "Shall we go for lunch?"

"We could, but then again it's Eric's—"

"—He's a douche."

"—housewarming party tonight at 1 OAK. Why don't you come along?"

"What time?"

"Can you pick me up at about seven?"

"Is that a real seven or a Soraya seven?"

"It's one Soraya hour, which is about two Earth hours!" she grinned. "See you later."

Having hired a car while he was in LA, Kam arrived in the latest, fastest Mercedes. He drove up to the curb and parked about two feet away from a nearby puddle to avoid splashing the paintwork. After greeting him and admiring the vehicle, Soraya jumped cheekily into the driving seat, glancing over to her cousin expectantly.

"We're running late!" she told Kam and put her foot down hard on the accelerator.

"I'm gonna die!" Kam yelled.

"Oh, come on. Is my driving really that bad?"

"Fuck my life," he screamed. "I'm gonna die!"

"Cuz, stop being so melodramatic. Just close your eyes and try to relax."

He was gripping the door handle as though letting go would be death itself.

"At least let me live till my twenty-ninth birthday!"

"Stop moaning."

His eyes snapped closed and his voice was shaky. "Are we there yet? Are we there yet?"

They got to 1 OAK in less than twenty minutes. Luckily, it was a calmer night, and they were quickly shown to the VIP section, which her cousin Eric had reserved for his birthday.

Despite her earlier hopes, Fate had one last trick to play on Soraya. On entering the club, she was greeted by the sight of Richard. He waved coyly as she passed their table. He was with his parents, and 1 OAK was clearly not one of their usual haunts. Realizing that this was just another matchmaking attempt, Soraya hissed in Kam's ear, "What the fuck are you playing at?"

"I owe you."

"You don't owe me!" Soraya replied, sitting down at the table. Kam slid into the seat next to hers.

"I hoped it would work out with Brian."

"Well, it didn't. Don't worry," Soraya said kindly, "it wasn't your fault."

"We thought he was a good bet."

"We?"

A deathly moment fell between them. Kam blushed and shifted his feet.

"Look, I wanted to tell you."

"Tell me what?" Soraya was sure she already knew.

"About Brian."

"What about Brian?"

"Sorry it didn't work out." He was fiddling with an empty glass, staring at it as though turning his glance away would lead to damnation. "Sorry… oh, fuck."

"Yeah, 'oh fuck'," Soraya replied, irately. "Did my mother put you up to it?"

He nodded miserably. "She's not any easy woman to refuse."

"I wouldn't have minded if you had simply told me."

"You'd never have met up with Brian if you thought your mother had picked him!"

Soraya paused, thinking back. "What about the gynecologist's son? And the ancient Texan?"

"What about them?"

"Has my mother picked them too?" her voice rose. "Oh, come on, Kam, tell me!"

"Yeah, all of them."

Soraya was finding it difficult to swallow. "So, while I was thinking that I was picking the men, or my friends were, my mother was pulling the strings all the time?"

"She said it was for the best."

"And you believed her?" Soraya snapped back. "Is everyone spineless in this fucking family?" She glanced across the room, her expression hardening as she saw Richard. "I didn't even know you knew Richard."

"I just know of him. Apparently, his mother cross-examined your mother after the basketball game and asked who the other guy was."

"The son of an Iranian gynecologist. Who, incidentally, is gay!"

Kam's large blue eyes widened in his tanned face. "Gay, huh?"

"Yeah, gay," Soraya replied dryly. "When did you last talk to my mother?"

He paused before answering. "This morning. She was the first one to ring me after I landed. She said I had to encourage you to get it together with Richard, as his mother thought her son was down to marry you. She said you were an ideal couple and that you were just being stubborn." Kam ordered small shots of vodka for himself and downed them quickly, aware that he was under scrutiny from the other table.

"I just can't get my head around this. This is twenty-first century LA, not the medieval Middle East. Richard's mother is trying to reserve me for her son like I was the last turkey in the shop." Kam shifted uncomfortably in his seat.

On the next table, Richard's mother looked as though she was in a state of shock, as she stared at Soraya and her cousin. What on earth's the matter now? Oh, Soraya realized, she thinks that Kam is my new love interest. Serves them right, she thought, grimly amused. About time she had a laugh at someone else's expense. Waving a cheery greeting to

Richard and his family, Soraya turned back to Kam as they continued to watch, mesmerized.

"Talk to me."

"I am talking to you,"

"No, I mean make a fuss of me. Lean towards me and talk and smile. Richard and his parents think you're my new boyfriend. Did you see the look on their faces? Priceless!"

Kam began cozying up to Soraya, both of them laughing and joking for several minutes before Soraya excused herself to go to the bathroom.

On the way, she stopped beside the next table.

"Hi, Richard. Hello, Mr and Mrs Parker."

"Hello, darling," his mother said stiffly.

"I'm with my cousin Kam from New York. He's staying for a few weeks."

She could see Mrs Parker exhale. "Oh, your cousin?" she said, relieved.

A few minutes later, Soraya returned to her table. Kam was mellow and relaxed.

"Did you set a date?" he asked.

"Go to hell. It's the Persian New Year Party soon," she said, changing the subject. About eight hundred Iranians all under one roof, checking one another out, and asking me if I'm married yet. I so look forward to those evenings."

"Why don't you move abroad? Or come back to New York with me and make a life there?"

"I don't know anyone."

"Looking around at this lot, that could count as a bonus," Kam said dryly. He stared hard at her. "Are you mad at me?"

"Would it matter if I was?"

"I couldn't refuse!" Kam yelped. "You know what your mother's like."

"I know, I know," Soraya replied, fiddling with her earring. "I just feel like such an idiot, thinking I was doing things my way when my family were running the show the entire time."

"We're Persian."

"Is that an explanation or an excuse?"

He downed another vodka shot. "Hey, cuz, say it's okay with us."

"It's okay," she sighed wearily. She stared across the room and felt oddly detached.

"I had a nightmare blind date last week."

She smiled, despite herself. "Go on."

"Her parents have been begging me to take their daughter out, so I succumbed. She's boring and average-looking. Did I mention boring?"

"You did."

"At some point, I was leaning my head against the wall about to fall asleep. Just so I wouldn't look like the biggest jerk, I occasionally pretended to look interested and nodded my head a few times. The girl calls me later to tell me what a wonderful time she had. I'm wondering if we were actually on the same date!" He puffed out his chest. "Turns out bored and disinterested is the new way to get the ladies! Bored is the new cool!"

"When's the wedding?"

"Thursday. Can you come? Wear a hat"

Looking across to the bar, Soraya spotted Niloofar and waved her over. The drinks were flowing, and Soraya was having such a good time she almost forgot about her marriage mission. Kam was such easy company and soon had her and Niloofar snorting in fits of laughter. Kam and Niloofar were getting on so well and Soraya could have sworn she felt a crackle of energy between them. Sighing, her mind reluctantly returned to the task in hand – would she ever feel that spark of desire with anyone other than the reprehensible Jean-Luc?

Distracted by fun and then the pressure of an unreasonable deadline, Soraya had almost forgotten who was sitting on the next table. But then it happened: Richard's mother suddenly grabbed her arm and jerked her out of her seat.

"You and Richard should be dancing. Why aren't you dancing?"

"My feet hurt," Soraya said. A lame excuse, she knew. "These Louboutin's are killing me."

"Nonsense, come and dance!" Mrs Parker persisted. Richard loomed into view as his mother launched into a determined marital bid.

"Richard thinks the world of you."

God help me, Soraya thought. Could my night get any worse?

"He would be a wonderful husband."

Shit.

"A man every woman would want on her arm."

Somebody shoot me now, she thought. Just finish it.

Finally back in her apartment, Soraya flopped onto the bed and stared up at the ceiling, wincing when the phone rang. For a moment she was tempted to ignore it. Then again, she risked missing an opportunity. It could be The One. Her Mr Right finally putting in an appearance.

But it wasn't. It was Aden.

"How are you?"

"Don't ask," she said dryly.

"That bad?"

"Much worse.

He laughed. "You know, I've been thinking about you a lot," he said. "You're lovely, even lovelier than your friend said you were."

Soraya kept her voice steady, her heart pounding queasily. "My friend?"

"Anya."

"You talked to her before we met?"

"Yeah, I spoke to her on the phone," Aden replied, without a hint of slyness. "She rang me after she'd spoken to your—"

Jesus, Soraya thought, don't let him say the next word. Please God, don't say it.

But he did.

"—mother. They arranged it between them for us to get together. It was a great idea, wasn't it?"

It took Soraya barely fifteen minutes to rush over to the Russian's house, and only seconds for her to be let in. Standing in the plush doorway of her home, Anya smiled stepped back to allow Soraya to enter.

"Hi, *dahling*, why the late visit?"

"I thought you were my friend," Soraya said coldly. "I thought I could trust you."

"What?"

"You've been talking to my mother, arranging for me to meet up with men she wanted. You've been working with her all this time!"

"*Dahling*."

"Don't fucking *dahling* me!" Soraya snapped.

"We both thought it was a good idea for you to meet Aden. Obviously, he's not right, but that should make you feel more kindly disposed toward Richard."

"You've been plotting with my mother!" Soraya glared at Anya. "How could you?"

"Stop being so melodramatic. You're such a drama queen, Soraya." With a sigh, Anya moved into the sitting room and leaned against the back of the couch. "I was just trying to help."

"You were going behind my back! I was relying on my friends to understand, to support me. I would have supported you."

"But I wouldn't have done something so ridiculous, sweetie," she countered. "Living in a tiny apartment, for God's sake! I've told you so many times, *dahling*, just give in to your family, and stop being so stubborn and rebellious."

Soraya felt like a child being scolded by an adult who knew better than she did.

"Give in? Are you crazy? If I give in, I'll be sacrificing my life, as well as any chance of being happy. Why would I do such a stupid thing?"

"They love you and want the best for you."

Dumbstruck, Soraya studied her glamorous, exotic friend. Anya, a woman who treated men like disposable goods. Anya, who was tough talking and took no prisoners. Anya, who had been one of her closest friends for years. A friend who had turned out to be devious and superficial. That Anya.

"No one's going to rule my life. Not my mother, and certainly not you."

"Soraya, unless you become a millionaire overnight, you're always going to be financially dependent on your family. You will never be free of their control, so you just need to grow up and accept it."

"Is that why you only date rich guys?"

She shrugged. "I gave into my family a long time ago. I do what makes them happy and put my own happiness aside. Granted, they don't know every detail of my personal life but I'm still financially dependent on them." She sighed indolently. "Your uncle is right. You and I daydream, but reality always remains. There is no way they'll let you date who you want. And, if I were a parent, I would be the same. Better to agree with your family. Compromise, and let go of finding Prince Charming."

Soraya was silent, spellbound, so much so that it took a moment for her to reply.

"Are you really telling me to give up everything I believe in?"

"It's a fantasy."

"It's not! I am independent and I will be free of my family."

Anya sighed again, almost impatient. "Sweetie, why do you have to be so stubborn? Your family must be so embarrassed by what you've done."

Soraya shook with rage. "So, working with my mother was your way of getting me back under my family's control, was it?"

She shrugged.

"Of course, Niloofar didn't agree with it. Although, like me, she thinks your little escapade is pathetic." Anya paused and lit a Russian cigarette. She looked elegant in her designer clothes. "We're not ordinary people, Soraya, we're the people everyone else envies. The world wants our money, our lives, and you – you – are throwing all that away! For what? So you can marry for love?" she sneered. "It's sweet, *dahling*, but not practical. If I were you, I'd marry Richard Parker and then have a lover on the side. He'll do the same, after all."

Enraged, Soraya stared at her, seeing her clearly for the first time. Over the past weeks she had realized that Anya had a cold streak, but she had not known just how freezing she really was. Devoid of compassion and empathy. Jesus, Soraya thought, had she been like that? Had she been one of a clique of bitches?

"I'm leaving before I say something I'll regret," Soraya said, turning.

"Good girl. Go home, *dahling*. With luck, in time, no one will remember this silly incident."

Shaken, Soraya rounded on her. "Was that all it was to you? A silly incident? Did you have a good laugh with my mother about it?"

She shrugged but didn't deny it.

"And you never realized what it meant to me? You never took it seriously?"

"No one does, *dahling*," Anya retorted coldly. "Anyway, I do agree with your mother. You should let your family pick the man for you. You've had no luck with the ones you've chosen." She laughed. "You can't succeed, Soraya! You're a rich girl, with rich friends and a rich way of life. You can't pretend to be something else. What for? No decent man would marry some woman who lives in a dump of an apartment and works for a living. I'm sorry, *dahling*, but everyone's laughing at you."

"You bitch!" Soraya lunged forward. "You absolute pathetic bitch!" Soraya continued. "Just because you do whatever your family tells you to do."

"And where has your defiance got you?" Anya retorted. Her glamour was gone, replaced by a flustered unease. Soraya was suddenly the stronger one with her determination undermining and intimidating Anya. "How dare you speak to me like that!"

"Maybe that's your problem. Maybe someone should have slapped some humanity into you a long time ago." Soraya walked to the door and turned. "What a revelation these months are turning out to be. The one thing I took for granted – the loyalty of my friends – came to nothing. Just smoke and mirrors." She fixed Anya with a warning look. "Be very careful, because looks fade and men leave. You think I'm a laughing stock? Take a glimpse into the future, honey, and see what the world will think of you in twenty years' time. How will the rich and powerful value a woman who's slept with everyone and lost her looks?"

"Get out!"

"I'm going," Soraya replied, chillingly. "You blew it, Anya. And although you think it doesn't matter, there'll come a time when you'll remember this. One night, years from now, when you're alone and without a friend to your name, you will think about what I've said."

The Final Month

EIGHTEEN

"One month to go!" Anahita said cheerfully, staring at her nails and wondering whether the color of her polish was too red. "Only one month left and my baby will be home."

She could hear her mother Parvaneh exhale as she turned an immaculately made-up face in her daughter's direction. "If I were Soraya, I would keep away."

"Mother!" Anahita replied, outraged. "How can you say that?"

"You pushed her away with all your nagging. Your own daughter."

"I pushed her away?"

"Yes, you!" Parvaneh replied, "If you had any sense, you would have handled all of this differently."

"Oh, really?"

"Yes, you would have pretended you weren't worried about her getting married. That you trusted her judgement, even if you thought it would be a disaster. If you'd left her alone, she would have settled down soon enough!"

"Oh, you think that would have worked?" Anahita's voice came close to a sneer.

"Well, it did on you," Parvaneh replied smartly, getting to her feet and walking out.

The next morning, Soraya was absentmindedly logging into Instagram when her cell rang.

"Hi, babe," Niloofar said cheerfully. "How are you?"

Immediately, Anya's words came back to her: "Niloofar didn't agree with it. Although, like me, she thinks your little escapade is pathetic."

"Soraya, are you there?"

"Yeah, I'm here."

"I saw Jean-Luc and his new girlfriend the other night at Soho House.

They're a pathetic bunch, that lot. And the girlfriend is too tanned, babe; she's practically orange."

Soraya said nothing.

"Have you heard from Anya?" Niloofar asked. "She was very odd on the phone yesterday."

"No."

"Still no man, babe?"

"Still no man."

"It's the last month," Niloofar said, before quickly changing the subject. "That cousin of yours, Kam. I think he likes me."

"He does," Soraya said, just realizing the same thing. "He hasn't stopped talking about you since the other night. But he's going back to New York tomorrow."

Niloofar's voice fell. "I know. So why don't we all get together tonight?" she suggested hopefully. "I'll book a table at Soho House."

Soraya had wanted to celebrate with her friends, but there was too much going on and now there was too much hidden between them for her to relax the way she used to in their company. Nevertheless, she agreed to meet them later that night. She wondered how Niloofar and Kam would manage a long-distance relationship. Maybe it would be exciting to fly back and forth to see each other. Or would it prove exhausting? But there's always video calling.

She smiled ruefully, wondering whether her recent experiences had made her cynical. To her surprise, Anya walked towards their table. Sitting down, she avoided Soraya's gaze.

"I don't want us to fight," she told Soraya in a voice clipped with tension.

"You could apologize."

"I'm sorry," Anya said. "I have some news."

"Yeah?"

"I'm moving to Monaco."

Expressionless, Soraya stared at her. Monaco? How did that happen? Here she was, sitting across the table from Niloofar, who looked like she would up sticks and leave for New York at a moment's notice. And now Anya was off too. Why the hell did her world keep shifting so quickly? Why were the people she had known for years suddenly changing? Was everyone leaving her behind.

"Monaco," Soraya said finally. "Why?"

"It's time, *dahling*," she purred. "I need a change of scenery and I need to get away from my family."

"Poor you," Soraya replied, her tone sour.

"I'm sorry I went behind your back."

"Have you told my mother about our argument?"

"Jesus, *dahling*, no!" she said, shocked. "Why would I?"

"Well, I know how much you two love to talk."

"Do you hate me?"

Soraya turned to look at her, shaking her head. "No, I don't hate you. But I don't understand you."

Shamefaced, Anya glanced away, then back to Soraya. "Oh god, he's here."

"Who's here?"

"Jean-Luc," she whispered.

"Damn it!" Soraya snapped, looking around. "Is he here with his girlfriend?"

"Sadly, he is."

At once, Soraya grabbed Anya's arm. "Let's go to the bar, I need a drink."

A moment later, shyly holding hands, Kam and Niloofar followed, with Soraya pointing out the Frenchman to her cousin: "You see that guy in the ridiculous diamante shirt with the orange girl? That's my ex."

"She looks like a cheap whore," Kam blurted out so loudly Niloofar had to hush him.

Nervously, Soraya watched Jean-Luc chat with his new girlfriend. She could feel a lump in her throat and wanted to cry. But she wasn't going to. Why was she so drawn to him? Why was he the only man who made her heart beat faster? Why? Why? Why? Waving her arm at the bartender, Soraya waited almost fifteen minutes before she was actually spotted. Anya slipped her titanium American Express card into her hand to pay for the drinks.

Knowing that it was meant as a peace offering, Soraya didn't reject it. But then she had another thought and handed the card back.

"You know, I'm really tempted to order our drinks on Jean-Luc's account."

"Go for it, *dahling*."

"Yeah, why not," Soraya said defiantly. "What shall we order? It's not like he'll notice an extra bottle or two of Dom Perignon.

"You're so bad, but I love it," Anya said huskily. "Besides, your cousin is quite careful with expenses, *dahling*. Kam will be thrilled to have his booze on someone else's tab!"

It took a while, but finally the bartender noticed Soraya. "Can I help you?"

"Yes, I'd like to order a bottle of your finest champagne, a passiontini, two lychee martinis, three large bottles of sparkling Voss, and a whiskey on the rocks."

"Member's name?"

"Jean-Luc Martinez. If you just put it on his tab that would be great and add a drink for yourself too."

Oh, this was genius! The bartender hadn't questioned her once and she was sure he would serve her much faster next time. Grabbing their drinks, they then headed to the dance floor. Jean-Luc walked past Soraya, giving her a nasty look. Stung, she turned to Niloofar, who said "Ignore him, he's crazy."

Unfortunately, the Frenchman overheard and started yelling at Soraya's group. "I'm crazy? She's the crazy bitch!"

Stunned, Soraya stared at Jean-Luc. What the hell had gotten into him? She had only ordered a few drinks on his account, which was hardly as damning as flashing a new lover in his face. But his face was livid, his rage obvious to everyone in the place.

"Crazy woman!" he cried.

"Fuck you!" Soraya snapped. "You're nothing but an asshole."

Slightly drunk, Jean-Luc staggered on his feet, but then, out of the blue, his girlfriend lunged at Soraya and slapped her across the face. Hardly able to keep his balance, Jean-Luc leapt towards Soraya, but the bouncer arrived just in time, escorting him and his permatanned whore out of the club. Stunned, Soraya stood in complete shock, wondering if she had imagined the whole episode.

"Are you ok?" Anya asked, shaken.

"What the hell happened?" Niloofar asked.

Kam was more to the point: "Are they both totally fucked up?"

With the party over, a pensive Anya drove Kam and Niloofar home, while Soraya sat in silence during the entire ride. She played the night's events over and over in her mind, her confusion mounting. Why had Jean-Luc's girlfriend hit her? Why had he been so angry? Putting some drinks on his tab was nothing compared to what he had put her through. If anything, he deserved to be slapped.

But, mostly, she kept wondering what had happened to the man she had once treasured. Jean-Luc had been so good-looking, so successful, but now he was slipping. He was getting sloppy and letting the wrong people into his orbit. What had gone wrong? Where was the charming, funny Frenchman she would have given her life to be with?

Slowly she turned to the window. The light had faded out of the sky and a dull moon rose above LA.

Fascinated to hear the evening's incident related in detail, Vince shared his own opinion with Jean-Luc – that he was a jerk and a "class A asshole." Why would he hang out with some slutty piece when he could be with Soraya?

"I don't want to settle down."

"Christ, you moron," Vince replied, "Why don't you just marry Soraya and have women on the side?"

"And what would be the point?" He was nursing a hangover and still recovering from the tongue-lashing he received from his new girlfriend. Soon to be ex-girlfriend. What did it matter that she was great in bed? She was clearly a maniac. God knows it had been hard enough to become a member of that club. He didn't need to get thrown out, and by that fucking gorilla of a bouncer, of all people!

Jean-Luc sipped his coffee tentatively. "She shouldn't have hit Soraya."

"You have to call her and apologize."

"Apologize? She put all those drinks on my account!"

"Like you can't afford it," Vince remarked coldly. "Wait until Amir Milani hears about this."

"I did not hit Soraya. That crazy woman hit her!"

"Ah, but you didn't stop it, did you?"

Jean-Luc slumped further down his seat. "I was wasted."

"Great excuse," Vince replied. "Send flowers."

"To Amir?"

"To Soraya, you fucking idiot!" Vince said impatiently. "It's nearly the end of her deadline and she's not found Mr Right. You could have been The One, but you've blown it. She's never loved anyone as much as you. I reckon her family will be polishing up their choice—"

"Who is he?"

"Richard Parker."

"Jerk."

"Well make your move then!"

"I don't want to be married!" Jean-Luc replied. "I can't commit. I don't want to be anyone's husband. I'm a lover more than a husband. I could offer Soraya a long-term relationship, but not marriage."

"And Amir will go for that big time," Vince replied sarcastically. "Face it, Jean-Luc, you've lost. You've lost Soraya and her dowry. Damn, even I could commit for two million."

"People think I'm an asshole but, if I really was one, I'd lie to her," Jean-Luc said sadly. "I'd promise anything, but it wouldn't be fair. If I were going to get married, I'd marry Soraya, but I don't want to get married. End of story."

"But you love her!"

"I always have," Jean-Luc said quietly. "But sometimes love isn't enough."

NINETEEN

The next morning Soraya woke up early, still half in a dream. Her left cheekbone felt sore, and then she remembered what happened. She recalled Jean-Luc's girlfriend hitting her, and she shuddered. Slowly, she got out of bed and began to dress for work. Her actions were automatic and her brain sluggish. Only three days were left before the deadline was up and then she would have to admit, publicly, that she had failed. Even worse, she realized that she had been waiting for Jean-Luc to eventually come forward. That he would come to his senses and realize that she was the woman he really wanted to marry.

Well, Soraya thought numbly, that wasn't going to happen, was it? Pulling on her coat, she thought of Brian, Richard, the gynecologist's son, the aged Texan, and Aden – and she felt sick of the whole business. Perhaps her family were right. Perhaps she should let them go ahead and pick a man for her. After all, looking at her track record, their choice could hardly be worse than hers. Feeling broken, she sat down at the bottom of the bed. Her efforts had been futile; her tiny rebellion inept. She didn't have what it takes to pull off an incredible triumph. Without her family and their financial support, she was just another pathetic damsel in distress.

But, as low as she felt, Soraya wasn't going to give in. She had three days left. Miracles could happen in twenty-four hours, so why shouldn't one happen for her? Sighing, she walked out of her apartment and paused to smile at Jenny next door, who had just returned from grocery shopping.

"Morning."

"Morning," Jenny replied, entering her apartment. "You look pale. Is everything okay?"

"I had a late night."

"I liked your friend, Mark Tehrani," she remarked. "He seems like such a genuine and lovely man."

But married, Soraya thought. Like all the good ones. Nodding, she changed the subject. "How are you feeling?"

"Good, really good! I'm looking forward to the baby now. My father's going to help me out. He won't know what to do, but he'll try," she laughed. She looked pale but pretty in the morning light. "We could all do with a new life in the home. It'll cheer the place up."

Amen to that, Soraya thought, waving and walking off.

That morning, by some miracle, Chloe kept her distance, and Madison watched a very subdued Soraya going through the motions at her desk. It was only after Chloe left for a meeting that Soraya turned to her own, personal emails.

From: kam@googlemail.com

Hey, Soraya, hope you're ok, you've gone very quiet, which is always a worry. You didn't respond to my last email, which I am re-sending. If you're not getting married, murdering your family, or jumping off a window ledge, then come and play tennis in the next U30s Tournament on March 14th! Teams are as below: Please can you confirm your availability ASAP.

She replied at once.

To: kam@googlemail.com

Hi, sorry, just in my own world, not quite sure how to deal with things at the moment. I've lost all my motivation and haven't played tennis for weeks. Put me down anyway. Basically, my time is running out in the marriage deadline stakes. Looks like I'll be forced to let my family find me a husband, after all!

Usually, she would have picked up the phone and talked to her cousin directly, but Soraya was feeling so choked up she feared she wouldn't be able to get her words out. But, within minutes of sending the email, her cell rang.

It was Kam.

"Hey, cuz, what's new?"

"Aside from being assaulted by Jean-Luc's girlfriend last night."

"Are you going to report it?"

"No. I just want to forget it. Put it down to a bad night. One of many lately. Did you get the pictures of Prada I sent you yesterday?"

"Hair up in a ponytail? Pink designer dog coat?" Kam replied. "Move over Paris Hilton, there's a new girl in town. That poor pup!"

Suddenly Soraya's voice fell. "You know something, cuz? I just don't understand men."

"So? I don't understand women!" He laughed. "I'm glad we had this talk. I feel better already."

"Seriously, I'm confused."

"Oh, we're pretty simple creatures really. Give us a beer, a pizza, and a naked woman, and we're happy." He paused, aware of the cold air coming down the phone. "What's the matter?"

"Why do I always attract the weirdos?"

He sighed expansively. "You're commitment phobic."

"Huh?" Soraya said, baffled.

"You're scared of committing to a man because you're terrified they're going to leave you, which means you purposefully go for guys that are unsuitable, because you believe you're not worthy of love and that it'll come to an end at some point. And, because you date the wrong guys, you always have an excuse to end things with them. Or you make it so difficult for them that they have to give up on you."

"God, Kam" she said dryly. "Where did all that come from? Anyway, you're wrong. What about Jean-Luc? I didn't have any commitment issues with him. I wanted him to commit."

"Perhaps because you knew all along that he would never commit, you felt totally safe committing to him, knowing he would never do the same. I reckon if Jean-Luc had committed to you, you would have panicked and found a way to wreck it. Like I said, on the surface you want to get someone to commit, but subconsciously you don't and, by acting this way, it perpetuates your own beliefs about men." He blew out his cheeks. "Fuck me, I'm impressive."

"You think that, whenever I enter a relationship, I actually hope that things will end?"

"Not necessarily, but you have to ask yourself if there's a pattern to your relationships. Do you go for men you can't have and avoid the ones who are willing to give you everything?"

"Or maybe I just like the attention."

"I didn't like to mention that you were a spoilt brat."

"Hey!"

"Oh, come on, Soraya. If you're serious you have to ask yourself why you need the attention."

"I don't know, but I just feel as soon as I start to really like someone things change."

"Do things change, or do you change?"

"Okay, I change!" she paused. "Maybe I'm just scared of getting too close to anyone after what happened with Jean-Luc."

"Ah, and we're back to the fucking Frenchman again!" Kam said impatiently. "Why does it always come down to Jean-Luc?"

"Because he's always been there."

"Because you're attracted to men with commitments issues! Like I've just told you!" Kam snapped, absentmindedly leaning over and picking up a magazine and flicking through it with one hand as he talked. Women! They had to analyze and endlessly repeat everything.

"This morning I even considered going home when the deadline's up."

"What?!" Kam interrupted her before she could finish the sentence. Impatient, he flung the magazine across the room. In all honesty the conversation was giving him a headache, but he also liked Soraya and thought she needed a break. Iranian men could play the field, but Iranian women were supposed to marry and shut up. The injustice wasn't lost on him.

"You can't give in to your family. You'd be stuck in a loveless marriage. Stay true to yourself."

"But I've tried it on my own. I thought I could pull it off, but I didn't and I'm hardly likely to meet The One in less than a month, am I?" She paused. "I don't want to go home. I'm not saying that I will. But surely my life would be easier if I just gave in to my family?"

"Maybe you shouldn't take them so seriously."

"What do you mean by that?"

"Next time your uncle makes a remark, just laugh it off. Or, better still, pretend to lose the plot."

Her eyebrows rose. "Pretend? My plot was lost a long time ago!"

"That's true! Well, just pretend to act crazier. I mean what's the worst religion a Muslim could go out with?"

"Jewish!"

"Well, tell them you've met a Jewish guy."

"I could pretend I've met someone even younger than Aden and that he's into Scientology."

"Brilliant! And tell your family that his father is a drug dealer and that his mother's a prostitute."

She laughed. "It has to be slightly believable, cuz!"

"Okay, you can go the other extreme and tell your family you've met a fifty-year-old married guy who's trying to get a divorce and has two kids, but at least he's graduated from university, has a job, and is fairly established working as a middle manager in some soulless insurance company. What is worse? Dating an eighteen-year-old or a fifty-year-old with three kids on the verge of paying all his money in alimony to his soon-to-be ex-wife?"

"And thanks to your genius master plan my family will probably back off, so long as I promise to go back to being normal." Soraya's good mood faded suddenly, with reality quickly taking its place. "I've failed, I admit it. I haven't found Mr Right, so maybe it is time to hand it all over to my family."

"This is the 21st century."

"And I'm Iranian!" Soraya countered. "Besides, I want the things they want for me. I want to be married. I want to have children. I want a home of my own. And if I can't find it, then why not let them find it for me?"

"Don't be so fucking defeatist!"

"The nagging would stop."

"I know your mother. The nagging will never stop," her cousin said dryly. "Come on, Soraya, it took balls to do what you did. How many girls in our circle would have left home, rented a shitty apartment, and got a job off their own bat? No one! Look at Anya, who, for all her tough talk, always does what her family wants."

"But where has this show of defiance got me?"

"Respect, cuz!" he replied, his tone sincere. "Even your uncle has to be impressed by what you did."

"No, he's only interested in money. All this would never have happened if I'd been financially independent. He belittles me in front of everyone because my parents are divorced, and my father is poor." She paused, unwelcome memories of childhood coming back. "With money comes respect, Kam, and with respect comes power. Something I don't have."

"Your family can't run your life for you."

"Well, they have done for nearly thirty years. Maybe I should have made a stand earlier."

He paused down the line. "You sound really pissed off."

"I am."

"Ah, stick with me and you'll be fine!" he said, cheering her along. "Spiritually I'm pretty in touch, although I can't see dead people! Emotionally? Not bad. Well, okay, you know, for a dude! Intellectually? A match for most people but might be outwitted when talking string theory with Stephen Hawking! Physically? No problem – I've got Sat-Nav!"

She laughed, despite herself. "You're cruel. None of this is funny!"

"So how many fiancés have you got this week? I forget."

"You mean real ones or phantoms? My mother keeps count. Or you could ask Prada's one and only groomer, as Dante usually knows more about it all than I do." She paused, thinking. "You know something? Perhaps I should fake my own engagement. Buy myself an engagement ring and tell them I've found someone. Think it would work?"

"Not a fucking chance, cuz. Not a chance."

Hanging up, Soraya was just turning back to her work when her cell rang again. She recognized the number at once. Checking that Chloe had not returned to her office, she took the call.

"Mark," she said, pleased – perhaps too pleased – to hear from him.

"I have to tell you something."

"This sounds bad."

"I got wind of the incident with Jean-Luc last night."

"How the hell—"

"Don't ask." Mark said hurriedly. "But when your mother hears about it, she'll want you to file a police report."

"I don't want to do that. I just want to forget it! Jesus, how did you find out about this anyway?" She paused. "Are my uncle and mother having me watched?"

"They're concerned about you."

"Right. So, I am being watched?"

"Oh, come on," Mark said simply. "Did you expect him to let you just walk away?"

She was unexpectedly disappointed, her voice strained when she spoke again. "All the times you've dropped by—"

"—to do the DIY."

"They weren't because my uncle asked you, were they? Because I'd feel pretty shitty about it if you were only being sympathetic because my uncle was paying you."

"How little you know me," he replied curtly. "I didn't call around because your uncle asked me to. And I've never been hired by him. I hire people. I don't get hired."

Aware that she had insulted him, Soraya softened her tone. "I was just... Look, I'm sorry."

"You must have a pretty low opinion of men if you think everyone does everything for money," Mark continued. "You're Amir's niece. Someone I've known for a long time. Surely, it would be natural for me to be interested in your welfare? We're friends. Or at least I thought we were."

She could feel the chill in his voice and was shaken by it. "Look, I didn't mean to insult you. I was tactless. Forgive me."

There was another long pause over the phone before Mark spoke again.

"Don't mistrust the wrong people."

"I'm sorry. Really, I'm sorry!" she said desperately, anxious that he shouldn't walk out of her life. She might have taken him for granted for years as Amir's friend, but lately Mark Tehrani had proved to have a powerful influence on her. She spent a lot of time thinking about what he had said to her when they talked, and considered his advice, which was something Soraya didn't do that often. And she had remembered how, over the years, he had always been willing to listen. Non-judgmental, calm, and his own man.

God, Soraya thought angrily, she couldn't offend Mark Tehrani.

"I do think of you as a friend," she said sincerely, "I'm really sorry if I've said anything inconsiderate."

"Okay," he replied, "Then, as a friend, I can make sure that your mother doesn't hear about what happened with Jean-Luc. That way you won't have to file a report and the whole thing can be kept a secret."

"But if my uncle finds out he'll be furious that you held it back from him. He demands loyalty above everything else. Why would you risk losing his friendship?"

"You're under a lot of pressure, Soraya. I don't think you need any more."

She was astonished. "But if my uncle heard about this later and found out that you'd sided with me—"

"—Yes?"

"He'd never forgive you."

There was a laugh down the phone. "How dramatic! He would never forgive me? Well, that would be his choice, wouldn't it?" Mark replied evenly. "I've told you, Soraya, I'm my own man. I make my own money, and I've never been under anyone's power or authority."

Her voice dropped. There was hope in every syllable. "Can you keep it quiet?"

"It happened in a club in front of everyone. But they won't hear it from me and I can underplay it if they hear it from anyone else."

"Can you?"

"Yes. Let's just say that some things should be kept hidden. It's not being secretive, it's being discreet. Too many people broadcast their lives to all. I don't. I never have. And I think you might like a little privacy too."

"Thanks," Soraya said, moved. "But I don't want to spoil your friendship with my uncle."

"Everyone has to pick a side in life, Soraya," Mark said enigmatically. "And you must think very carefully about who you want to throw your lot in with. Because when you do, you have to stick to it."

TWENTY

Soraya's energy had got up and left the building. She hadn't given up, but she was exhausted and unsure of where to turn next. She was also unexpectedly homesick. As she entered the apartment, she heard Jenny moving next door and thought about the coming weekend and the end of the deadline. If she did have to go home, would it really be so bad? She missed her old bedroom. She missed the familiar belongings and sights and smells, as well as her clothes, jewelry, and car. Living in cramped conditions with limited comfort had been a culture shock, but endurable because most of her attention had been on finding The One. But, although the apartment wasn't swanky by any means, it had become special to her. What it lacked in glamour, it made up for with heart. No opulence, but plenty of hope. The wallpaper was fading, but there was always music playing, or baking smells coming from next door. Even her failures had become precious to Soraya. The hair straighteners finally worked, the oven timer had been mastered, and the washing machine in the laundry room no longer shrank her jumpers from a size six to a size zero. They were all such small triumphs, so simple, so ordinary, and yet so indicative of the journey she had taken and the progress she had made.

If Soraya went home, she would never see the apartment again. Would that be so bad? Yes, she realized with surprise. She had been independent here, thrown her housewarming party here, daydreamed about Mr Right here, and made silly plans about her future here. She had been so sure that she would triumph and head home with her prize, proving everyone wrong.

Idly, Soraya thought of the email that she had received from Anya the previous night. She had been living in Monaco for nearly a week and she already had a new number, a new email, and a new life. Their argument was over from her perspective, but not from Soraya's. She might have forgiven her oldest friend, but had she forgotten? No, never. Their closeness had been shattered and could never be fully repaired.

From: anya@monaco.net

How are you, darling? I haven't heard from you for three days – what's happening?

Anya

After some thought, Soraya replied.

Hi, how's Monaco? Looking good? Are you happy?

Well, you asked how I was, so here goes. I'm feeling confused. I spoke to Kam the other night and he thinks that I may have commitment issues when it comes to relationships and that's why I choose guys I can't really have a future with. Maybe it's time to go back into therapy!

Seriously, the deadline is nearly up, and I feel rather stupid. Did I really think I could pull this off? Maybe I should have listened to you, but hey, Anya, I'm not you and I can't give in.

S

Surprisingly, a reply came almost immediately.

Darling, maybe it would be a good idea for you to see a therapist to sort you out and give you some kind of direction. You've been under this pressure from your family for ages and leaving home has only put you under more stress. Did you really think you could find the man of your dreams in four months? No one could have done that, so don't beat yourself up for failing.

Love you

"Bitch," Soraya thought, reading the email twice. She gave a carefully judged response.

You know something? I've been thinking, and actually I'm not confused at all. Scared, yes, a bit. Anxious, sure. But not confused because I know what I want.

It hasn't been easy, and I don't suppose it will get any easier, but I'm determined. I'm not running away from my family or my past. I'm running toward my future and whatever's waiting for me there.

S

She then hit send. But, despite her determined words, the reality was that the deadline was approaching, and all she had was several disastrous dates, a handful of faux Romeos, and the disappointment that was Jean-Luc. Reality has a foot in two camps – her Persian heritage and her LA life. Reality was having to choose.

Damn that Cupid Index, Soraya thought. If she saw that little fucker she'd blow him out of the sky! Romeo, Romeo, I don't know where the fuck thou art, but wherever thou art, you're late. Extremely late.

Moments later, she was leaving for work. The clouds opened and a storm started. Soraya knocked on Jenny's door. Jenny opened it and motioned for Soraya to come inside. She handed her a set of car keys.

"What are these?"

"Keys to the Mini Cooper," Jenny replied, "Honestly, I hardly ever drive it now. Being this pregnant makes it a bit difficult, and I couldn't see you struggling through this rainstorm." She jiggled the keys lightly. "Go on, it's not a great car, but at least you'll be dry."

"Hey, thanks for that," Soraya smiled, kissing her on the cheek. "I'll look after it."

It was only after work had finished for the day that Soraya realized how much of a blessing the Mini was. It meant that she was able to take Vince up on his invitation to play tennis, which would be a welcome distraction. Making sure to leave by five-thirty in order to get to the club by six, Soraya set off without realizing that the police had closed the main route. To avoid getting stuck in traffic, she used Google maps to find another way to get to the club, which was on La Cienega Boulevard. Although she was a member of the prestigious Riviera Tennis Club in Pacific Palisades, Soraya was laying low and avoiding the family friends who frequented the club.

As she stopped at some traffic lights her cell rang. It was a short text, apologetic, but to the point: Vince couldn't make it and he was sorry, but something had come up. It meant that Soraya was way over the other side of Brentwood, on a wild goose chase. Annoyed, she looked at the dashboard and noticed that the oil warning light was an angry red. Damn!

Deciding that she had no choice but to enter the club and then turn around, Soraya inched along. But, as she approached, not a single car gave way to allow her to enter. She started pushing her way into the road until some guy who had pretended not to see her jammed her in. Stuck, Soraya's temper flared.

"What are you doing?" she shouted across to the man.

"I'm sorry, but I have ten cars behind me," he replied.

"And I'm in someone else's car and it's going to break down at any minute and you've jammed me in!"

"And I've been waiting here for the past ten minutes trying to get through!"

Eventually, after several awkward maneuvers, they managed to squeeze past each other, but then a woman in a jeep decided not to let Soraya get through. This time she was really trapped. She couldn't reverse or move forwards, and the oil warning light was still angry. Close to panic, Soraya looked behind her only to see a police car reflected in her rearview mirror.

Oh great.

Slowly the police officer walked over to Soraya as she wound down her window.

"Excuse me ma'am, is there a problem?"

She told herself to be cool, but her frustration got the better of her.

"Yes, actually. These people won't let me through, and I've been waiting for ten minutes giving way. I believe it's my turn now!"

The police officer looked at her as though she was mad. "Do you realize that your front tire is worn out? There will be a penalty charge."

What the fuck?

"Excuse me?" Soraya sputtered.

"There isn't sufficient tread depth in your front tire. That's breaking the law."

Oh my god, this can't be happening.

"But… but...," Soraya tried to think of something to say without telling the police officer that it wasn't her car (which would create even more problems and complications). She wondered whether she should cry or make a run for it when a collision occurred further down the roadblock.

Sighing, the officer looked at her. "This is your lucky day, but get that tire fixed," he warned, before hurrying towards the crash. Soraya was sweating with nerves and her hands were gripped so tightly around the steering wheel she could feel her bones cracking.

Slowly, very slowly, Soraya crept back to Brentwood, expecting at any moment for the Mini to cough to a halt. After all, it would have been in keeping with the day. But by the time she finally parked the car in the building's car park the oil light, tired from its melodramatics, had gone to sleep.

As soon as Soraya reached her apartment Jenny was in the hallway, opening the door.

"So, how did you get on?"

"It was a breeze," Soraya said woodenly, giving her back the keys.

"Well, they aren't Ferraris but, like my husband used to say, you can't beat a Mini for reliability."

Smiling distantly, Soraya turned to go. Jenny called after her.

"You had a visitor."

"A visitor?"

"Yes, a little while ago. I said you were out but that I'd take a message."

"Who was it?" Soraya asked, hoping that it was Mark.

Walking into the kitchen, Jenny reached for the notepad where she had written down the visitor's details.

"He said he was called…," she paused, reading out the name, "Jean-Luc."

"Jean-Luc?"

"Yes," Jenny said, putting her head on one side as she looked into Soraya's ashen face. "He wanted to speak to you. Looked pretty upset actually. He said it was urgent."

TWENTY-ONE

His thoughts occupied, Dante combed through Prada's hair and tied a pink bow in her top knot. She had refused to wear the Gucci dog coat he had bought for her, preferring to have all the attention on her diamante leash and collar. He would miss the little dog when Soraya took her home. Her deadline was on Saturday. In a way, Dante was disappointed. He hadn't expected Soraya to find a suitable man in four months, but it had been fun watching all the excitement. His mischievous streak had relished hearing all the gossip from Angelo. It was deliciously convenient that Anahita and her daughter went to the other salon where his lover worked, and even better that some of the Persian matrons also frequented the same place.

"Oh, tell me again!" Dante said, glancing over his shoulder to where Angelo was sitting, one leg bent over the arm of the chair, his head resting back against the cushions. What a poseur, Dante thought. But what a handsome poseur. "Go on, tell me what she said again!"

"Mona Sattari said to Ariana Amanpour that Anahita was an idiot if she thought anyone really believed her story about Soraya getting married."

"And?"

"Mrs Amanpour laughed and said that Anahita couldn't find a husband for her daughter because she was unmarriageable."

"Ooooh," Dante said, baffled. "Why?"

"She's too demanding."

"I thought that was a good thing, if you were rich," Dante replied, confused.

"Demanding emotionally."

"Oooooh, like how?"

"Soraya wants to marry for love, everyone knows that. And then the older bitchy women laughed and said that nobody who's rich married for love. They couldn't afford it!"

"Never!" Dante replied, kissing Prada loudly and cuddling her.

"They then went on to say that Soraya was turning thirty and likely to end up single, with nothing to look forward to as she got older, except a lot of facial hair. Which, I might add, Soraya doesn't have. As for Mona Sattari

– Jesus, that woman's an ape!"

"They're just jealous, bitter women."

"Anyway," Angelo said, keen to carry on with his narrative. "A moment later Anahita walked in. Some idiot had booked her appointment to coincide with Ariana Amanpour and Mona Sattari! Fuck! You should have seen her face fall. All the carefully applied makeup in the world couldn't hide the shock. But, to her credit, Anahita acted all nonchalant, sat down and chatted very loudly to her neighbor about their huge house in Palm Springs."

"Then?"

"Well, the two women weren't going to let her get away with it, were they? So, Ariana Amanpour leaned across and asked Anahita if Soraya and her new husband were going to live there!"

Dante's eyes widened. "What did she say to that?"

"That they wouldn't need to, because Soraya's fiancé had a place of his own in Palm Springs! And a home in The Hamptons."

"Fuck me," Dante said, impressed. "That is some wealthy phantom!"

"But what happens," Angelo asked languidly, "when the deadline's over and there is no fiancé? Soraya will find it tough enough having to go home. But how will Anahita live it down? Everyone will know that she was bluffing. I mean, Soraya's uncle will just put it down to his sister being female – he thinks every woman's an idiot – but Anahita won't take it well. Not well at all. She'll be a laughingstock."

"Yeah, and she'll need someone to blame."

They both looked at each other and said in unison: "Soraya!"

Pushing aside the papers on his desk, Amir Milani stared ahead, thinking of his niece. He would have never believed that she could have fended for herself for a day, let alone four months. Of course, she had had some savings, some money put aside, but not much (most of it having already found its way to the shops on Rodeo Drive). In fact, if he was honest, Amir had long expected a panicked phone call from his niece asking him to bail her out. But the phone call had never come. His admiration was growing.

Perhaps he had underestimated her. Perhaps all of them had done so, apart from Parvaneh who had believed in her granddaughter from the start. Parvaneh, the old-school Persian, throwing her support behind Soraya, the modern, LA woman. Who would have thought it? But perhaps Parvaneh knew something they didn't. Or maybe she was just smarter than they were. Amir sighed, thinking of the reports he had received on Soraya's activities over the last month. She had stuck to the job, which was a miracle, and made a temporary home for herself in an apartment owned by a heavily pregnant widow. Amir cringed. Of all the places to choose.

Still, he reassured himself, it would be over soon. And, when Soraya was settled, she would soon forget about her stab at liberty. Rich women didn't need to be independent. They needed to be wives and mothers, nothing more, otherwise they turned into Women's Liberationists! They would start wanting to have opinions and make changes and think for themselves. No, Amir thought, it was dangerous for a woman to think for herself. That was a husband's job.

"I've just been humiliated!" Anahita said, walking in and sitting down at her brother's desk.

"Gone up a dress size?"

"Amir! It's not funny!" she snapped. "Some of our friends – I use the word lightly – were grilling me in the salon again. It's amazing that women who normally forget everything have this deadline tattooed on their minds!" she sighed, "So many questions. They never stop."

"You started it with that lie," Amir said, not unreasonably. "You've no one to blame but yourself, Anahita."

"It was Soraya who walked out!"

"It was you who made her walk out!"

Sniffing, Anahita fiddled with the bracelet on her right arm. "She will come home, won't she?"

"I don't know."

Her eyes filled with a mixture of unhappiness and threatened exposure. "But if she doesn't, what happens then?"

"Say she eloped," Amir suggested, "then we can pretend we're all estranged, and no one will ever know whether Soraya got married or not."

"Is that a serious suggestion?" Anahita blazed. "I thought you'd have found some way to sort this out. You're supposed to be a genius, Amir. Fix it!"

"Soraya is an adult, I can't force her to do anything," he replied, curtly. He watched her shoulders slump. He would be glad when all this was over. Maybe then he could pack his sister off to Hawaii for a long vacation. Somewhere far away. Without a phone.

"Are you listening to me?"

"Look, I can't kidnap Soraya and bring her home."

"Then go and see her!"

"I don't know where she is."

"If you expect me to believe that," Anahita said, her eyes narrowing, "then you must think I'm a fool. I know you, Amir. Nothing gets past you."

He left the comment unchallenged.

"What do you really want for Soraya? I mean, if she comes home do you really think she'll marry Richard? Or maybe she'll get back with Jean-Luc?"

Anahita rolled her eyes. The Frenchman certainly wouldn't have been her first choice, but then again, he was successful and, if Soraya could nail him down, he would suffice. At this point, anyone would do.

"I don't care who she chooses so long as she comes back to marry someone."

Amir finished for his sister: "And rescues you from an embarrassing situation."

With a hostile pout, Anahita walked to the door, paused, then turned back to her brother.

"I can't understand why you're taking all this so calmly."

"Because, unlike you, dear sister," he replied. "I only panic when I have reason to."

TWENTY-TWO

Walking into the apartment in Brentwood, Jean-Luc hesitated for a moment before Soraya gestured for him to sit down. Naturally, he took the most comfortable chair, lowered himself into it, and crossed his long legs. He was looking sheepish. Although her heart rate had escalated alarmingly, Soraya was keeping a tight check on her emotions. This was Jean-Luc – the asshole who had messed her around for four years. Jean-Luc, who had wormed his way into her family's affections, only to fail The Interview. Jean-Luc, to whom commitment was as toxic as garlic was to a vampire. Jean-Luc, the man she had always loved. Despite herself.

"So..."

Soraya waited, sitting with her arms folded. What the hell was he going to say now? That he was sorry? Or maybe he was coming to tell her that he was getting married to that tart.

"Yes?" she nudged him.

"Ma chérie."

"Piss off!" Soraya snapped. "Don't come here and 'ma chérie' me after what happened that night."

"I've finished with her," he said, cutting across Soraya's outpouring. "I was so sorry about what happened in the club. She should never have hit you."

"Shame you didn't rise to my defense at the time."

"No excuse, but I was pretty drunk," Jean-Luc replied, looking like a lost little boy. "Soraya, I've been thinking very hard, and I've realized how much I care for you."

"You've said that before. You told my family that!" she snapped heatedly. "But where does it get me? The next minute you're off with some orange bimbo."

"You hurt me."

"I hurt you?" she said, open-mouthed for an instant. "You put me through hell, Jean-Luc. It took me ages to get over you, and every time I do, you come back."

"I love you."

"No," she said, although she wanted the words to be true, more than anything. "You don't, or you'd act like you loved me instead of just saying meaningless words."

His head bowed, he ran his finger along the crease of his trousers, deep in thought. For an instant, Soraya wanted nothing more than to reach out and touch his hair. She wanted to lie beside him in bed, and smell the scent of his skin, and feel his body against hers. She wanted to remember all the kindnesses and fun they had shared.

But caution stopped her. He had been so kind and considerate when they first met, especially when she told him about her anxiety and panic attacks. On their first weekend away, when Soraya was feeling anxious before going to sleep, Jean-Luc held her in his arms and watched her till her eyes closed. The next day, Soraya began to realize she was falling in love with him. There was the time he thoughtfully took her to a top neurologist in Boston to try and help with her bad migraines. When she was going to get her dog Prada, he took her shopping and bought a bed, toys, food and water bowls, shampoo, clothes, and blankets. He bought half the store for the little pooch. And all the times they had laughed over silly things like when Soraya would pinch his nose in his sleep to stop him snoring and he would wake up startled. Or when Soraya would make fun of his strong French accent and they would both laugh hysterically. How he would do the sweetest things for Valentine's Day or birthdays. He always remembered what Soraya liked when window shopping, and he'd surprise her with the shoes she had singled out, or the handbag she had her eye on. He'd make little cards and write, "You are the sunshine of my life." How could this have been the same person? Did he just suddenly change and turn into an asshole? Or had he always been an asshole and played a character for the first few months? Did she do something wrong? She couldn't get her head around it all. It didn't seem real.

This was Jean-Luc, and kindness came hand-in-hand with cruelty. Kindness was extended only so far, and never far enough.

"I want to be with you."

She paused, her breath catching in her throat.

"Soraya, I know this deadline is over on Saturday. I want to offer myself."

"As what?"

"Your husband."

Fuck, Soraya thought, where did that come from? She shook her head certain she had misunderstood. "My husband! You always said you didn't want to get married. Only the other week you said you couldn't commit. So why the sudden change?"

"Well," he began, avoiding her glance. "We could get engaged. That would please your family."

Engaged? Had she actually managed to find a fiancé? And as luck would have it, it had turned out to be Jean-Luc? The man she had loved for so long? The man she had ached to be with? She wanted to pinch herself, but instead remained impressively cool.

"You want us to get married?"

"Not yet."

Shit. Here comes the crash.

"I don't understand, Jean-Luc."

"Well, you want to take home a fiancé at the end of the deadline. That way you'll have succeeded, and you'll keep your family happy. And you won't have to marry someone they choose." He paused. "We could get engaged."

Soraya felt as though she was walking along a very thin edge, and she might fall at any minute.

"And when exactly would we get married?"

"There's no rush."

"No rush?"

"You would have a fiancé."

"For life? You're offering me a permanent fiancé?"

"You wanted to take a fiancé home."

"I wanted to take home a man who would marry me!" Soraya replied hotly. "Why can't you do that?"

"You don't understand," Jean-Luc said, in all seriousness. "This is a very big step for me. I have never thought of getting engaged to anyone, but I will do this for you."

"And I'm supposed to act as your fiancée?"

"Of course."

"Living together?"

"Of course," he said, amazed that she would ask. "We could live in my house in France. You'd love it there. We could have a wonderful life, Soraya. Think about it. You would be free of your family and we could love each other."

She stared at him blankly. Of course, to Jean-Luc it would seem as though he was taking a huge step. Becoming engaged to someone was like putting an ankle monitor on him, permanently. He had asked her to be his fiancée. She wanted to laugh, to accept, to kiss him, and say yes, yes. But something stopped her. Why was she only good enough for a fiancée, and not good enough for a bride? How long would she have to wait for the marriage? How long would she be hoping, uneasily, worried he might change his mind? She loved him. She had always loved Jean-Luc, and every part of her wanted to run away with him. Yes, they would have a wonderful life in France. Free of her family, free of restrictions, free of being controlled. But where was the wedding ring? Where was the security? If he loved her as he said he did, why wouldn't he go the whole way?

"When would we marry?"

"In time. Somewhere down the line."

"I'm nearly thirty," Soraya replied softly. "You know my family. They'd never approve of me living with you without being married. And I want children."

"Why does your family have the last word on everything you do?" Jean-Luc snapped, his face frowning in irritation. "Can't you just be happy with what I am offering? We can make a life, and then, in time, get married and have a family. Stop wanting so much so fast, Soraya. I've told you that this is as far as I can go at the moment. I love you, you love me, stop making problems."

Was she making problems? Soraya wondered, confused. People said that when you got what you wanted in life, you didn't want it anymore. Was that true of Jean-Luc? Here he was telling her that he loved her and that they would get married one day. It was always what she had longed to hear, so why wasn't it enough? Soraya stared at the coffee table in front of her, trying to settle her thoughts. This was the miracle she had been looking for. Her way to triumph by proving to everyone that she had found her man by herself. No one had believed she could pull it off, but now she was going to bring home the biggest prize – Jean-Luc. No other woman in LA had managed to do that. And if the commitment he was making was only partial, couldn't it be enough? Couldn't she trust him? Fate? Herself?

"I love you," Jean-Luc said again.

"I have to think this out," Soraya replied, surprised at her words. "I wasn't expecting… I just wasn't expecting you to come here tonight. Or for you to say any of this." She rubbed her forehead. "It's so sudden, so unexpected."

He leaned forward, kissing her gently on her lips. The same old thrill went through her. Jean-Luc smiled.

"I'll come for you on Saturday," he said. "We can go to your uncle's and tell everyone that we're engaged."

She nodded, but something still worried her. Some unease beneath the excitement, some hesitancy she pushed to the back of her mind.

"Be ready for me, hey?" he kissed her again. "I'll be here at seven. Pack your things and, after we've seen your family, we'll go to my house in France." He wrapped his arms around her, and Soraya clung to him like a falling child.

TWENTY-THREE

Only two more days to go until the deadline was officially over. The evening after the conversation with Jean-Luc, Soraya was walking Prada, before returning her to Dante for safekeeping. Despite all his pressuring and nagging, she did not tell him about Jean-Luc. It would be better for it to come as a surprise to everyone, Soraya told herself, moving down the quiet streets of Brentwood near her apartment block. Her heels clacked on the sidewalk. Suddenly she noticed a fancy car with blacked-out windows driving in her direction. It slowed down and pulled up right beside her.

"Excuse me, young lady, could you tell me the way to Bel Air?" The driver asked Soraya, in what sounded like a New York accent.

Bel Air, of all places. He must be going to some fancy party in one of the houses. Bending down, she gave him directions.

"It's about a fifteen-minute drive from here, a few turns here and there. You need to drive in the direction of Sunset Boulevard, past UCLA and Bel Air Country Club, which is on Bellagio Road. Keep going straight till you reach Stradella Road and Bel Air is at the end."

As the driver of the plush Aston Martin Vanquish was about to say something else, a police van screeched to a halt right in front of his car. Soraya looked up, startled. Twelve police officers jumped out of the van, several of them running in her direction.

"This is a police raid, stay where you are!"

A raid? Soraya thought. A raid for what? She watched as the cops arrested some other woman across the street. She was wearing a micromini dress and knee-high, patent leather boots. Oh shit, they think I'm a prostitute, Soraya thought in horror. The man in the car panicked at that same instant. Only he reversed his car to escape. He caught Soraya off guard and the strap of her bag got caught in the door handle. Jerked off her feet, she fell to the ground. Dazed, hurt, and bloodied, she lay on the road as a police officer ran over to her.

"Are you okay?"

She tried to speak, but the words wouldn't come out. All Soraya could feel was pain, in every part of her body. Her gaze went out of focus and she shivered, bitterly cold, and with blood on her tongue as she slid, mercifully, into unconsciousness.

Ashen faced, Anahita sat down, clutching the arms of her chair as Amir gave her the news. Her eyes were enormous in her face, and her tears threatening to choke her. Somehow, she kept her composure until they reached the hospital but, on seeing Soraya, all control dissolved.

"Darling!" Anahita said, throwing her arms around her daughter, and then drawing back to study her bruised face. "Are you alright?"

"They want to keep me in tonight for observation."

"Not in this fucking dump!" Amir replied, glancing around for a member of staff. He then turned to Soraya. "So, how's my favorite niece doing?"

"Uncle, I'm your only niece."

"Yes, and you are still my favorite."

Soraya could feel her head pounding. "I'm fine, uncle."

"You need a specialist. The best! You need to be taken to Cedars immediately!"

"Uncle, please!" she pleaded. Anahita gave her brother a fierce look.

"Amir stop fussing. Can't you see Soraya's upset?" She turned back to her daughter. "How bad is it?"

"I'm okay, just bruised. No broken bones," she explained, torn between wanting to have her mother there and wanting to stop her fussing. "I banged my head on the ground."

"Dear God!"

"Mom, relax," she pleaded, glancing over to Amir for help. Catching her look, he sat down on a plastic chair beside the bed and continued watching out for a nurse.

Stroking Soraya's hair, Anahita was almost serenading her. "You come home, darling, and we'll look after you."

Tempted, Soraya felt her mother's touch and wanted to cling to her, to become a child again. To let her mother and the rest of her family make all the decisions. To be back home among the money, the luxury, and the safety. Back in her own bed, with her own expensive clothes, and her diamond white Mercedes E-Class Coupé convertible. If she went home, she would have her allowance back, her Platinum card, her membership to all the best clubs, and her invitations to private yachts and planes. She wouldn't have to work or think for herself or take on any responsibility. All she would have to do was accept the life of a traditional Persian woman.

But that was also the last thing she wanted to do. Not now, not after all this time. It had been hard working for the sex-mad bitch Chloe; hard being humiliated. Worse to be dumped by the likes of Brian. Discovering that her family had still managed to manipulate her, even from a distance, had been a revelation. And it had been a bitter, painful blow to discover that Anya had sided with her mother behind her back. But having her own door, with her own key, had been sweet for Soraya. Struggling on public transport, as well as with old, borrowed cars and an uninspiring apartment had given her an insight into another way of life. Sure, it was one without lots of advantages, but there was a sense of pride in being independent. Soraya had made a stand, and it had sparked an irrevocable change in her.

"Mom, I don't want to come home just yet."

"Of course, you have to come home now!" Amir replied, his cell phone ringing. Impatiently, he took it out and answered. "Hello, Mark. Yes, we're at the hospital now. I've spoken to one doctor. What an idiot. He's assured me that Soraya's not in any danger. They just want to keep her in overnight because she banged her head."

Ignoring the conversation going on across the room, Anahita turned back to Soraya.

"You've no idea how worried we've been, darling. Everyone, me, your uncle, your grandparents. These months have been hell for us all."

"Mom, don't. Please…"

"Sorry, sorry!" she said hurriedly, "I just don't want you to worry about a thing. We'll sort it all out when you get home." Sliding on to the side of the bed, she smiled at Amir as he finished his call. "I was just telling Soraya how she hasn't got to worry."

"The damn police let the man get away! Mark's just told me they're still looking for the guy." He turned back to Soraya. "So, sweetheart, how did this happen?"

"Well..." she mumbled, trying to organize her thoughts. "I was just walking along, and this guy asked me for some directions and, before I knew it, a police officer came over and said it was a raid. He thought I was a prostitute."

"God!" Anahita said, in a strangled voice. "Does anyone know? Did anyone see you?"

"Yes, Mom, the whole thing was filmed by CNN," Soraya replied, exasperated. "Look, the police thought the man was curb crawling! That's why they stopped me. And him." Soraya hurried on. "Not that I knew it then – that he was curb crawling, I mean. But now I think back, it was obvious. I just didn't realize it at the time." She sighed, her head banging. "When the police tried to block his car to stop him getting away, he reversed, and the strap of my bag got caught in the door handle."

"You could have been killed."

"Amir!"

"Well," he rounded on his sister, "she could have been killed. All this fucking independence was bound to lead to something like this." He turned back to Soraya. "You're not the kind of girl who should live alone. You need looking after."

"It could have happened to anyone!" Soraya cried. "It wasn't my fault!"

"Darling, we know that, but this has made one thing clear to me – you need your family."

"I've been coping," she insisted, injured by the suggestion that she had somehow failed. "I've done well. I've—"

"—nearly been killed," Amir said, interrupting her. "Soraya, this has got to stop! I've spoken to the rest of the family and we've decided that you have to come home now."

"But the deadline isn't until Saturday."

"The deadline?" Anahita said, almost dismissively. "Who cares about that? Just come home and marry Richard."

"What?!"

"It's the perfect solution," Amir went on. "He's the right person for you,

Soraya. He thinks the world of you and his parents are very eager for you two to get together. And, of course, we approve."

"You always thought Richard was something special," Soraya murmured bitterly.

Amir ignored the comment. "It's time you settled down. It was brave of you to try and find your own man, Soraya, but obviously it's not worked out."

Her expression was defiant as she turned to her uncle. "But you're wrong. I have a fiancé."

Anahita opened her mouth then closed it, unable to speak. Blinking slowly, Amir stared at his niece.

"What?"

"Jean-Luc."

"What about Jean-Luc?"

"He's my fiancé." Soraya felt like her brain had been plunged into a tub of boiling water, as she flushed with a mixture of triumph and terror.

Her indecision had been suddenly wiped out, forced out by her mother and uncle's pressure tactics. Within minutes of talking to them, Soraya had realized that, if she went home, her life would go back to how it had been before: controlled, planned out, and her husband chosen for her. Indeed, it had been their very certainty that had forced her into deciding that anything was better than going back to her old life.

"Okay," Anahita whispered, deep in shock, but rallying. After all, there was now a fiancé. Maybe not her choice, but a fiancé nonetheless. "Jean-Luc has been around for a while. And we all know him and like him."

Amir gave her a look that said it all. "Jean-Luc is an asshole."

"But he was on your list," Soraya smiled coolly, her head thumping. Shit, why wouldn't they go and leave her in peace! What did she have to do to get them to back off?

"Soraya," Amir intoned patiently, paternally. "Jean-Luc has made it very clear that he doesn't want to commit."

"He does now."

"He might just be saying it."

"No!" she said firmly. "We're engaged."

"Richard would be better for you."

"Oh my god!" she groaned. "We agreed that I had four months to find a fiancé. Now that I've found him, you want to change the rules! Well, you can't, it's settled. I found my man and I'm sticking with it. Jean-Luc and I are engaged. In fact, on Saturday we're coming and seeing you before going to his home in France for a vacation."

"Just like that!" Amir howled.

But for once it was Anahita who kept a cool head. In fact, she thought it was all working out rather well. Her daughter had actually managed to find herself a fiancé, and now her grandiose lie would never be exposed. So much for Mona Sattari and the grande dame of gossip, Ariana Amanpour. So much for all those chattering Persian matrons – Soraya was getting married.

"Why the hell are you grinning?" Amir asked, noticing the smile on his sister's face. "You can't approve of this!"

"Surely that's not the important question," Anahita replied, turning to her daughter. "Do you love Jean-Luc?"

"Of course I do! I always have." But, despite her declaration, Soraya wasn't as sure anymore.

"He treated you like shit!" Amir roared. "You were ill because of him. You took to your bed and had to have therapy because of that moron. Four years you suffered. Four years we suffered. How do you know he's really changed?"

"Last time you met, he apologized for the way he treated me in the past," Soraya said hurriedly, rubbing her temples to relieve the pain. "He also said that if he was going to marry anyone, it would be me."

"Okay," Amir said, nodding. "When's the wedding?"

SHIT.

Soraya leaned back against the pillows, playing for time. Her face was pale, her hands shaking. Desperate not to be interrogated any further, she looked at her mother pleadingly.

"Mom, I can't talk anymore tonight."

"No, darling," she said hurriedly, "We'll talk tomorrow. When you come home."

"I'm not coming home."

"Soraya!" Amir warned.

"No, I'm not coming home!" she insisted. "You told me I had four months and I'm taking four months. The deadline's not until Saturday." She closed her eyes. "Please, you owe me this. I've kept my side of the deal. I've got a fiancé. The least you can do is let me have my last two days in peace."

"But we have to talk."

"Mom, we can talk, but not now," Soraya said, with finality. "Now, I want to sleep. Please go home. I'll call you in the morning."

Ten minutes later, Soraya was just about to doze off when she heard the door open again. Ready for another run-in with her uncle or her mother, Soraya's eyes snapped open.

"Oh, it's you," she said, smiling at Mark.

"How are you?"

"Fine. They just want to keep me in for observation overnight," she grimaced. "But then you already know that, don't you?"

He nodded. "Amir told me. He wanted to have you transferred to Cedars."

"No point. I'm going back to the apartment in the morning."

If he was surprised, he didn't show it. "It must have been terrible, what happened to you."

"It was all so fast," Soraya said, trying to make light of it. "One minute I was giving directions, the next I was on the sidewalk seeing stars." She paused, suddenly tearful. Embarrassed, she wiped her eyes. "Sorry."

"It's a shock," Mark replied. "Better get it out of your system."

"It's not just the accident! My family have already been hassling me again. Come home. Do what we say. Nothing changes with them. Nothing." She paused, but the words took their time coming. "I'm engaged to Jean-Luc."

"Congratulations."

She smiled, relieved and disappointed at the same time. For a moment, she was tempted to confide in him, to explain her reservations. Mark, of all people, would give her sound advice. After all, he was married and had experience. But, then again, would it be fair to him? He had helped her so much already. Maybe it would be too much to ask for his romantic opinion. And, besides, wouldn't that divide his loyalties between her and her uncle? No, Soraya decided, she had made her choice. She was going to marry Jean-Luc. Well, she was going to become engaged to him, at least.

"I did it."

Mark knew at once what she meant. "Yes, you did. You found Mr Right, and within the deadline."

"Not bad, hey?" she said, grinning. "I don't think anyone thought I'd pull it off. Especially my uncle."

"Amir will have to admire you now."

"As for my mother," Soraya went on, "she's just delighted. Honestly, I could have married a silverback gorilla and that would have been okay. Now her little lie will never be discovered." Suddenly, she started crying again, mortified. "Oh my god, what's the matter with me?"

"You had an accident and just got engaged," Mark replied, "that's enough to make anyone emotional."

"But why am I crying?"

"You had an accident."

"And I got engaged!" she shrieked. "So why am I crying?"

Mark shrugged, but he was smiling at the same time. "You'll feel better in the morning. It's just been a lot to cope with all at once." As he stood up to go, Soraya looked at him.

"Stay for a while," she asked him.

"You should rest."

"I don't want to," she said, confused and afraid to sleep, afraid of the dreams that might come. Dreams of a man in a car who wouldn't stop, and an engagement that was also spiraling out of control. "What do you think of him?"

"Who? Your uncle?"

"Jean-Luc."

"Oh, he's very handsome," Mark said tactfully. "And he was your first love."

"He treated me like shit," Soraya replied. "But he's changed now. He really wants to be with me. I believe him."

"Of course, he did say something like that before."

"He wasn't sure then!" Soraya shouted back, then dropped her voice. "I've always loved Jean-Luc. Everyone knows that."

The tears came unforced, pouring down her cheeks. Mark gave her a brief comforting hug. She'd never known anyone to make her feel so safe and she could have stayed in his arms forever. He's married, she reminded herself.

"You need sleep more than anything, Soraya," he said, walking to the door, then turning back to her. "I'm proud of you."

She looked up, surprised: "What?"

"I'm proud of what you've done. Going it alone. That took guts. And you found The One – the man of your dreams," he smiled distantly. "Be happy."

TWENTY-FOUR

It was a very subdued Soraya who returned to the apartment in Brentwood the following afternoon. Parked outside the entrance was Jenny's car. Her father was carrying in groceries from the boot as she unlocked the main door and walked to the elevator. An hour after Mark had left, Jean-Luc had visited her, but Soraya had been asleep and so he had left a message next to her bed.

I will call in the morning.
Love you.

When Soraya finally woke, she had smiled as she read the note, then felt an odd sense of relief that she had missed him. What the hell had that been about? She unlocked the door of the apartment and walked in. Jenny had put some flowers on her coffee table, next to a get well soon card. Puzzled, Soraya looked at them. Who had told her about the accident? Then she realized it would have been Mark. Of course.

The apartment seemed curiously comforting and inviting, with the latest copy of Vogue waiting for her on the bed and the heating humming in the pipes. And from next door came the familiar sound of Jenny's radio playing, and her feet shuffling.

Having been given medication, Soraya wasn't in any pain. All the tests had come back, and she was relieved to be told that she had sustained nothing other than bruises.

"You're a lucky girl," the doctor had told her.

She had quietly smiled back at him. "Yes, yes, I am. I suppose. And I've just got engaged."

"Congratulations," he said, smiling in return. "I hope you'll be very happy."

Wow! Soraya began to feel a glow from inside. So, this was what it was like to be among the emotional elite! This was how it felt to be one of the chosen. A success! From now on, there would be no pitying looks from the Persian matrons. Soraya would have a ring on her finger to prove she

"*Dahling*, congratulations. I never believed Jean-Luc would settle down."

"We're engaged."

"Niloofar told me."

"That was quick."

"Good news travels fast, *dahling*," she replied in an even tone. "You happy with this?"

"Of course, I'm happy," Soraya replied. "I proved myself to everyone. No one thought I could pull it off and find a man in four months. Be honest. You didn't. You always told me to go home and, if I had gone home, I'd be getting married to Richard now. My family's choice, not mine."

"Richard instead of Jean-Luc?"

"Yeah, Richard instead of Jean-Luc."

Anya paused for a long moment. "When is this marriage, *dahling*?"

"I'll let you know."

She made a clicking sound with her tongue. "Soraya, this man will never marry you. He's an asshole, and he will always be an asshole."

"People change. Sometimes they do things you'd never expect," Soraya said pointedly. "We're going to get married, and I'll be with Jean-Luc for the rest of my life."

And, with that, she switched off her cell and began to pack.

Soraya kept herself busy for the next few hours. Only once did she pause and eat something, composing a note to Jenny to explain that she was leaving. When she had finally finished, she put the envelope outside Jenny's door, along with a teddy bear for when the baby was born. She would keep her promise and pay the full three months' rent so that Jenny wouldn't be out of pocket. It was only fair. Her landlady had been kind to her, and God knows she needed the money.

Soraya got dressed, taking great pains with her appearance and using concealer to cover the bruising on her face and neck. Her hands were shaking with excitement. Jean-Luc was coming for her! Jean-Luc, the man who had never really left her life. The ever-present specter who had overshadowed every other man. From that night onwards, Jean-Luc was going to be hers. Her lover, her fiancé. But not her damn husband.

Glancing at her watch, Soraya checked the time. It was 6.45pm. Only fifteen minutes to go. In a quarter of an hour, her life would be transformed. In fifteen minutes, she would be with Jean-Luc. No going back to her mother and uncle. No more being single. She had done it.

"Shit!" Soraya exclaimed, startled by a thump directly next door. Surprised, she went into the hallway and knocked on Jenny's door. "Jenny, are you okay? Jenny!"

There was no answer.

Worried, Soraya left her coat and suitcase on the bed in her apartment. She grabbed the spare key that Jenny had given her just in case. She quickly opened the door and found Jenny lying on the kitchen floor, her dress bloodied.

"Oh, God!" Soraya said, hurrying in. Gently, she took Jenny's hand. "What happened? Are you OK?"

"I fell… the baby..."

"Is your father here?"

"No," she was pale, sweating, "he… had… to go out."

"Okay," Soraya replied. "I'm going to call for help." Gently pushing a cushion under Jenny's head, she grabbed her cell and called 911. Calmly, she explained what had happened and said she needed an ambulance urgently as Jenny's baby was due and she was bleeding.

"Help is coming," Soraya said, rubbing Jenny's hands to warm them. "They'll be here really soon. How are you feeling?"

"Scared," she said, clinging onto Soraya's hands.

"I'm here for you" she reassured her. "Stay calm, Jenny, I'm just going to run downstairs and see where the ambulance is."

Hurrying out onto the main road, Soraya glanced around and sighed. Where the hell were they? She looked at her watch – nearly ten minutes had passed. Jenny was bleeding and the baby might be in trouble. She desperately muttered: Come on! Come on! Suddenly a sleek car turned into the top of the street. Relieved, Soraya waved at Jean-Luc, who drew up at the side of the curb next to her.

"Hello, ma chérie."

"Thank God! Jean-Luc, I need help," she said, hurrying on. "Jenny's fallen and she might lose her baby. I've rung for help, but it hasn't arrived yet."

He got out of the car, slightly impatient. "We have to go now."

"I can't leave her!" Soraya cried out, "she's frightened."

"But you have rung the EMS, they will be here soon."

"Jenny's on her own. I can't leave her!" Soraya looked at Jean-Luc's car. "We could take her to the hospital!"

"What?"

"We could take her in your car. It would be quicker than waiting for an ambulance," Soraya suggested, turning to re-enter the building. But Jean-Luc immediately called after her.

"Not in my car! I don't want some sick messy woman in my car!"

Stunned, Soraya turned to face him; her expression was incredulous. "Jean-Luc, she needs help! She might lose her baby!"

"This is a Ferrari," he replied, "you think I'm going to use it as an ambulance?"

Lost for words, Soraya stood by the entrance, staring at the man she had loved passionately for years.

"We have to go," he insisted. "We have to go now."

"You go."

"What?"

Soraya shook her head. "You heard me. You go, Jean-Luc."

"I can't go without you."

"Fuck off, Jean-Luc! Go and find another orange bitch to sleep with. I've got more important things to deal with right now! I've no time for a waste of space like you!"

"I'm a waste of space?!" he hurled back. "Look at you! Thirty years old and even with a million-dollar dowry you can't find a husband! You're lucky I offered what I did. And you know something, Soraya? I would never have married you."

"Goodbye, Jean-Luc." Slamming the entrance door closed behind her, Soraya ran back to Jenny's side, sitting on the kitchen floor beside her.

"The ambulance is on its way. Hold on."

"Stay with me, Soraya."

"Of course I will," she said gently. "I'm not going anywhere."

TWENTY-FIVE

For reasons that only the gods could explain, the ambulance went to the wrong address. When her cell rang, Soraya snatched it up, and was surprised to hear Mark on the other end.

"Amir's trying to get hold of you. Where are you?"

"Still at the apartment," Soraya replied. "I need help. Can you come over? Jenny's collapsed and the ambulance still hasn't come."

"Be there in ten."

True to his word, he arrived before the ambulance. Picking Jenny up, Mark carried her to the elevator and into his car. He put her gently on the back seat. Soraya placed a blanket over her then jumped into the passenger side. Leaning over, she took Jenny's hand as Mark drove through the traffic and finally drew up outside the entrance of Cedars-Sinai Hospital. Moments later, Jenny was on a stretcher. Soraya finally let go of her hand as she was wheeled into the operating theatre.

"Will she be all right?"

"I think so but, without you, probably not," Mark replied. "Thank God you were there."

Taking a seat in the waiting area, Soraya held her head in her hands.

"Here, drink this," Mark said, passing her a black coffee.

She sipped it and winced, burning her lip. "It's hot!"

"Which means you can't taste it, which is probably an advantage," he replied, sitting down. "Amir couldn't get you on your cell."

"No? I probably left it inside the apartment when I went out on the street to look for the ambulance," she explained. "What did my uncle want?"

"To know where you and Jean-Luc were. Apparently, you were all meeting up for a chat before you left for France."

Soraya said nothing.

"He never came?"

"Oh, he came," Soraya replied, "and showed his true colors. I told him to get lost."

Laughing, Mark leaned back in his seat, both of them looking up as a doctor came over to them.

"Is Jenny going to be alright?" Soraya asked anxiously.

"She was lucky you got to her so quickly," he replied. "We could have lost her. She's sleeping now, so there's no point staying. You can come back tomorrow."

"And the baby? How's the baby?"

"We had to perform a Caesarean. It's a little boy. And he's strong. He'll do well."

Soraya's eyes filled with tears; her head bowing as the doctor walked off.

"A little boy," she said dreamily. "And she could have lost him. All for a fucking Ferrari."

"What?"

"Jean-Luc didn't want blood on his car seats."

"Well, valeting's expensive these days," Mark replied, smiling wryly. Soraya giggled.

"The deadline's up. And I failed. But you know what?" she asked, turning to him. "That baby's alive and I don't really give a shit that I'm single. Maybe I'm supposed to be. Maybe that's my Fate, my destiny."

"Do you believe that?"

She looked at him and shrugged. "I don't know. But I'll tell you one thing: however much my family pressure me, I'm not marrying Richard!"

They both laughed. Mark stared down the corridor. "My son was born here."

"Your son? Was he really?" Soraya asked, surprised. "You've never wanted to talk about what happened to him, have you?"

"Some things are best not talked about," he replied simply. "Sometimes you can make a mistake if you speak too soon. Sometimes it's better to wait and bide your time. If the right moment comes, then you can put it all into words."

She sighed. "I've learnt a lot these last months. Grown up, I suppose. Certainly found out about people."

"Disappointed?"

"In some," she said, then added shyly, "but not in others."

A moment flickered between them. Soraya felt a pull towards Mark but glanced away, knowing he was unavailable.

"God, what a day."

"Did it really mean so much to you to have a fiancé to take home?" he asked. "To have someone by your side? Or was it really just to prove that you were worth loving? Not just to your family, but to yourself?"

She nodded, embarrassed. "Stupid, hey?"

"No, not at all." He stood up and offered her his hand. "I'll take you home."

"Thanks. I could do with a ride."

"No. I mean I'll take you home to your family."

"What?"

"Soraya, my marriage has been over for nearly a year. We're still close and I care about my wife, but we're getting divorced. I care about her still, but we couldn't get past what happened and we are both ready to move on to our next separate chapters. I haven't told anyone because it's no-one's business, and you of all people should understand that." Mark took her hand in his. "I've known you for a long time. Seen all your ups and downs, God knows, there have been enough! But recently," he paused, smiling, "seeing how you struggled and wanted so much to make a life for yourself. I've seen how brave you are. And I realized how much I wanted you. As a wife. My wife…"

She tried to speak but couldn't.

"I love you, Soraya. But if you'd gone with Jean-Luc, I'd never have said any of this, but you didn't. You stayed to help Jenny, and you saw him for what he was. Which has given me an opportunity." Mark paused, staring into her pale face. "Jesus, you're not going to faint, are you?"

His eyes were so blue, Soraya thought; his mouth much fuller than she had ever noticed before. Oh God.

"You want to marry me?"

"As soon as the divorce comes through," Mark replied, leaning down and kissing her on the lips, gently, but with real feeling. Soraya was momentarily dizzy. Jean-Luc, she thought deliriously. Who the fuck is that?

TWENTY-SIX

Immaculately dressed and styled, Anahita sat in Amir's living room and glanced over to her brother. "Where's Soraya?"

"I don't know. I didn't know a minute ago when you asked, and I don't know now." He spoke sourly and wondered why Mark hadn't returned his last call.

"We were supposed to be meeting them."

"Enough!" Parvaneh said, exasperated as she studied her daughter. "They'll come when they arrive. Be patient. They have other things on their minds. Jean-Luc will want to be with his girl."

"Like he'll want to be with her dowry," Amir said, under his breath.

"These months have aged me," Anahita moaned. "I look in the mirror and see how much it's cost me."

"It was all your fault! Your stupid lie was the reason behind all this drama."

"Good!" she replied defiantly. "If my lie forced my daughter to go out and find herself a husband, then I'm glad I lied."

"Even more glad that no one will find out what you did."

She ignored the insult. "I can't wait to announce the engagement."

"And what are you going to tell Mr and Mrs Parker? That their son, Richard, has been replaced at the last minute by a French gigolo?"

"Don't be so dramatic!" Anahita replied, adjusting her hair even though not a strand was out of place. "Richard was never the front runner."

"Hah!"

"We all like Jean-Luc."

Parvaneh sighed, ignoring the comment. "The important thing is that Soraya's getting married."

"A married daughter, at last," Anahita said dreamily.

She shushed everyone as she heard the front door open. Anahita, Amir, and Parvaneh all held their breaths and waited. Gamely, Amir was trying to smile in welcome, preparing himself for Jean-Luc, while Anahita was making a wedding list in her head, with Ariana Amanpour and Mona Sattari at the top of the guest list.

A second passed.

Then another.

Finally, the handle turned, the door opened, and Soraya walked in.

"Darling!" her mother said, hugging her. "I'm so happy for you." She looked over her daughter's shoulder expectantly. "So, where's the lucky man?"

"He's just coming," Soraya said, turning to the door.

She would always remember her mother's expression in the seconds that followed. Anahita's skin paled beneath her makeup; her mouth opening and closing without uttering a syllable. For a second she looked as though she might faint; her eyes huge as she watched Mark Tehrani enter and stand beside her daughter.

"This is my fiancé," Soraya said, happily. "I think you all know each other."

EPILOGUE

When Anahita recovered, she immediately screamed for a phone, then began ringing everyone she knew, her words tripping over themselves as she hurried to pass on the news. Her daughter was marrying Mark Tehrani. He was getting an amicable divorce and then he would be Soraya's husband. Mark Tehrani, Amir's closest friend. Mark Tehrani, half-Iranian, successful, good-looking, and his own man. The perfect husband. The perfect partner. The man they all knew and liked. The man who knew everything about Soraya and loved her deeply.

Hearing Anahita's high-pitched, excited voice in the background, Amir glanced over to his niece, who was talking to her grandmother. Oh yes, he thought, Soraya had done well. Very well indeed. Persian society would be talking about this match for years to come. He liked the idea of Mark marrying into the family. He was smart and business savvy, and no one's fool. Even Amir couldn't push him around.

Walking over to his friend, Mark nodded to Amir. "Quite a night."

"It's a good thing I like surprises. As for Jean-Luc, what a moron." He turned to Mark. "Make her happy, you hear? I don't want her coming back."

They both laughed. Mark took in a deep, contented breath.

"This is wonderful."

"Not bad."

"I'm a lucky man."

Amir raised his eyebrows. "You after the dowry?"

"Give it to charity," Mark replied, smiling broadly. "Soraya is all I want."

Printed in Great Britain
by Amazon